T0095459

CISS-STORIES

Concordia International School Shanghai

iUniverse, Inc.
Bloomington

CISS-STORIES

iUniverse books may be ordered through booksellers or by contacting:

iUniverse
1663 Liberty Drive
Bloomington, IN 47403
www.iuniverse.com
1-800-Authors (1-800-288-4677)

ISBN: 978-1-4697-3259-6 (sc)
ISBN: 978-1-4697-3260-2 (e)

Printed in the United States of America

iUniverse rev. date: 1/9/2012

Contents

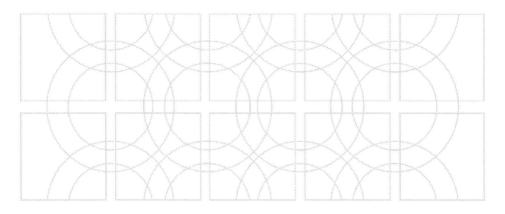

Foreword

By

Terry Umphenour

CISS-STORIES IS A BOOK FILLED WITH DELIGHTFUL TALES, THROUGH which imagination takes both the reader and the writer on an adventurous tour of the writing experience. For a third year, this project exposed the minds of eighth grade student writers from Concordia International School Shanghai (Concordia) to the demanding challenge of writing and refining a 5000-word story for publication. Collectively, the stories printed on the following pages take the reader on imaginary adventures conceived from the adolescent minds.

Brainstorming to determine the genre and story parameters started the process. Students expressed excitement at the freedom to write about a topic of their choosing. Some students expressed concerns about writing such a long story and the time it would take. The second phase of the assignment found students struggling to introduce their characters, set the scene, and make their characters come alive with individual characteristics. After considerable thought, a first tentative outline, and a brief introduction, each student read and revised the plot and the storyline that provided the conflicts needed to bring the story to its climax and conclusion.

Usually the eighth grade writing process includes an outline, a rough draft, a final draft, and proofreading. *CISS-STORIES* required students to write an outline, an initial introduction, a first draft, and three additional drafts.

After finishing the story's first draft, each student revised the story ensuring that the facts remained consistent, that the story used the same tense throughout the manuscript, and that correct paragraph and sentence structure kept the story moving forward. Next each young writer edited his or her own story to make sure that the story used active voice and that pronouns, adjectives, and verbs used the correct tense. The final draft provided an opportunity for each writer to proofread. Proofreading such a long story, one that needed every mistake corrected, provided many opportunities to teach the conventions necessary to bring a story to publication.

Becoming insightful learners and effective communicators remains one of the expected student learning results at Concordia. *CISS-STORIES* tests Concordia's curriculum to see if it provides students the skills necessary to reach this expected result. As in our previous books, *Stories from Room 113: International Adventures* and *Stories from Room 113:More International Adventures*, only you—the reader—can determine the degree of success that each of these young writers has reached toward achieving that goal. The final stories are printed exactly as the students submitted them and may include errors or even missed comments that should have been deleted. In order to make this work a continuing education resource, no teacher or professional editing was added to the final submitted stories.

It is with great pride that I present *CISS-STORIES* for your enjoyment. I hope that you enjoy reading these imaginative, adventurous stories as much the students enjoyed writing and editing them. To learn more about this writing process and its authors or to comment on this work, contact Terry Umphenour at the following email address: terry. umphenour@concordiashanghai.org.

The Chaos of the Future World

By

Aryn Aiken

"Why can't I go to the funeral?" Laila's timid seventeen-year-old voice cried into the phone. "He was my grandfather, your father. You get to go even though you don't care."

"I do care sweetie," Laila's mom replied from her cell phone in Chicago. "I just think that your education is more important right now."

"You don't care about your dad dying, so you don't want me to care either," Laila screamed, trying to contain her tears. " But guess what? You might have control over what I do, but you can't make me not care. I STILL CARE!"

Drenched with rage and hatred towards her mother, she punched the red, "end" button on her dorm room's portable phone. Laila walked out from her isolation in the bathroom to be bombarded with questioning stares from her roommates. She ignored them. Laila didn't really want to see anyone at that moment, except her grandfather who always knew the right thing to say to her. Paw Paw understood that she wasn't like everyone else in her family and her life.

Lost in thought, Laila simply passed her three roommates and went out onto the grounds of the elite boarding school her mother forced her to attend. The crisp, fresh North Carolina breeze greeted her when she opened the door. Finally, free to express her emotions, she broke down and cried. The first tear, of many, rolled down her cheek as she thought about living her life without Paw Paw, the one person who genuinely understood her.

Sitting below the old oak tree in the center of the courtyard, she let her ginger hair fall over her face, hiding her tears from all passersby. Thankfully most people didn't ask Laila what was wrong, so she submerged herself in thoughts. How could her mother not let her go to her grandfather's funeral? Why wasn't her mother going? Paw Paw was her father. Did her mom care about anything other than shopping in Chicago and staying away from her only daughter? She really didn't care. Ever since Laila was little, her mother had ignored her and dragged her father down the same path. Laila often compared herself to Mary from a book titled *The Secret Garden*. Her parents didn't care about her either.

Laila didn't know how she would survive on the Egypt archaeology field trip that departed in just three days. On that note she realized that her loving Paw Paw would have wanted her to remember him but not spend too long crying over him when she had the rest of her life ahead of her.

Laila stood up straight and tall. She wiped the tears from her eyes, ready to march her way back to her room and face any questions her snobby roommates asked. She had nothing to hide.

Laila fixed her navy blue shirt, brushed the dirt off the back pockets of her jeans, and flipped her hair so that she might not appear too torn. Although she felt like her heart had been ripped into millions of pieces, she left the tree, determined to move forward while she grieved quietly. With Egypt ahead, it couldn't be that hard. *I miss you Paw Paw*, she thought, and a final tear rolled down her face.

"Life was too short to put on hold. If you wait too long, your world turns into living chaos," Paw Paw's words rang in her head as she walked away from her sorrows. Laila didn't like chaos.

*   *   *

Egypt, the land of pyramids and historical mysteries, surrounded Laila. She breathed in the dusty desert air and leaned on her shovel.

Laila's school offered an AP course in archaeology, which included a "once-in-a-lifetime" trip to Egypt to help on a real excavation site. For the first two days they had only dug holes really slowly so they wouldn't ruin any remains. *I guess when they said help, they really meant just help,* Laila thought as she started back to work.

Everything went the same way for another hour until the boy next to Laila, Mark, yelled, "I found something."

Dr. Raskavi, a professional archaeologist, ran over to the site and started uncovering what looked like a femur bone as all of the student "helpers" watched him—all of them—except Laila. She backed away from that hole and slowly made her way to the top of a small mound of sand. The sight of lifeless bones swept away all thoughts except one, *Paw Paw, Paw Paw, Paw Paw.*

Laila looked back down at the excavation. *How could no one feel sorrowful at the sight of the barren bones they were uncovering that once walked as people and had families?*

Laila couldn't stand it anymore. She wanted to move on, not to be reminded of her recent past. All she could do was run away from the cause of her misery. She turned away from the scene below and took one humble step that turned into a sprint. She ran until her teacher, Dr. Maricai, stopped her.

"Laila," she shouted from a few feet away. "Where might you be going? The excavation isn't even close to being done for the day."

"I know this is a once-in-a-lifetime thing, but I can't stand there and watch them pull a lifeless skeleton out of the ground."

"I know your grandfather's death was a great loss for you, but you have to move on and leave your past behind you."

"I know, but seeing the tombs and the skeletons of these people only makes me think about last month. Please, just give me a different place to dig holes."

"Go ahead and work over by Dr. Cavicia."

"Yes, ma'am," Laila replied. She detoured around the other excavations to where Dr. Cavicia tried to uncover a clay pot in a sea of dirt. Laila asked what she could do. Dr. Cavicia told her to start digging a hole with a paintbrush and a toothpick. Go figure!

After only fifteen minutes, Laila found something. It had a metallic, blue-gray color and was clean, unlike the other pots that had been found that morning. Its shiny and opaque exterior insured that nothing could ever be seen if it were placed inside it. The thing moved. Part of the thing jumped up to make a finger pointing straight at Laila. It moved like a gear. The edges stuck out and then it started to rotate. It moved around Laila's feet. This was no ordinary pot. It had no shape, and it moved randomly as if it lived but couldn't decide where to go. First it twitched left, then right. Then it suddenly had spikes.

Puzzled, Laila reached out to pick "it" up. She wanted to know what it could be, and she figured Dr. Maricai would have the answers. Right as her fingertips touched the smooth, cold surface of "it" all of her surroundings disappeared as if, suddenly, they evaporated. A black sky– as dark as crow's feathers–replaced the serene, blue Egyptian sky, and harsh, black concrete replaced the sandy ground. A floating motorcycle passed her, headed towards a downtrodden shack. The shack sat at the end of a long road of black pavement. Trash littered the entire area. Even areas capable of growing grass were covered, held back, and polluted. Out in the distance, she saw a clean floating city-like skyline.

What was this place where motorcycles and cities floated and shacks were in the middle of trash instead of in the middle of nowhere? Surrounded by no one but the worms eating at the trash and whoever passed her on the floating motorbike and lived in that shack, Laila stared out at the polluted sky and wondered. *What is "it?" Where am I? What am I here to do besides just look dumbfounded? How will I get home?*

Laila held "it" tightly and thought, *Why am I not home. Please take me home. Home. Home. HOME!*

Nothing happened.

Laila lay herself down on the pavement and closed her eyes. "It" flattened itself, and she decided to use "it" as a pillow. Soon she sat in a chair in her grandfather's house surrounded by his antique furniture and dusty old pictures. He told her a story about a nice little kangaroo that lived in Australia and loved to eat grass. He and his friend, the koala bear, were taking a trip to the desert so they could pick cactus flowers…

She heard another engine moving towards her. When it floated right beside her, it stopped. She opened her eyes, and she could only see the face of a young boy, about her age. His deep brown eyes stared right at her.

"WHAT ARE YOU DOING LAYING DOWN IN THE CREATURE'S TERRITORY?" the boy yelled.

"Well if I can't lie down here, why does someone live here?" asked Laila, referring to the shack at the end of the black, paved road.

"For your information that person was just leaving."

"So you live here, and you are yelling at me because I'm temporarily laying on the ground."

"I'm moving so it doesn't matter anymore," he said with a large frown on his face.

Laila placed her hands on the cement to push herself up, and the boy extended his hand to help her. Laila willingly accepted his act of "chivalry" as her grandfather would have called it. She stared at him, noticing his charmingly handsome, striking features. His eyes glistened without a single beam of sunlight shining down on him.

With his hand in hers, she pulled herself up and stood next to him wondering, daydreaming. *Who is he?* she thought. *Who are the creatures? Why did he live here if it was so dangerous? Why is he leaving?*

"What is that?" he asked pointing at "it."

"I'm not sure," replied Laila. " All I know is I was in Egypt until I touched it, but now I'm here, wherever here is."

The boy picked "it" up. "Come with me." He grabbed her arm and pulled her to his floating motorcycle.

"You know, if you're going keep on getting mad at me and then helping me and then forcing me to go somewhere against my will, it would help if I at least knew your name."

"David," the boy replied. "David Number 18. I'm seventeen years old. I go to Fotcite High, and my dad is in jail for no reason. Wanna know anything else, nosey?"

Feeling ashamed, Laila swung her leg over the seat of David's motorcycle, and David started the engine. Laila leaned forward and whispered in his ear, "I'm sorry."

"It's okay," David replied. "How did you find this?"

Laila recalled her experience in Egypt with "it", and how she just appeared here. David stared at her like she didn't belong.

"What's your name?"

"Laila Servaine."

"Who is your grandfather?"

"It should be who was my grandfather."

"He died!"

"What is it to you?"

"You see this power source." David held "it" above his head for Laila to see. "It is set to find your grandfather's DNA, but I guess it thinks you are the closest thing."

"Well I'm not him, so can I please go home," Laila said. She found herself very annoyed that wherever she went, the memory of her grandfather haunted her. "I live in Gastonia, North Carolina, at a boarding school, 2533 Lawrun Drive."

"You think I can just drive you back home? Do you even know where you are?"

"No, but I know where I want to be, and you can take me there. Just find the highway and drive."

"Have you even noticed that my motorcycle is floating?"

"Yeah," Laila replied. "It's 2010. I want a flying car too, and you were one of the lucky ones who got one."

"Laila," David said, treating her naively. "You're in 2112."

"Oh." A tear started to form in the corner of her eye.

"I know that's hard to grasp, so I'll let you get used to it seeing as you're from the past and everything. I'll explain everything else later."

Laila didn't want to know anything else. The more information she got, the more it hurt. She only wanted to curl up in a ball and cry, but she couldn't––at least not with David around.

*   *   *

David stopped the motorcycle in front of a run-down warehouse. They got off the motorcycle, and David heaved the door open revealing a large room with a mattress, a fridge, and a collection of chemical experiments. Laila walked in and asked, "Do you live here?"

"Yes," David replied. "But that isn't the issue right now. You have to know what you need to do, and you won't have much time at the rate we're going."

"So I actually have a purpose here?" Laila wondered.

"Of course. You wouldn't have been sent here if you were useless, and right now you have one of the most important jobs ever."

"Okay… What is this 'job'?" Laila asked, sitting down on the dirty floor of the warehouse.

David picked up the power source and said, "You have to take this fuel to the power house."

Laila stared at him completely puzzled, "HOW? WHERE? WHY? ME? NOW? PLEASE TELL ME WHY?"

"Whoa! Why are you so scared? It won't be that hard. I'll go with you."

"I'm sorry, but I just got here, and you've made this place seem so cruel and unjust and…uh… I…I just don't understand. If this thing was supposed to get to my grandfather why did I have to find it after he died?"

"Now, the last question I can't answer, but I have most of the answers. This place is cruel and unjust, but if you play you're cards right you can get through with some rewards. Now for you to understand everything, I'll have to start at the beginning. When I was growing up, the world was pretty much the same as it is for you except we had higher technology. A man by the name of Luke Servaine was the chief of our civilization and had the power to lock all of our important buildings with passwords, including the powerhouse. Everything went wrong about five years ago when Luke became a greedy man who lead our people into starvation. Many people died, and this city is one of ten all around the globe that still remains. Luke had become a creature. Later that same year we lost our last bit of power. The creatures took it. Laila, Luke is your great, great, great grandson."

"But, he destroyed your world. Well, almost."

"It gets worse. About three years ago it was gradually getting darker all over the world, and my father proved that the sun was losing its power too and would explode, destroying our world with it if we didn't have the power to stop it. Immediately, my dad started looking for a source of power to save our world."

"And he found one," Laila filled in the blanks.

"Right, but the new chief found out that he had discovered a power source and wanted it to use for his pleasure. When the chief came to retrieve it my father had destroyed all evidence of it and sent the actual source to the past so that your grandfather could come here and get it into the power house."

"Okay," Laila stated. "Wait… But why send it to my grandfather. Why not the president? He probably could've done a lot better than anybody else"

"Well, that's because the only clue we have for the password to get into the powerhouse is great, great, great, great grandfather."

"Okay," Laila muttered. "That isn't creepy. So how do *I* save the world and stuff?"

"You're really that up for this."

"If this is what I'm here for, I'm gonna get it done."

"Well the first thing we need to do is break my dad out of jail because he's the only one who will know what to do with the source when you get into the powerhouse. Then…"

"Do you have like a white board and markers or something in this dump?"

"No! We don't have time to draw. The sun is predicted to blow up in twenty-three hours"

"Well can I at least have a pen to write this down?"

"Here." David gave Laila a pen and a piece of scrap paper from his pocket. "After rescuing my dad, we need to teach you how to move across creature territory because we'll have to go through their zone to get to the powerhouse. Plus, they're guarding it, so that could be a problem. Then we'll go out and save the world."

"Next time, don't make it sound so simple. That can mislead people."

"Not you it seems like. So, we'll need to break my dad out at night when it's pitch black, and no one does anything at the jailhouse. They got a new guard to do the night shift, and he can sleep through anything. So we'll just weld through the bars, and let him out."

"Couldn't you just take the keys and open the door."

"Go ahead, ruin all the fun. Killjoy."

"I was just saying."

"It's okay. We could," David said. "Right now it's ten o'clock in the morning so we can start getting you used to a jet pack."

"COOL!"

David walked across the room to a small cupboard and took out two jet packs. Laila looked at them in awe. They weren't any bigger that her Biology textbook back home, and they weren't any heavier either. Laila chose the bright orange one and put the thick straps on her back and buckled a second set of straps across her waist.

"So where's the on button," Laila asked.

"Just say… ON," David's jet pack spit flames from its end, and he shot up to the top of the warehouse. "FLOAT." David floated above Laila's head. He almost touched the ceiling of the tall warehouse.

"OKAY. THIS IS OFFICIALLY THE COOLEST THING EVER. ON." Laila rose up to the ceiling. "FLOAT." She floated in the air next to David.

Wind rushed by her. Laila looked down, and the ground crept closer to her. "DAVID."

Her cry reached his ears too late, and she crashed to the ground. Surprised by a soft landing, Laila found herself on a mattress. She collapsed back down onto its fluffiness. For what seemed to be no reason she let herself start to cry, but she wasn't hurt. She just wasn't sure anymore. She wasn't sure that she was really excited to be in the future. She wasn't sure if she wanted to save the world anymore. She wasn't sure if she could ever do anything that her grandfather was meant to do. She wasn't ready to fit into his shoes. She didn't know if she would ever be.

Why couldn't she have time to grieve? Why couldn't she just come back another time? Why did God make life unfair? Why? WHY? WHY!

"Are you okay?" David rushed to her side. "I'm really sorry. I wasn't paying attention when you fell. You must have lost your concentration. You have to think about flying when you're up in the air."

Laila stood up and muttered, "I'm going home." And she walked away while wiping the tears off her cheeks.

David stood still watching as she walked away.

Right as Laila reached the door of the warehouse she heard, "But you're our only chance. How will you be able to live knowing that in 2112 everyone on Earth will die, and you could have stopped it?"

"I just can't help you right now." Laila started to cry again. "I can't move on right now."

"We need you," David screamed. "I need you… My dad needs you. Everyone here needs *you*."

"I just can't," Laila managed to say as she ran out of the warehouse.

She could go into town and get some time machine thing or something. She would do anything to get out of 2112.

As she started to mount David's motorcycle, a hand fell onto her shoulder. "Don't go. I know that sounds pathetic, but not doing this will haunt you for the rest of your life, and you know it. Please. I don't want to die."

Laila turned around and just looked at him. Tears streamed down her face, and she reached out to hug him.

While they were embracing she managed to say through her weeping, "I won't go anywhere."

Laila and David walked back into the warehouse and cried away their sorrows through the rest of the afternoon and evening. At six-thirty, Laila came back down to earth and wanted food. She got up from her spot on the floor and walked over to the small refrigerator.

"How are you supposed to eat any of this?" Laila asked. "Your cheese has mold on it, your milk has chunks in it, and your bread has GUM on it!"

"I'm a guy and it's called a restaurant."

"Well can we go to one?"

"Sure," David said while getting up. "All you had to do was say 'I'm hungry.' But no. You had to criticize my food supply."

"Hey, if you get any meaner, I will leave."

"Okay, okay," David agreed as they left the warehouse. "The restaurant is just on the edge of town, but we can't waste much more time. Only fifteen hours left."

"I can eat fast."

"Hey. If you get much ruder I'll let you save the world alone."

Laila and David mounted the motorcycle and they were off.

*   *   *

The darkness became unbearable as night crawled closer. Even at nine-thirty the sky had already turned black. The ground had become an even darker shade of black. There was no moon, nor were there stars to guide a man's way through the shadows. Laila saw no street lamps, no energy, and no light.

Laila and David grabbed their jet packs and one of those really cool spy gadgets that cut through stuff with fire. "On," they whispered.

Fire flared from the bottoms of the jet packs, and they set off into the unknown darkness of unknown cruelty.

David and Laila flew across the unlit sky, managing to bypass crashing into several trees. By ten fifteen they arrived at the dull jailhouse. Laila could hear the guard snoring inside and figured the plan would work swimmingly.

Mini-welder in hand, David opened the door. As it creaked the guard flinched but didn't awaken. Laila thought the jailhouse was pretty pathetic compared to the large jails in North Carolina. It had only one-room with a chair and desk for the guard and receptionist, who wasn't there. Behind the guards desk a safe lay on the floor. It had a piece of tape on it that said keys. The safe had a keyhole, and in it the key had already been placed. Laila walked towards the safe, turned the key, and it opened revealing the keys to the jail cells.

"Three keys. Three jail cells," Laila stated. "Now all we have to find is your dad."

The jail cells were guarded with thick, gray doors and had small windows in the tops. David jumped up to look in the first cell. "Not my dad," he said. Then he looked in the second and said "Give me the keys."

"Here," Laila said as she handed the keys to him. David immediately put a random key in the door, and it worked. He swung the door open to reveal a man with an unruly beard and strangely round spectacles sleeping on the floor of a room with nothing in it.

David kneeled to the floor and shook the man's elbow. "Dad," he whispered. "Dad, wake up."

"David," the man cried. "How did you get through?"

"HEY!" The guard woke.

"Put this on," David told his dad as he shoved a jet pack into his hands.

David's dad fit it clumsily on his back as Laila stood dumbfounded staring at the guard. He fumbled through his desk trying to find a gun.

"Now is our chance," David yelled at Laila. "ON."

"What's going on?" David's dad asked. His jet pack turned on, and he flew.

"ON," Laila cried. As she flew up in the air, the guard caught her leg. "Let go of me," she screamed. The guard only gripped her ankle tighter. Laila wiggled her foot and tried to set it free, but that didn't work. Then she remembered taking karate as a child. *Back kick,* she thought. She lifted her free foot and kicked it right against the guard's nose.

His hands automatically let go of her foot to comfort his now bleeding nose, and Laila shot out of the door of the jailhouse.

As Laila flew a light flashed on the strap of her jet pack. BEEP. BEEP. BEEP. BEEP. The noise it made reminded Laila of the beeping of a large truck when it drove in reverse. Laila didn't know what it meant, but from all her knowledge she figured that beeping must mean something bad. "DAVID," she cried.

Off in the distance Laila could her David's dad ask, "Who is she?"

David started to answer but Laila screamed, "MY JET PACK IS BEEPING. WHAT DOES THAT MEAN!"

"Darn," David said. "Keep flying, Dad. She's losing fuel." He turned around to fly back Laila.

"LOSING FUEL," she screamed. "WHAT DO YOU MEAN LOSING FUEL?" The beeping went faster and faster, and Laila started to fall slowly. The beeping still rang faster like a bomb before it explodes. Laila fell faster and faster, and then the beeping stopped.

Laila fell, and as she did she could see David flying fast towards her, but he didn't catch up in time, and Laila fell onto a pile of trash in the middle of nowhere. Then nowhere started to fade to black as her eyes closed. Laila could have sworn that she heard someone crying off in the distance, but she wasn't sure.

*   *   *

"Who was she?"

"The creatures probably have her by now, and we only have eight hours to get her back if we want to have anytime left to stop the sun."

"Could I at least know who she was?"

"Laila."

"Who's Laila?"

"The key to unlock the powerhouse." David paced as time ran out.

"No she's not. An old man was supposed to get the energy."

"Well she got it, and she's the old man's granddaughter. That old man is dead."

"We've gotta go save her. Nobody else has any chance of knowing the password."

"Really, Dad. We need to save her?" David inquired sarcastically.

"She's our only hope."

"I know."

"I know where they took her. I was there before. Son, I never told you this, but I was once captured by the creatures. It was a terrifying experience. One day…"

"Now is NOT the time for reminiscing. Just tell me what you know."

"There are guards set up only on the ground, two at the front gate and two at the back. Then another twenty or so are scattered inside the building."

"Okay, so where are prisoners kept?"

"In the dungeon. Where else?"

"Wait, is this like a castle or something?"

"It's a castle of trash."

"Weird."

"We could sneak in at night by flying in one of the lower windows on the side of the castle. Then we'll have to wing it. There's no way to know what will happen. We might not even make it in time to stop the sun, but what's life without taking risks."

"Well it's still dark out so we'd better get going. How long will it take us to get there?"

"Three hours max."

"Get the lasers, and let's go before we only have seven hours left."

*   *   *

Laila lifted her head to rub her back. It hurt like she had just fallen a thousand feet. When she thought about it falling fifty feet or a thousand feet doesn't make a difference.

Her bed poked her. She looked down at it. "Wow," she said still looking at the pile of trash that had served as her bed for the night. "This is such a lame excuse for a bed, David."

When no one answered, Laila looked around. "David? *David.* Putting me in a trash box isn't funny." Laila ran to one of the walls and beat on them. "DAVID LET ME OUT." No one answered, and it occurred to her that she couldn't still be in a warehouse. Then where could she be?

"HELP!" No answer. No David. Nobody.

Laila went to a corner of the "box" and curled herself up into a ball. "Where am I?" she cried, seeking answers about her dreadful situation. No one answered.

She felt like she was talking to her mom on the phone while she shopped. She would say "Hi Mom." And then her mom would pretend excited to get a call from her. When Laila would try to tell her about something funny or sad or happy that happened at school she could hear her mother talking to one of her stupid friends.

"That is an amazing dress. You should get it."

Laila would say, "Mom are you listening"

And her mother would just say, "Yes, but I'm quite busy. I'll call you back later." Laila never got any calls from her mother.

She lay on the floor of her confinement and cried for hours and hours. She had nothing better to do.

* * *

Hours had passed, but Laila didn't care. She just wanted to be back home in her world not the world of trash jails or where ever she was. Then she heard a noise. "Hello," she yelled. She saw a red semicircle appearing on the wall in front of her. "Who's there?" she cried.

"Shhh. It's me, David. The creatures are after me so be ready to get out of here."

So that's where I am, Laila thought. She stayed silent, and a few minutes later a small opening appeared. She crawled through, and David gave her a jet pack. David's dad was there too.

Laila took a moment to look around, and she saw trash surrounding her. She also noticed a small hallway and at the end, a broken window. She looked at David and saw his bleeding hands and the scratches on his face from when he had crashed through the window.

They heard footsteps. "Put the jet pack *on*," David whispered.

"Oh, right."

"Only an hour left, and the creatures are coming," David's dad said.

They all ran over to the door, but were stopped by a fierce creature. He looked like a man, but then again he didn't. He had trash built into his body and a third eye where his nose should have been.

"AHHHHH," Laila screamed. "ON."

With her jet pack exploding with life, Laila rose high enough to look right at the face of the creature.

"Laila," David said. "They heard you."

"You will not destroy the world!" Laila yelled at the creature and punched him in the face. Like a kid who had played in a bounce castle too long, the creature collapsed.

"LET'S GO," David screamed. They all flew out the window as four more creatures turned the corner.

"We have forty minutes left, and it'll take thirty to get to the powerhouse," David's dad said, "It'll take me about five minutes to set the power to stop the sun from exploding. You'd better start thinking of that password right now."

Laila thought and thought and thought, but nothing came to her. What would be so important that her grandfather did or said that would have been remembered over one hundred years after his death? Still nothing. Nothing was the worst thing ever.

*   *   *

"Almost there," David said. "Please tell me you've thought of something."

"I'm really trying, but I can't think of anything."

Laila looked at the powerhouse. There were three creatures guarding the entrance. *This part should be easy.* Laila flew right up to one and punched him twice, while David used his awesome laser gun to kill the other two and the one Laila had knocked out. They heard a buzzing sound and saw the creatures coming towards them with their jet packs.

"There are too many to shoot all of them," David yelled. "I'm running out of laser power already, and I've only gotten seven."

"I've got one," David's dad said. "Laila get over to the password lock, and we'll guard you."

"Umm," Laila muttered. "Okay."

She ran over to a small little box beside the door of the powerhouse. *So five letters. Think. Sweet. No. Elder. No. What else am I supposed to try?* Laila thought. She turned around and saw all the creatures coming and falling after being shot. "Man this is chaos," she said to herself. "The future world is chaos. WAIT! CHAOS." Laila remembered what her grandfather used to say, "Life was too short to put on hold… If you wait too long, your world turns into living chaos." That had to be the key She typed it in.

"Access granted."

"Hey, Mr. David's dad. How much time do we have?"

"Four minutes!" he cried. "You have to password in right?"

"Sure do. So give me your gun and go save the world."

He walked inside. Trying to find the device that they had used to stop meteors from falling to the Earth by using a force field. A joystick in the corner of the room controlled it. "Sun. Sun. Need to find the Sun," he muttered to himself. "How much longer?"

"Two minutes," David cried. "Can you do it, Dad?"

Laila could see the sun becoming a menacing scarlet brown color and knew that they had to stop the sun.

"I'm almost done," David's dad said.

"Only thirty more seconds," David yelled.

Laila looked back up to the sky and saw a ray of blue light shoot towards the sun and surround it with a blue glow. Laila had been a part of saving the world. She smiled at Daniel as they continued to shoot the incoming creatures. Then his face disappeared and changed into a blue sky. The gun in her hand changed into a brush and a toothpick, and the pavement below her transformed into sand and what looked like the start of a hole.

Back in Egypt, she thought. Laila wished she could've have stayed longer, but she had done her duty so she had to go back to her own time. That's just the way life works. kneeled down in the sand and put her had in her pocket. She felt something in it. Laila grabbed it and pulled it out of her pocket. In her hand she held a box. Laila opened it to find a note and a little red button. *Come visit anytime. Just press the button, and it'll take you to whatever time I'm in. I miss you already. David.*

Laila took his advice. In an instant she stood in the warehouse with

David after they had saved the world. They grabbed some jet packs and went out to the new, improved, and better future.

"Thanks for being my saviour," David told Laila.

I love futuristic happily ever afters, Laila thought. She felt happy again. Even though her grandfather wasn't on Earth she knew he still lived on through her. He never left her, and he never would. Paw Paw stayed with her, and now she had David too.

A Change for the Better

By

Evan Burton

"HEY KID, STOP!"

The distancing authoritative voice and the stop of the clinking of the keys assured me that the security officer had stopped chasing me. This was the third time in a month that I had been caught at a bar, under age. Since I couldn't get my car that I left at the bar, I decided to walk home. When I got there, a dark figure greeted me on the porch.

"You smell like a bar. Have you been drinking?" exclaimed the shaded figure.

"It was just a little celebration after the baseball game. I only had a little," I replied in a hasty tone.

"You are just like your father. You know that? If you don't change, then you are going to end up next to your father in that cemetery."

Without a word, I stomped down the stairs to my room in the basement and gently drifted to sleep. The next morning I overslept. Mom woke me by banging pots and pans next to my ears. After a quick morning breakfast, I raced off to weekend baseball practice at Meadowbrook High.

Practice was already going when I got to the field. I knew coach Matheson would be angry, but I would think that he would be more careful about how he treated kids. Since his wife had died, he had not been the same. He became a heavy drinker and has had a hard time being nice to his high schoolers as well.

"Hey, Coppiellie; you're late. This is the fourth practice in a row that you have been late. You have one more time to be late, and then I will be forced to start benching you during games," Coach Matheson yelled in a very aggravated tone. Coincidentally this was the fourth time I had heard this little lecture.

"Sorry coach, I had a rough night last night, and I overslept my alarm clock. If you want, I can stay after practice and make up for being late." The truth was, that I wanted to stay after to practice anyway. After practice, I didn't want to go home and have to face my mother today as well.

"You kidding me. I don't want to waste my Saturday afternoon working with you little brats."

A few players couldn't handle the pressure and quit the team. So today we had tryouts for new players. The day was a complete failure except for the handful of players that actually looked decent. Once practice ended, I jumped in the back of Brian Richy's truck and headed for the nearest Quickmart. Brian and I had been friends since fourth grade. Ever since then, Brian and me had been buds.

When we got to the Quickmart, I grabbed my wallet containing thirty dollars and my fake I.D. When I entered the store, I recognized one of the freshmen kids that tried out for the team. He grabbed a bottle of Mountain Dew and a bag of Beef Jerky. Then left the small store without a word.

When I was done, I had a case of beer and a bag of potato chips. When checking out, the cashier saw my I.D and gave me a dirty look. Dodging his look, I grabbed the beer and rushed out the door. Without noticing the figure standing at the exit, I shoved open the door.

Falling over the figure, I was forced to drop everything in my hands to save my face from hitting the ground. Noticing the figure was the boy from practice, I found myself gathering the beer while he grabbed the chips. He told me his name was Curt. I turned to look at him, when I noticed his eyes locked on the beer in my hand.

"Your underage, but of course you know that," he exclaimed. "If you are caught with that, your high school baseball career will be over."

"You going to rat me out. You're just a freshmen. You're treading dangerous waters here," I replied, feeling ashamed.

"Don't think I am just going to sit here and let you do this."

At this point I knew I was in trouble. The look on his face told me that he was not joking. I signaled for Brian to back me up. He came out with a baseball bat. Sensing the fear in Curt's eyes, I slipped by him and got into Brian's truck.

Brian and I didn't speak the whole way back to the field. After sitting in the dugouts. I grabbed my keys hidden under the dugout seat and drove home.

*   *   *

It was the first practice since the Quickmart incident. When I arrived, Coach Matheson walked straight for me. I knew by the way he looked that he was angry. He was six foot two with short buzzed blond hair, and when he was mad, his face turned a cherry red. The next few seconds happened pretty quickly. Matheson picked me up by my shirt and slammed me into my black Nissan.

I was not too worried about my car. It had a pretty good number of dents and bumps in it already. Matheson screaming in my ears made for a bad beginning of practice. After I regained my composure, I tried to fight back; but his two hundred pounds of muscle were no match for my one-hundred and forty pounds of average American teenage body, filled with movie tray dinners and soda. I couldn't make out what he was saying in complete sentences. However, after a quick minute he released me and walked to practice. He walked in such a manner that you couldn't help but laugh at him.

From the scene that had just unfolded, I was not going to go to practice today. I suppose if I did, Curt would feel the wrath of Dan Coppiellie. That would just make for more trouble.

I spent the walk home thinking about the rest of the day. Odds are my mom will find out about everything that has happened. The Quickmart incident and today's practice, and as always she will bring something totally irrelevant into play, so that she can get more mad at me. I was sadly wrong.

As I neared my driveway, I noticed immediately that my Nissan was missing on the driveway. My walk home turned into a jog. 300 feet from the driveway, my walk turned into a jog. Around 250 feet from the house, my feet couldn't move faster.

I was now at a sprint. My anger was now at the point where I was about to snap. At 150 feet, I could see my mom standing at the window peering out at me. At the house, the hinges that connected the door and the wall were no match for me. I ripped the door from the already weak hinges and entered, leaving the door on the front porch.

"Mom! Where is my car?" This had been the angriest I had been in a long time.

"I sold your car." Somehow, her tone was calm and showed no sense of anger. However this did not take away how angry the words made me.

"You sold my car, how am I supposed to get to school and to my baseball games?" I usually didn't take my car to school anyway. I usually just hopped into the back of Brian's truck and we carpooled to school, but I wanted to have a reason to get mad at my mom.

"I will drive you to school from now on, on my way to work. As for baseball, you will not be going anymore. Not until your attitude changes."

The words came out of her like she was trying to ruin my life. I could have argued with her, but there was no use. I grabbed the clothes that she was folding out of the laundry room and threw them out the front door in anger.

"Oh, and you now are taking a course on anger management after schools on Mondays and Wednesdays."

I ran outside hoping to see somewhere I could go. The closest thing was my mom's suburban. It wasn't the place I was hoping to go, but as of right now. Anywhere was better than heading back into the house and having to talk to my mother. Twisting and turning in the back seat, I tried to find a comfortable position to sleep in. What seemed like hours went by and nothing seemed to be working until I finally gave up and fell asleep rather uncomfortably.

Light, light is what woke me up the next morning, and man was I in pain. I fell asleep with my neck drooping over the armrests. This meant that I had a very bad pain in my neck and a killer headache. I went into the house and grabbed the toolbox. I felt bad for what had happened last night, and for some reason I keep thinking that if I fix the door, my darn headache will go away.

*   *   *

When school came around, I decided to take my dads rusty bike rathr than accepting my mom's offer to take me to school. However it didn't take long to notice that I was the subject of most people's conversations.

Apparently the baseball team told everyone that Matheson had attacked me. I would have been more mad, but I noticed the principal talking to Coach Matheson. Form the gestures that kept appearing, I could tell that it was a heated discussion as well.

At the end of the day, I was just about to leave to head home when I noticed my mother was at my locker. That's when it hit me. I heard the words anger management course come out of her mouth. At that time, it felt like someone had dropped a car on me.

I really didn't want to go, but my mom said if I cooperate than she will buy my car back. I entered room 101 and I could tell that this was not going to be something that I would enjoy. The room was filled with misfits and bullies that no one liked. Either because they were mean to them, or they thought that the kids were just weird. Taking a seat, it was my turn and I was forced to say it.

"Hi, my name is Dan and I have an anger management problem."

I had my expectations low for this class already, but now I realized even the low expectations were too high. Through the class we learned about each other and brainstormed goals for our anger. I couldn't take it anymore, halfway through the class I got up and left. I never wanted to go to that stupid class again. The idea of not returning was quickly shot down.

My mother got the police chef on the phone to try and encourage me to stay with the class. I'd like to say that it was the first time, but it wasn't. The police chief told me that if I didn't take this class, my future wasn't looking too bright. My mother also helped out and said that if I do the classes, she will let me join baseball for my senior year.

*   *   *

Every day that I went to school, I would hear stories about the baseball team. The more stories I heard the harder it gets to just stop playing. Then the day came, Coach Matheson was replaced and the replacement coach wanted me on the team. As much as I wanted to say yes, I had to say no. After the meeting with the replacement coach, coach Goodman, Brian met up with me to talk.

"You joining the team again," Brian said enthusiastically.

"I can't, you know how my mom is. I have to listen to her otherwise I can't play baseball senior year," I said with my head hanging low.

"Your mom has never stopped you from doing anything before. So what if she took your car, then ride with me." I could tell that that Brian was serious about this.

"Ok, I'll talk to coach and set something up. Ill sneak out for games, but weekend practices will be hard to get to."

After the second meeting with coach, I had to go to anger management class. After the first meeting I went to, it got a little bit better. I didn't have to say my name and my problem anymore. I still didn't want to go. When I got home, I noticed something was out of the ordinary. I entered the house and my mom was waiting for me with a smile on her face and a blindfold in her hand. With the blindfold on she guided me to the backyard.

"Ok, now open your eyes," said my mom.

"My eyes are open, but can I take off the blind fold?" I said with a little laugh.

Slipping out of the blindfold, I was staring at a convertible black Dodge Challenger.

"I bought it off of a couple down the street. They just had a baby girl and needed a safer car. This is for how hard you are trying in the anger management class and how well you are doing in school. Also, I have noticed you haven't come home drunk since you started the class." She said still carrying the smile in her face. Speechless. I nodded and thought about what I had told coach Goodman. I like the car but I am still going to go to practice.

*　　　　*　　　　*

The first game of the season was about to play out, and I was stuck watching Desperate Housewives with my mom. I had to think of something to get out of here, the game will start in five minutes with or without me. Four minutes till game time.

"Mom, I'm going to go over to Brian's house if that's OK."

"Sure honey, just be back by nine o'clock. On the way back can you stop by the store and grab some tomatoes?"

I nodded and ran up the stairs to grab my bag. Three minutes till game time. I rush out of the house and sprint for the school. Two minutes till game time. I take off my shirt and begin changing in the middle of the street.

One minute till game time, I reach the dugout and find out the game started five minutes early. Ricky Hamilton was out in centerfield, where I usually play.

I took a seat in the dugout and waited for the inning to end. I don't know what was worse, having to sit for an inning, or the fact that the inning seemed to straggle on and on.

Finally, we had batted and we were ready to go take the field when coach told me to sit this one out. With a sense of question and anger I blurted out.

"But coach we are taking the filed again," I said having one foot on the field and one in the dugout.

"If you planned on playing today, you should of gotten here on time and came to practice," said coach Goodman with no uncertainty.

I sat out the rest of the game thinking. Thinking about my mom, thinking about the car, baseball, Bryan, Coach Goodman, just thinking. Back to reality, I realized I was staring at a poster for a club after school that looks into why the brain does what it does. The best part about this poster was that it was on the same days as baseball. The downfall to this was that it was on Tuesdays and Fridays, which meant a day after my anger management classes, and that the only day of the week I had off was now taken up.

The game finally ended with a score of 15 to 6, our win. I went to talk to the activities director. I made my point and had signed up for "Brain Club." It was nearly eight o'clock by the time I was done at the school. I packed up my unused baseball bag and slowly headed in the direction of my house. On the way home, I saw the people who traded my mom cars and gave her the Dodge Challenger.

I went up and introduced myself to them. They introduced

themselves as the Austin's. The father works at the local hospital as a neurologist. After catching a glimpse of my watch, I noticed that my wristwatch read the numbers 9:15. I was late, and in the middle of a conversation with the people who sold me my car. After an awkward goodbye, I jolted out the door down the street to my house. Then it hit me, I had forgotten my bag at the Austin's.

At this time I was sprinting back towards the Austin's house. Dodging fire hydrants and trees, I reached the door, grabbed my bag from the front porch, and then was off, again. Where my angered mother is now waiting to yell at me and call me a loser.

The feeling that I got running towards my house, it felt all too familiar. Running to my house, expecting to see my angered mother. This was it, the time that it all ended. By now, my mom has found out that I am playing baseball. She'll get me off the team, and give me a life lecture about my father. As I reached the front porch, I turned to see my mom on the swing. No sign of her. I entered the house cautiously, still no sign of my mother. I walked into my living room to find my mother asleep on the couch.

The credits of "Desperate Housewives" were rolling. I turned off the TV and carried my mother up the stairs. After I placed her on the bed, I tried to sneak back out of the room. When I heard it,

"Wait, don't go. We still need to talk about tonight," the words slipped out of her lips in an exhausted tone.

"I know, and I'm sorry for." I was cut off.

"I just wanted to thank you, again. You have really became a young man that I would want to be my son." Not quite what I expected, but I'm not one to complain about compliments.

With a nod, a simple nod and a good night. I turned off the lights and went back to my bedroom in the basement. As I went down the stairs, I couldn't help but letting a tear run down my cheek. This was something I hadn't done since the fourth grade when my father died. I wasn't sure if I was crying because I was sad for lying to my mom or if I was sad because I actually felt proud of myself.

The rest of the night, I spent on my bed, thinking. Thinking about my mom, baseball, brain club and my father. Eventually I entered the sanctum of sleep. Sweet sleep where nothing bad ever happened.

Saturday couldn't have started out any worse. I started the day with a greeting from my sister Michelle. She made breakfast for me and brought it to my room. My mother also came down to my room. The attempt on her part to surprise me ended as soon as it began. The lack of cleanliness in my room side tracked her. She began folding clothes and picking up everything on the ground, including the carpet. Michelle and I stared at each other and then broke into laughter. As my mother came out of her brief need to clean, she came and joined me on my bed.

"Happy Birthday Mike!" The words came out of my mom and sister simultaneously.

The fact that this was my seventeenth birthday and I had nothing planned for my birthday was making me sick to my stomach. But that's okay, because I got to go shopping all day with Michelle, courtesy of my mom. My mom dropped us off at the Meadowbrook mall and told us that she would pick us up at three o'clock. That meant two hours of shopping with my sister. As much as I hate to say it, it actually sounded fun.

My sister always had a way to make things interesting anywhere she went. Surprisingly instead of going straight to all the girls' stores first, we went to the glow in the dark mini golf course in the middle of the mall. Baseball may be my sport, but miniature golf certainly came close. After a "miraculous" ten-stroke down comeback from my sister, she quickly ripped up the card and claimed she won. I just chuckled and continued on.

Around 1:45 PM, I began to get hungry. We stopped by the food court to pick up a hot dog. My sister told the vendor that it was my birthday and we received to free hotdogs as long as we told people how good the mans hot dogs were. As two o'clock rolled by, my sister begged me to go check out the Abercrombie store on the other side of the mall. Michele challenged me to a race across the mall, shortcuts included of course. This was a slight problem, since I had officially no idea where the store was actually located.

"On your marks, get set. Go!" My sister jolted into the crowd of people and left me wondering how to get to the clothing store.

I headed in the direction that I saw my sister head off in when I noticed some of Michelle's friends gossiping on the benches near me. I paid one of the friends five dollars to take me to the Abercrombie store in the shortest time possible. To my disbelief, it wore me out to get to the store.

The thought of somebody memorizing the specific location of every store made me laugh. When I reached the store, to no surprise Michelle was already in line with her cart all ready filled with stuff. Since she was fifth or sixth in line, I pointed to the sporting good store and walked over with her approval. As soon as I was in the store, I saw the big letters. "Sale on all baseball goods." The sign made me want to melt.

I immediately walked over to the baseball section. Then I spotted him Coach Matheson was shopping as well. It had been close to a month since he was fired. I stood next to him and began rummaging through the baseballs. Coach Matheson smiled softly and then left. Shocked that he didn't think of something snotty to say, I dropped my basket of baseballs on the ground and the rolled all over the place. I bent down to pick the balls up when someone pushed me over. Standing up to see who had pushed me I saw Brian.

"Hey man, what's up?" Brian said in a joyful tone.

"Nothing happening man, just shopping with my sister," I replied in a slightly embarrassed voice.

"Oh, sounds like fun. Anyway, there is a party at my house tonight. My parents are gone and my little bro is at his friend's house. Can you come?" His voice sounded slightly threatening.

"Sure, I'll stop by for a bit." I replied, slightly confused.

"Cool, my house at nine tonight." With a slight nod, he left.

I continued to clean up the balls when my sister came in. She had three stuffed bags in her hand, filled with clothes.

"Was that Brian?" She looked confused.

"Yeah, you ready to go?"

She didn't answer, and instead walked out of the store.

Things were very weird. I had a feeling that something was going on. When I was outside, I saw my mom's car. I got into the car and questioned my sister.

"What's wrong with Brian?" I asked. She didn't answer. Instead she just stared out the window. A tear rolled down her cheek. I knew something was up, and I needed to find out what.

At eight-thirty I left for Brian's house. The whole way to his house, I could only think about what upset my sister. When I arrived at Brian's house, I could already tell that there was going to be a problem. Music blared, and there was a bunch of beer cans in the front yard.

I would have not entered the house, but I decided that I would go in for the soul purpose of figuring out what happened between him and my sister. After zig-zagging between the drunken seniors and the passed out juniors, I found Brian passed out on the staircase. I grabbed a fruit punch from the drink table and then went to talk to Brian.

"What did you do to my sister?" I asked, at this time I was furious, I was not supposed to be around alcohol and wanted to get out. Brian motioned me to go to his room. In his room, he answered the question.

"I dated your sister for about two months behind your back." I could tell he was wasted by the way he slurred his words together.

"You dated my sister, why didn't you tell me. What happened?" I was infuriated. My best friend went behind my back and dated my sister who was four years younger than him.

"About a month in a half in, we went to a party. I was drunk, and I told her that I would tell you about me and her if she would try marijuana with me. She said no, so I tried to force her to smoke the pot." Brian said and showed no shame.

I just stared at him for a minute to take it all in. With all the anger built up, I couldn't stop myself from unloading on Brian. I tackled him and then punched him multiple times in the face. He grabbed a cup of beer and threw it at me. I got off of him and tried to clear my eyes of the alcohol.

"You tried to get my sister to smoke pot with you," I was burning with anger. Or it could have been the burn of the alcohol in my eyes.

"That's right; the way she fought was pathetic. It felt more as if she was squirming and crying for more."

At this point, all boundaries had been crossed. We fought it out for a whole ten minutes when a strong force hit me on the head. When I finally came to, my head was killing me. I was in an ambulance cuffed to a bar. Brian was over talking to the police officials. My mom came over to me and slapped me. As Michelle walked over to me, she wound up for the slap and then gave me a big hug and thanked me. The officer noticed that I had come to and came to talk to me.

"Were you under the influence of alcohol, son?" The deep voice demanded respect.

"No sir. I came over to talk to that guy over there when we got in a fight." I shot a dirty look at Brian who was still talking to a different officer.

"He told me that you came into his house under the influence, gave everyone a beer, spiked the punch and then brutally attacked him, is that true?" The officer looked at me as though Brian was his kid, and that I would be wrong anyway.

"No sir, the only thing I had to drink tonight was some punch from the punch bowl in the house. As for the attacking Brian part, Brian provoked me to, and he fought back." I knew that saying he fought back was like saying I stole the cookie because it told me to steal it. The officer cuffed my hands together, held a breathalyzer up to me and said blow. Fragment. The reading was high. The officer didn't believe me about the punch.

"You're under arrest for being under the influence of alcohol, giving alcohol to other minors, and assault for attacking Brian."

I couldn't believe it, I was going to jail for things I didn't do. A short ride later I was at the jail. I found out that Brian was just going to be held overnight at the police station. I would have to stand a court session and spend a few weeks in jail. What a great birthday present.

* * *

Finally, no more bad food, angry cell mates, or mean guards. I had pled innocent to all charges against me. The drawbacks would I would have to have one- hundred and fifty hours of community service and miss out on all extracurricular activities while I was in court. Meadowbrook had won all their the playoff games and would go onto win the championship game. My one chance of getting into a decent school was ruined. No scholarship for sports, community college here I come. The community service would be spent tutoring middle schoolers and cleaning garbage off of the highway.

Three more weeks of school and then summer. I can make it until summer. Then I can focus on senior year and the community service that I would have to do. As for now, I will try and regain my respect from my family and work hard in school.

As summer came, I was proud. Brian being a senior had left to go work with his dad in Alabama as a car mechanic. Community service was as hard as I thought it was. I caught a break though. Instead of having to work on the highway. I was offered to go work for the church. My mother after hearing this began making me go to church to find my value through God.

As I finished up community service, I also received God as my savior and was baptized in the name of the Holy Spirit. With the consent of the judge, jury, and the pastor, I was allowed to be team captain for Meadowbrook's baseball team. Even though I was finished with my services, I still decided to help out tutoring middle schoolers and helping with the church. The first practices of baseball did not focus on baseball at all. But the team focused on sportsmanship and keeping a good clean conscience.

The beginning of the season started out rough. We lost most players because they were focused on wining rather than being good sports. We were left with freshmen, sophomores, two juniors and me being the only senior on the team. We lost every game of the preseason.

When the normal season started we won fifteen games and miraculously lost no games. We took home the championship trophy and were voted the team with the best sportsmanship. I brought my grade point average up to a 3.6, however the grade point average form the previous year's brought that down to a 3.0.

I applied to Meadowbrook Community College. I was accepted. However, I got a 20,000 dollar scholarship to USC for my baseball. I majored in psychology and human science. I visit my mom every weekend, to check up on her and tell her how much I appreciate her for everything she has ever done for me, and everything she will do for me.

I attend church every Sunday and help out the Meadowbrook baseball team whenever I can. Not sure what I am gonna do after college, or how many years I'll be in college. There were two things that I were sure of: playing baseball for USC was like a dream, and I was not going back to my old ways, ever.

The Greater Secrets

By

Ashleigh Carroll

THE MUSTY ODOR OF THE SHABBY ATTIC FILLED TWELVE-YEAR-OLD Hayley Ramirez's nose, bringing about a sneeze. The round, grimy window showed a glimpse of the shimmering Pacific Ocean and palm trees that dotted the shoreline and trickled up towards the hills. She adored Laguna Beach more than any other place on Earth. Not only did she call Laguna Beach home, but she also loved its sunny, year-round cloudless skies that made her feel like the world went on forever.

"Black chest with the gold latch," Hayley recalled as she repeated her mother's instructions. The chest contained some clothing for Hayley that were once too big, yet her recent growth spurt resulted in the demand for some new attire. Because of all the sports she played, it seemed that she never gained much weight, only grew taller.

Scanning the dim attic, Hayley soon found the chest and lifted its heavy lid, disturbing the thin layer of dust that lay on the chest. As she knelt down, her strawberry blonde hair fell around her like a veil. She dug through the chest but found no clothes, except a threadbare, Christmas sweater and a key ring holding numerous gold keys. Puzzled, she rummaged through the rest of the chest's contents, curious about what might be stored inside. Other than some old books and records, there were several compact wooden boxes that lay there, enticing her to reach for one.

Hayley opened one of the boxes and stumbled upon a photograph and a few tangled pearl necklaces, seemingly untouched for many years. As she smoothed out the crinkles on the old photograph over her tanned legs, it revealed a man standing with a backpack slung over one shoulder. Hayley's aqua eyes scrutinized the photograph, but she didn't recognize the man as her father or any of her relatives. She read the short caption scrawled on the back which said: "My sweet Paul, standing on Four Corners during our vacation. Summer of '93."

Hayley whispered, "Paul? My dad's name isn't..." and then it hit her. "My 'father' isn't my father at all. My 'dad' is my stepfather, and this man is my biological father!"

A wave of emotions came over Hayley, and her heart pounded. She pondered for a minute and then began to question everything. "When did he leave? Why did he leave? Did he and my mother ever marry?" Frustrated, she couldn't understand why, after all these years, that neither her mother nor her stepfather informed of this. Perhaps they thought it would make her life easier. Were they planning on keeping all of this a secret for the rest of her life?

Anger bubbled inside as she thought of all the possibilities. She searched through all the other wooden boxes for more items that could provide any insight on her parents' relationships. To her dismay, she only found her mother's old ring, the ruby in the center still gleaming as if it were new. "Obviously they were married or at least engaged," Hayley said to herself while she slipped it on and examined it. "At least that's a start."

Hayley sifted through everything surrounding her, seeing if she'd missed anything important. Finding nothing, she sighed and sat there for a moment, debating what to do. Her choices were to pry information out of her mother and stepfather, unsuspectingly, or to use her resources here in the attic. Frowning, she glanced at the photograph again and noticed the man in the picture looked like her. Their noses and eyes looked identical. She stared at her father's still image and sighed, letting everything sink in. It would be difficult for Hayley to treat her stepfather the same way after this astounding discovery.

Eventually, she packed everything up so that she could find it again later. She decided to reunite with her father, no matter what difficulties she might face. She was responsible for locating him now. And, although keeping it a secret might be wiser, Hayley needed to tell her best friend, Samantha Knox. Trustworthy may well have been Sam's middle name because the two girls told each other absolutely everything. She made plans to call Sam this afternoon…

The sound of her mother's voice pulled her out of her deep thought.

"Hayley? Hayley, are you still up there? We are getting ready to go out for lunch with the Timmons."

Realizing that her findings had interrupted her search for clothes, Hayley panicked and slammed the chest shut. Racing around, she located the right chest, selected several items, and rushed down the stairs to grab her favorite hoodie. For the moment, she didn't care what she picked. Eventually, she'd hunt for the new clothing she bought last summer. Hayley needed to make sure her family wouldn't figure out her realization.

Her mother called out to her again, "Hayley?"

"Coming! I'll be there in a moment!"

"Dad is waiting in the car for you. I'm going out there now as well."

"Okay!"

To neaten up a bit, she dusted off her jeans, tied up her hair, and changed her shoes. She didn't have enough time to do anything else because her stepfather honked the car horn. Hayley dashed out to the car as quickly as she could in sandals and slid into the back without saying a word. Thoughts of her dad continually ran through her mind.

Once they settled in at Dalton's Deli with the Timmons, Hayley forgot about her father and what she'd learned. She chatted to the Timmons's son, Adrian, who went to school with her. While they ate grilled chicken sandwiches, they discussed the recent math exam, the upcoming school dance, and their latest ski trip to Big Bear Mountain. Sitting on stools near the open window, Hayley admired her magnificent view of nearby cliffs and the ocean beyond. As Adrian talked, Hayley watched a seagull dive in the air, parallel to the cliffs. Normally she enjoyed Adrian's company, but today she didn't pay much attention to him. Suddenly, she remembered Samantha knew nothing of her findings. What would Sam think?

Hayley excused herself as quickly as she could and went to the bathroom. Once safe in a stall, she texted Sam and said to be at Joe's Frozen Yogurt in twenty minutes. Joe's Frozen Yogurt had become their favorite hangout, as well as their meeting place to share important news. When she came out, everyone's plate looked spotless, and Mr. Timmons asked for the bill. "Good," she thought, "less time to wait before I meet Sam." She sat back down and twiddled her thumbs, waiting impatiently for the bill to arrive. A couple times when the waiter neared their table, Hayley rose off her chair. She grew more restless each time he strolled by.

"Hayley, is everything okay?" Mrs. Timmons questioned.

"Um, yes. Just feeling a bit under the weather. I think it's all the stress from school."

"Hayley has worked very diligently lately, as her grades show." While Hayley's mother continued to brag about Hayley's improving grades, the waiter came by and dropped off the bill. As soon as he did, Hayley whispered to her mother that she would be with Sam.

"Excuse me," Hayley apologized, but I'm not feeling great, and I wouldn't want you to catch something. Besides, I have a lot of studying to do." With that, she raced across the busy street and towards the frozen yogurt place.

When Hayley arrived at Joe's, she could tell that Sam wanted to know what important event had spurred this last-minute meeting. Sam followed her around like a dog while Hayley purchased her strawberry yogurt, adding sprinkles, M & M's, and Hershey's Chocolate Syrup to it. Sliding into a booth, Hayley nibbled at her yogurt while Sam stared at her.

"What?" Hayley asked nonchalantly.

Sam glanced at her and simply said, "Spill."

"All right, all right," answered Hayley, "but I highly doubt you will believe me." She proceeded to tell the story about how she'd come to learn that her stepfather wasn't her father, and that she had a long lost father. Sam devoured her yogurt as she listened intently, but before long her gobbles turned into nibbles, and her jaw dropped. "My real father's name is Paul," Hayley stated, "and apparently he left two months before my birth."

The color drained from Sam's face as Hayley's words hung in the air around them. Then she whispered, "So you mean to tell me that Rob isn't your real dad; he is your stepdad. Your real dad is out there somewhere," Sam swept her hand towards the windows "And neither your mother nor stepfather has said anything about him since you were born."

"Nope, not a word," Hayley responded. "I don't remember my real father, which is probably why they didn't tell me and pretended all along."

"So they weren't planning on telling you? Ever?" Sam questioned.

"Not that I know of," Hayley muttered.

"You have a right to know!" Sam shouted.

"Shhhh!" Hayley replied. "I might have a right to, but the world doesn't. I told you because you're my best friend, you're trustworthy, and you've been sucked into this lie like I have."

"So what have you found since then? Have you gone back up and looked around again?"

"Other than his photograph and my mother's ring, nothing else in the chest helped me with my finding. I didn't have time to have a thorough look through the other chests because my mother called me soon after."

"I just don't understand why they wouldn't tell you. It doesn't make sense. Anyway, you should look for hints until you know enough that we can sit down and fit the pieces of this insane puzzle together."

"Thanks so much Sam!" They hugged over the table and scarfed down the remainder of their yogurt.

Sam offered to give Hayley a ride home, so long as they stopped by the beach on the way. Hayley agreed, happy for the chance to go to the beach and hopped up on Sam's handlebars. They rode together through the side streets that crisscrossed down the hill and then sped across the Pacific Highway. Laughing, Hayley jumped off the sturdy handlebars into the sand while Sam locked her teal bike. Sam wore her bathing suit under her clothes, so she peeled off her T-shirt and shorts, adjusted her bikini, and raced for the water. Hayley simply took off her hoodie and sprinted after Sam in her shorts and T-shirt. Off they went, splashing in the cool water and floating over the waves. They giggled when two boys paddled by on their surfboards and winked at them. Sam's eyes glittered and she stared in awe as they watched the boys skillfully ride the waves, showing off all their neat tricks. Hayley splashed Sam with a ton of salty water and hooted with laughter while Sam coughed and spluttered.

"What," Sam shrieked, "was that for?"

"One, you were in a trance watching those boys, and two, it's almost five-thirty. We ought to get moving." They dragged themselves out of the water and walked up the beach.

"Well, I'm sorry that I took an interest in them. You have Adrian, but I have no one, Hales. Adrian, the tall boy with the tanned skin, mocha brown hair, hazel eyes, and muscular legs…"

"Oh for Pete's sake," Hayley grunted, "he liked me in fifth grade, Sammy. Two years ago."

"Sure, whatever," Sam teased as she dried herself off and gave the towel to Hayley.

*   *   *

The next afternoon, Hayley returned home from a morning of grocery shopping and visiting her grandparents. The heat of the day made her feel sweaty. Stepping into the bathroom, the cool water beckoned to her as she placed her towel upon the bench and stepped into the shower. Humming a tune, Hayley hurriedly washed her hair and cleansed her face. Before long, she turned off the water and squeezed the dregs of conditioner out of her hair. When she reached around the shower curtain for her towel, an orange paw appeared and pushed her hand away.

Adie, her stepfather's male tabby cat, crouched upon her towel, his enlarged pupils gazing up at her. Smiling, Hayley shoved the big ball of fur off her towel and wrapped the towel around herself. Adie remained seated on the bench and uttered an irritated meow. "Oh, stop it Adie," Hayley scolded. She changed and logged onto her laptop to chat with friends. She flopped onto her bed, chatting to her cousin Emily and two of her classmates. Adie ambled into the room and leaped up onto the bed beside her, demanding attention. Hayley stroked Adie as he lay curled at the foot of her bed. He meowed at her when she stopped, as if to ask why the patting ceased. Scratching under his chin, Hayley listened to his loud purr. Her mother abruptly appeared and leaned against the doorframe.

"Hales, Dad and I are going out for dinner. We should be back between nine and ten."

"Okay," Hayley replied, her mind calculating how much time she would be home alone. Three hours would be plenty of time to return to the attic and continue her search.

"Remember to feed Adie because you know that stubborn feline really hates waiting," her mother mentioned, pointing to the fat tabby as she spoke.

"I always do," Hayley replied. Her mother came over to her bed and caressed her freckled cheek. After kissing Hayley on the forehead, her mother left the room. She wished that her mother had been truthful all along so that they're close relationship wouldn't be damaged. She returned to checking her email and chatting.

"Hales, we're going now," her stepfather shouted from downstairs.

"Hales," Hayley hissed quietly, "you don't have the right to call me Hales, stepfather." She silently counted down the seconds until her parents locked the door. "Five, four, three, two…one!" Then, Hayley raced up the flight of stairs to where the attic's creaky ladder lowered from. She felt slightly uneasy about going up there at night, in the dark, alone. "Stop it," Hayley scolded herself, "it's your dad or the dark." Taking in a deep breath, she pulled down the latch that swung open the "hole-in-the-ceiling" attic door and unfolded the ladder attached to it.

Clambering up the ladder, she pulled herself up into blackness. As her eyes adjusted to the dim room, she gazed at the luminous full moon, its brightness filtering through the interstices of the filth on the window. She returned to the old chest where she first discovered her father, knelt down, and removed its contents to analyze everything again. Coming across her father's photo triggered a smile, and Hayley felt, at that moment, that he wanted to reunite with her as much as she wanted with him. Yet try as she might, Hayley found little in the chest that could help her with the research.

Closing the lid, she moved on to the chest next to it, a moss-green rectangular one with several chips that revealed its old age. The lid wouldn't budge, confusing Hayley, until she spotted the keyhole. She rolled her eyes, frustrated that her search seemed static. Without the key, the chest couldn't help at all. There were approximately two hours before her parents returned, and she needed to absorb as much information about her father as possible.

Not wanting to waste any more time, Hayley opened up another chest, this time similar to the first one. There lay the clothes that she bought last summer, the clothing she wanted to come back and get. For the next half an hour, Hayley hunted through the pile of "next-size-up" items to choose some stylish garments for the season. There were mini-skirts, T-shirts, jeans, shorts, and camisoles of every color in the chest. After much elimination, Hayley finally selected twelve pieces of new clothing that fit her well. She placed them by the hole in the floor and decided to hunt for the key.

Opening a cupboard, Hayley squinted in the dark to make out the shapes within the closet. She reached for something that resembled a key; however, picked up a rusty thimble. "Where is this key?" thought Hayley. "Why does the stupid chest require a key anyway?" Frustrated, Hayley plopped down on the rough, wooden floor. "Looking for clues in the attic just isn't enough, is it? But I'll search far and wide to locate Dad." She flashed back to yesterday morning, when she first found out that Rob wasn't her real father. Less than forty-eight hours ago. The neon glow of her watch showed eight forty-five, giving her a maximum of an hour before she must leave the attic. It comforted her to be able to see the driveway from the attic. She remembered the shock when she noticed the tattered Christmas sweater with several keys on top, instead of a chest filled with chic attire.

"That's it!" Hayley shouted as she jumped up, scraping the backs of her thighs on the sandpapery wood. Hurrying to the black chest, Hayley pulled the top open and saw the tarnished keys lying on the off-white sweater with the Christmas tree on the front. She smirked while picking them up, impressed at herself for recalling where they were. "Here goes," whispered Hayley as she held her breath. She tried one key with no success. The second slid into the keyhole but wouldn't turn. "C'mon, please work," Hayley begged. The third key slid into the keyhole...and turned.

"Yes!" Hayley yelled. She flung open the lid in her excitement and what lay in the chest thrilled her even more. Memoirs from her mother's time with her father filled a third of the chest. Love letters, gifts, and even a photo album in pristine condition lay within. "No wonder Mama keeps all this locked up," Hayley muttered. She spent the next hour or so reading every letter and sifting through the pages of the album, examining each photo.

By the time she finished, Hayley knew where they had holidayed and when, as well as a number of their most memorable moments together. She located evidence of several major events that her parents took part in, such as a naming competition for the town square that her father won. These events could help her gather knowledge of her father's life. She placed the album back into the chest and began to clean up. Just then, the moonlight disappeared and beams of bright yellow shone through the window.

"Their back!" Hayley yelped and raced to finish tidying up. Scampering down the ladder, she folded it into the attic floor and locked its door. Racing to her room, she slumped into her beanbag chair when she heard footsteps coming up the stairs. Her stepfather opened the door cautiously, but upon seeing light, strolled into the room.

"Hm, I thought you might have been asleep," said Rob, looking at the lime walls covered with a myriad of posters and photographs.

"Nope, not me," she replied, forcing a smile.

"Go to sleep, okay? You've got school tomorrow."

"Okay...Dad," Hayley choked the word out.

"Goodnight, sweetheart," he murmured, planting a kiss on the top of her head. "I love you."

As soon as Rob left, Hayley jumped on to her bed, turned over, and let her head hang over the edge. "Why does this have to happen to me? I love Dad–I mean Rob–and if none of this occurred I wouldn't feel so torn. If I meet my real dad, can my relationship with Dad still remain the same? We are so close..." A single tear rolled down her cheek as she thought about how life would be without her stepfather to guide her. The thoughts whirled in her head as emotions drained her energy and tears began to spill over her eyelids. She shut down the computer, changed into pajamas, and crawled under the striped covers. Adie leapt up onto the bed, mewing softly and pushing his nose beneath Hayley's hand. She pulled Adie close and buried her face in his fur, soaking him in tears. With Adie in her arms, Hayley cried herself to sleep.

After a stressful morning of rushing, Hayley slid into an empty desk at school and placed her math books on the table. Adrian, who happened to be sitting beside her, turned to her.

"Here comes the Hitchkins," he declared, mocking Ms. Hitchkins nagging voice.

The laughter muffled when Ms. Hitchkins strode into class and started to write lengthy equations on the dusty army green chalkboard. Sam kicked Hayley's heel and leaned forward.

"Tanned skin, tall, sporty, smart, et cetera."

"Annoying, boy-crazy, obsessive, and did I mention desperate?" hissed Hayley, pinching Sam's elbow at the same time.

"Girls, is there something you'd like to share with the class? It must be extremely amusing judging by the giggling going on over there."

"Not at all, Ms. Hitchkins," Sam replied casually, rolling her eyes once Ms. Hitchkins turned around to the whiteboard.

"Just that Sam's boy-crazy," murmured Hayley teasingly.

After school the next day, Hayley rode two blocks to the public library. She'd gotten this far with her research and if she gave up now, she would certainly regret it. Besides, without the research she would have to hide the secret for the rest of her life. Now that would make life utterly miserable. Two men chatted by the library entrance as Hayley sauntered by.

"Did you see that there has been a drug crime?" said one man.

"Really? Another one?"

"Yes, I heard it on the radio coming here. Apparently, they have several suspects that they wish to question."

"I heard about that one. It's been on the news for a while now," Hayley thought to herself. Once inside, she wandered around trying to locate the newspaper rack. "Hm," thought Hayley, "where is this section?" Suddenly, someone tapped her on the shoulder. There stood Mrs. Wiggs, the librarian, her glasses balanced precariously on the tip of her nose, as if the slightest bump would send them flying.

"What are you looking for, dear child?"

"Oh, I'm just looking for the newspaper shelf, where they keep news from years ago."

"I see. Well, you're almost there. See that orange sign above the shelf? Turn right there, and you should see it in front of you. Why, some of the stuff there is almost as old as me!" Mrs. Wiggs chuckled to herself as Hayley thanked her.

Hayley chose one a newspaper dated 1993, the year written on the picture in the attic. "January...January," she muttered as she flipped through the papers. Hayley read through all the headlines of each paper in 1993, from January to July, but nothing appeared that caught her attention.

"How about we try closer to my birth?" Hayley said as she looked for papers from 1996, the year prior to her birth. She skimmed the headlines of these papers, right through to September. She came across an obituary for a Carris. The title stated: Obituary–Alexander Christian Carris. Her eyes moistened as she read the heartfelt obituary. She squinted to make out the faded name scrawled underneath the eulogy. Paul Carris. Her father had written the eulogy. Shocked, Hayley whispered, "He lost his brother around the time we left him!"

Stuffing the paper back on the rack, Hayley left the library's newspaper section. Her family would want her home before it got dark. She smiled at the librarian as she walked by. The librarian asked, "Did you find what you were looking for?"

"Yes, thank you for your help." Hayley smiled and opened the wide mahogany doors into the chilly breeze. Shivering, she unlocked her snow-colored bike and rode off into the twilight.

Hayley opened the front door to see both her parents standing there in the living room. Her mother crossed her arms while her stepfather stood there, a bewildered expression on his face. "Hayley Elizabeth Ramirez," her mother said.

"Shoot," Hayley thought, "I am in serious trouble now."

"What is it?" Hayley replied hesitantly.

"We all know how secrets have zero tolerance in this household. You've broken this rule and damaged the relationship we all share."

Hayley rolled her eyes, "Okay, I'm a smart enough girl to figure out where this is leading. Yes, I found Dad's picture in the attic. Yes, I know you lied to me by making me believe that Rob is my dad. And yes, I have been trying to find things to lead me to my real dad."

Rob's eyes widened at Hayley's remark. She felt bad about being so harsh, especially to her stepfather, but they kept her from knowing the truth. "Stephanie, what do you suppose we do?" said Rob. "I mean all she's sure of now is that you're her mother."

"I'll tell you what we'll do," Hayley snapped. "We'll explain this situation to me so I don't feel like I've been cheated my entire life by the two people I adore most."

"Hayley, stop that right now!" Stephanie growled.

"How can I?" cried Hayley. "The main adults in my family lead me to believe that my stepfather is my father. What would have taken place if I never found out? I know you weren't planning on telling me. I have a right to know who my real father is, even if I don't choose to include him in my life. I'd like to meet him, which is why Sam and I have been trying so hard to find clues in the attic and around town. He's my dad! Why should a girl be punished for wanting to meet her dad?" Hayley covered her face with her hands and wept. Rob breathed deeply and studied Hayley, a look of sympathy in his eyes. Then he bent down and brushed away some of the curls from her face.

"Hayley, please listen to me," Rob whispered. "I can't even begin to imagine how difficult this must be for you. But honey, we had a reason for it––a good one. When I was slightly younger than you, my parents decided to split up after months of terrible fighting and arguing. Witnessing this transpire between my parents broke my heart and when my mother married another man, I couldn't ever able to love my stepfather."

Hayley understood that feeling completely, remembering her attitude about the situation the other night.

"Hayley," her mother broke in, "don't think that Rob decided this. I chose it because I wanted you to be able to love your stepfather and feel that you lived in a caring family. Besides, your dad wasn't a very glorious time of my life, and I don't think he has the values that I desire for my own daughter."

Hayley gave a loud sniff and remained obstinate. "He's my father and I should have a right to meet him," she insisted. "Rob, you got to meet your father. Heck, you got to live with him. You loved him. I want the chance to at least meet mine."

Rob nodded and seemed to empathize with her. "Okay Hayley, you made a good point and I acknowledge how difficult all this must be for you. If you really want to meet your father, it's fine by me." Rob turned to Stephanie and stated. "What do you think?"

Stephanie paused for a moment and Hayley could tell that she felt worried. "Mama, what is it? What's the matter?"

"I just don't think it is a good idea. I mean, if he treated you the same way he…no Hayley. I won't let you."

"Stephanie," Rob coaxed, "you know she has a right to meet her father. It's not like he'll harm his own daughter."

Hayley gazed up at her mother and saw a flustered look upon her face. "Please," Hayley implored, "one day——whether it's now or later——I will meet him. You can't expect me not to be curious now that I know he exists."

"Fine, but you are really pushing me out of my comfort zone. Let me just say this: he's not what you think he is." At this, Hayley's mother left the room. Rob gave Hayley a bear hug and followed Stephanie upstairs. As Hayley expected, their bedroom door closed quietly and a muffled conversation began. "There's no doubt about what they are debating," Hayley thought to herself, "so I'm gonna eavesdrop. And so much for not keeping secrets, Mother."

Silent as a mouse, Hayley crept up the wood stairs and tiptoed into the guest bathroom next to her parent's bedroom. Eavesdropping on her parents from the bathroom seemed second nature to her, for she'd done this since the age of five.

"How could she have found it?" Rob asked. "And what's more, why aren't you comfortable with Hayley reuniting with her real father? She'll be a mess if we forbid her from meeting him because she knows that he's out there somewhere. She is aware that he exists."

"It's all perfectly clear to me now. When I gave her the directions to get clothing, she would have looked in the other black and gold chest rather than the one with her next-size-up clothing. That's how she came across it."

Rob repeated his pressing question again. "Why are you so worried?"

"Look Rob," sighed Stephanie, "when I dated him—true love. Until I realized that he dealt in small crimes. I noticed it by the substantial amounts of cash he kept depositing into the bank. He received money from the men leading the felonies. They were minor involvements, but

I felt betrayed and angry all the same. I threatened to split up with him if he didn't stop. He tried to, but couldn't manage it. He begged me to stay yet I still left because I knew that it would be impossible to raise Hayley with a criminal in the house."

The rest of her mother's talk became a jumble of words as Hayley began to fathom what her mother said. "No," Hayley hissed, "I refuse to let that get in the way. He won't be anything like a criminal now. When my mother left him, pregnant with me, he would have been heartbroken and stopped these misdemeanors immediately. I mean, imagine losing your fiancée or wife and your first daughter. Your unborn baby! Yes, he would have given up his crime life the minute we left to try to make amends. That's what my father would do."

Just then Adie scratched at the bathroom door, crying so loudly that all of America could probably hear him. "Shut up Adie!" thought Hayley, rolling her eyes. She listened intently and heard the conversation die down and footsteps approach the door.

"Hayley? Are you in there?" Rob's voice called out.

"Yes, and the cat wants in."

"Well, I gather that. New Zealand can probably hear him. Well, we are going to bed. Go to bed soon, too. I have a surprise for you tomorrow morning."

"Okay, thanks. Goodnight." Hayley replied. "A surprise? What kind of surprise?" she pondered, leaving the bathroom after brushing her teeth.

Hayley, awakened by the sound of her cell phone alarm, got dressed and trudged down the stairs to breakfast. The smell of pancakes wafted up to her and she trembled because of the delicious aroma. What a lovely surprise. Hayley sat down at the table and waited for her father to put a plate of pancakes drowned in syrup in front of her. Seconds later, Hayley's pancakes arrived. As she wiped her eyes groggily, she noticed a slip of syrupy paper lying across her breakfast. She picked it up and read it. It said:

Paul Carris–79 Redwood Street, Costa Mesa. Tel. # 6342 - 9081

Hayley gasped and stared at her stepfather. "Rob, are you serious?"

"Don't thank me, thank your mother. She gave me the information."

Hayley leapt and gave Rob and her mother a hug and jumped up and down with excitement.

"It is a half-day at school today, so she called him and told him that we'd bring you at one. Is that all right?"

"Perfect! Thanks so much!"

Hayley quickly went and got ready so she could tell Sam the great news. She dashed outside once she grabbed her backpack and bike, flying down the street. Dodging cars and pedestrians, Hayley pedaled to school as fast she could and threw her bike into the rack, not bothering to lock it up. "Sam!" she screamed while she dashed up the hallway.

"What?" shouted Sam.

"You'll…never believe…it!" Hayley stammered, out of breath from running and riding.

"Oh my goodness! Did Adrian asked you out?"

"No, Sammy. Not everything is about Adrian. Anyway, I'm meeting my father after school at one!"

"Seriously? Can I––no, that would be rude."

"It's fine. You can come along and Rob will drop you at home after a little. Rob isn't going into the office today."

"I'm so happy for you!"

The rest of the morning seemed to creep by slowly and Hayley found herself constantly looking at the clock. At twelve, the bell rung so Hayley and Sam bolted to their bikes and sped to Hayley's house. They shared a lunch of potato salad and chicken breast while predicting what meeting Paul would be like.

"I've never seen you girls so excited." Stephanie laughed. "Calm down so you don't give yourselves stomach aches."

Shortly after lunch, they all piled into the car and drove to Costa Mesa. As they neared, Hayley's heart began to beat faster and faster. "This is it," she thought, "this is the moment I've waited for." They eventually found the house and climbed out of the car.

"We'll stay here, but you two go ahead. Go on, you chose this, Hales." Nerves certainly weren't going to keep Hayley from her dream. Arm in arm, the two girls walked up to the door and Hayley rang the doorbell. Suddenly, the door opened and there stood Paul Christopher Carris, Hayley's father.

"Wow, I wasn't expecting a second daughter." Paul joked. Hayley gazed up at him and he held his arms out to her. "Hales. Hayley Elizabeth Carris." As they stood there embracing, Hayley felt relieved of all her previous premonitions. "You must be Sam," Paul said to Sam over Hayley's shoulder.

"That's me," Sam grinned. "Look, I'm going to go now and let you to catch up, but it was lovely to meet you Mr. Carris.

"Please, call me Paul."

"Bye Hales," Sam shouted as she jumped into the car with Stephanie and Rob.

After they left, Hayley and her dad got in his car and drove to the nearby mall.

"I figured I should take you out to buy you some presents for you thirteenth birthday and all the other birthdays I missed. What do you want?"

"I already got my present. I got to meet my dad. That's a priceless present."

For the remainder of the afternoon, they shopped and snacked while finding out everything about each other. At four o'clock, they decided to go for a stroll in the afternoon sun. As they wandered down the street, Hayley heard police sirens in the distance. Her father looked in the direction of the sirens with a slightly distressed look. Hayley brushed it away. He probably interested in what caused the sirens.

"Let's go back to the mall now," he suggested. Their pace increased until they were almost running. The sirens began to get louder and Hayley worried. Why were they running? All of a sudden, a couple of police cars zoomed up the street and parked in front of them.

"Stop right there, you two!"

"Dad, what's going on?" Hayley asked, now terrified of the situation.

"I'll answer that," replied the police man who caught up to them. "Your father's been involved in a major drug dealing case that's run across all of California. A partner of your father turned him in when we questioned the man. He kept going on about how if he'd be thrown in jail, then so should his accomplices. Very convenient for us."

"What? That's not—possible," her voice quieted down as she recalled the words her mother had spoken. "...impossible to raise Hayley with a criminal in the house." She shuddered as the comment echoed in her mind.

"Dad, why?" Hayley asked. However, Paul only looked away and she watched several tears trickle down his face. Paul put his hands out for the cop to handcuff him.

Leaning forward, he murmured to the police officer, "This is my almost thirteen-year-old daughter. We reunited today after her mother left me years ago for this very same reason. It's an addiction that I can't control. Please Officer," he begged, "take her home to her mother and stepfather and explain the situation to them. Take her home and make sure she is safe." Her father looked sorrowfully at Hayley while tears of agony ran down his troubled face.

Another officer kindly took Hayley home, and her mother sobbed when she heard what occurred and confessed to them all that his criminal past was the reason behind her worries.

"I know," Hayley responded, "I heard you talking about it that night while I went to the bathroom. I heard you say that he'd been involved in delinquency, but I highly doubted that he still committed offenses."

"Hayley, I don't ever want you to see him again. He's not a good influence on you and I don't want you around him," declared Stephanie.

"Mama, why? He needs me in his life. Without someone to love, he will return to crime and never get a second chance. I still love him, and I know he still loves me because he felt ashamed. Please, let me be the positive influence in his life. Let me help him grow."

"Wow Hayley, you really have matured since this began. You're almost a teenager now and it shows, in a good way" Rob joked. "I'm extremely proud of your selflessness." Hayley blushed at her stepfather's compliment; however, her mother was not as easily persuaded.

"I'm reluctant to give him another chance, Hales," her mother explained. "It's transpired too many times before."

"Here's a proposal. How about you give me and him one chance, and if anything arises, all connections are cut? Please? I just want to give him another chance."

"Okay, one more chance. That's it. If he blows this, you'll never see him again."

Hayley breathed a sigh of relief. "Perfect. I—we—won't let you down."

The following afternoon, Hayley came home immediately and her stepfather drove her to the Costa Mesa police station and temporary prison. After organizing what would happen with the office at the front desk, Hayley waved good-bye to Rob and walked to the back of the station with the officer.

"We don't normally allow this kind of thing, but I can see that this is an extremely rare circumstance."

"Thank you so much," Hayley said.

"Hayley?" called Paul.

"I'm coming." The officer unlocked the door and let Hayley in. She ran into her father's arms and he wept.

"Hayley, I'm so sorry. I never meant for you to see me like this. I am addicted and I can't stop. With you, I stuffed things up but without you, I'm a total mess. Let me be part of your life or I won't remain sane. Please forgive me."

"Dad, I fought Mama and Rob to let me come back here and see you again. I'm not going to let you down by leaving you, that I can promise."

"I promise I won't ever commit another felony again, Hayley. I love you and you won't regret giving me this second chance."

"I love you too, Dad." With this, they embraced again and at that moment, Hayley knew she did the right thing.

CIA

By

Gershom Chan

BANG! BANG! BANG! THE SOUND OUTSIDE WAS SO LOUD, I HEARD THE sounds of the guards shooting at the two people who were running for the fence. I suddenly realized that if my brother, I, and my best friend were ever to make a jailbreak; and escape the death sentence that we had received, we would have to be very careful. But there was only one huge problem; the execution date was only six days away, so death was only footsteps away from us.

I lived in cell 52. It was as larger than the normal ones cuz of the prison shaping. It had three beds and a window, which was unfortunately barred, on both sides. The room was cold. The light in the dark corner was rather dim, even from the window it was dim. The life in the cell we did not deserve, we did not do anything. We were just on our usual CIA mission and fate chose us to be framed for the deaths of all the peoplein the building. *Knock, Knock, Knock,* The door was being knocked by the CO. Mr. Robert Black. A big fat cold stupid prison CO.

"Wake up prison rats," he hollered at us. I got out of my cold stone and rock hard bed; and walked out the door for the daily prisoner check, it was part of the daily routine. Next we all had to go to breakfast to eat.

Steven Got in line in between his brother Jacob and his best friend Zander, They grabbed their disgusting looking food and sat at their usual table. As soon as they sat down Steven said, "We need to break out as soon as possible."

"Don't you think we know that." replied Jacob.

"Yes I know that Jacob but I think I might have a plan, I spent the past month that we have been here, creating a plan and I."

"How was your day yesterday." Zander interrupted when he saw the Co. Robert walking their way.

"So", Steven continued when Robert was out of sight. "My plan will work fine if we all do our jobs."

"And what might that be?" Jacob replied.

"Well we will have to do a bunch of work but it is worth our freedom."

"Great." Zander replied in a rather sleepy tone.

I will tell you the rest of the plan back in the room.

So they talked for a little while longer *Ring! Ring! Ring!* the breakfast bell rang loud, breakfast was over and it was time for the boys to get back to their cell. On the way back to their cell, they heard a huge popping noise it was in the kitchen resulting in a sudden fire alarm. Everyone made a run for it in different directions. we all attempt to make an escape. Suddenly out of nowhere a huge banging sound came from Robert, "Quiet all you prison rats he yelled. No one is getting out of the mess got it."

So Steven and all of the other prisoners stopped running and making noise. When they made a head count of the prisoners none were missing. Robert discovered the alarm was set of by the smoke detector in the kitchen. Someone rigged the stove to smoke to make a feeble escape which failed. As Steven returned to the Cell he was reminded of the unpleasant thought of the escape being hard and near impossible. Finally back at their cell Steven began to lay the cards on the table, (or in this case the bed).

"So." Steven began. "Here is what we will have to do.

We first need to break the bars on our windows and yes I have already come up with how we are going to do that. We first need to get in to the mess hall that will be the first and easy job. Second I need one of you to plant a piece of plastic on the night shift heaters so it will make smoke. Step two we need to retrieve a chainsaw from the machine shop to cut the bars on our windows because that is our exit. Step four We need to run across the field right behind the spotlight so that we will have a minute to burn the fence with the tools we get. Finally we use the contraption you mad Jacob and we get over the fence."

"Hold on, Hold on, just say that we can actually pull this off, and it is a big if, how will we get away on foot?" Asked Jacob.

"Well," Replied Steven, "Before we were arrested I thought we might go to Prison so I stashed weapons, clothes, a car, and money all in a storage down the road. So once we get past the fence all we need to do is run down the road to the storage get the things and get out of town. Finally once we are out of this despicable place we can give the old boys a call they can get us a private jet out of the country in less than a day.

"This Plan of yours sounds great, a bit nuts, but none the less great." replied Zander.

"I agree, let's try it. after all we don't have much to lose. Jacob followed.

"Your plan won't work." Said Robert. A sudden panic came through the three. There was a brief moment of silence. Then they herd Tim's loud voice talking to Robert. Tim was one of Robert's friends and coworkers. They were playing chess.

"Man I thought for a minute that we were dead meat" Said Zander in relief.

*   *   *

Later on that day we all gathered in the workroom to fix the pipes which were broken, they had just found out what was Tim's plan to fix the pipes it would take at least a week. All of us were given tools to use to fix the dirty and rusty pipes under the prison. We would be mending the mendable and replacing the ones that cannot be mended.

We worked in the sewers for three hours or so and figured out when to swipe some of the equipment for our plan . "What do we do now Steve?" Said Jacob.

"We will need to gather the supplies that we can first and then we should gather the ones we can't later." Replied Steven.

"So what will we need?" Asked Zander.

"We will first need a bottle of antirust. I think we can get that tomorrow at work hour. We will also need toothpaste. Finally we will need a bottle of soda. With those we will have our first step to freedom."

So it was dark and damp in the cell that they prepared it all in the cell which was soon going to be emptied. While they decided that the best course of action was. They had many problems to solve "We have a problem," Said Zander, "We have been moved to F block so we Do not have Access to the windows."

"That is bad relay bad."

"I also discovered that our plan to get that tool during PI is not going to happen."

"Why."

"Because they also switched PI officers, We now have Peter running PI."

"That is bad, very bad, there is no way we are getting out of here."

As Steven walked around the empty dark and stone cold cell, he pondered the thought of not being to escape the unjust judgment.

Time passed on the day went by with not much excitement. The rest of the day he considered the thought of having to really face death without a doubt the thought of death was an unpleasant thought to think about.

He thought of the possibilities of escaping and finally came to the number ten to one of succeeding on this crazy endeavor that he planned. The next morning as the sun rose they could hear the ever defining noise of the other prisoners waling at the bright morning light.

"Shut your wailing" I could hear the Guards yell.

"This is such a pain" My brother said in a low and steady voice.

"Yes it is." I responded with no enthusiasm. Today is the day they were going to be moved to another block the transfer was taking place during the afternoon right after lunch-break. So they had to figure out how to not get transferred. I saw a prisoner reading a poem, which read…

Thank you
Thank you for each and every day,
For the house in which play;
For the green out my door,
And the warmth on the floor.
Thank thee for the food,
For my very good mood;
Thank you for my mother,
And especially my little brother.
Thank you for the stars,
And the planet of mars;
How I thank you for the sky,
And also the birds that fly.
Thank you for my dad,
A man who is never sad;
Thank you for the cross,
By the way do you floss.
Thank thee lord!
Thank you for everything each and every day;
the sun's amazing ray,
Thank you for the trees,
And the helpful bees.
I thank you every day,
In this I pray,
Amen.

I did not know why he was thanking the lord in his reading this prayer, I figured that everyone would hate God for letting them end up in here. But he was thanking God for his life I did not understand. As I sat down I thought about the day and what could happen I knew that if we got switched we would never get out of prison so we had to think of something. As I pondered those thoughts the guards took us out for breakfast.

"So what's the plan." Zander inquired of me.

"Well, I think I figured it out."

"So?"

"First we will need to get into F block during lunch. Second we'll need to mess up the F block to make sure that we do not get moved there. Finally we need to get back to lunch without getting noticed."

"That's a lot of work"

"I know Zander, But we don't have a choice."

"Okay, so how will we get out of the lunch room?"

"Well, I think that we can bypass the guards on the way to the lunch hall through the guards restroom. Then we can go to F block during the guard shift the guards will not catch us than we destroy F block so we cannot be moved."

"I like the idea."

"So do I." Said my brother.

"Let's eat now." I said.

"Okay," Said Zander.

As the day continued on I was thinking of how I ever got in this mess, I wish I did not have to go through all this. I wish that I could have taken it all back I wish that I never shot the guy I wish I could have stopped but now I am stuck with prison unless I get out.

After breakfast I went to the yard for work duty. The Job today was to dig a hole ten feet deep and five feet wide with your partner. We dug for such a long time, the pain in my hands was nearly unbearable. If I did not have the breaks in between shifts my hands would be gone.

After the work duty we got an hour before lunch in which I returned to my dark and cold stone cell and lay on my bed thinking about the plan. I decided that if we were to ever get out it would be a miracle but I also it would even be a greater miracle if we stayed out of prison. It was time for lunch we headed down the hall as planned we slipped F block when the guards switched as planned with not many problems once in F block we tampered with everything the toilets the cell doors the rooms. The cameras were not online yet because there was no one living in there yet, which was good for us because we did not have a problem messing up the whole place.

We spent a good load of time messing up the whole place and right when lunch ended we slipped back into lines going back to the cells.

"Who in the name of heaven dared to mess up F Block?" Yelled Robert.

There was a Silent pause no one spoke. "That's it, I have had it with you people You will be cleaning up F Block until it is spotless. No basketball, no break. Until this cell is pure clean you will only sleep eat and clean. Do you got that!”

“Yes sir,” We all replied.

“Good.” He said in a lower voice this time. “Get to work. Now!!!”

We worked and worked and worked but because we made sure the destruction was thorough, The cells would not be clean any time soon. So we would not be moving.

“Good job boys.” I said to Zander and Jacob “We got what we wanted. “Perfect”

“Nice thinking Steven”

“Thanks Zander.”

“ No prob.”

“You two shut up and get back to work” Hollered one of the guards.

“Okay, sorry sir.” I said.

“It won’t happen again” Yelled Zander.

“Good” He hollered back.

The day continued, we worked for such a long time when it was time for dinner we all were egger to get off work. The food was especially good today, because we had worked for such a long time it felt so good to eat warm (kind of) good food. The plan was falling together. We knew that working in F block would help us get the tools to get out.

The next day was the same working and eating. “Take a break.” yelled one of the guards. “We need to find out why Robert disappears every day at 10:07.” I told Zander. “I will follow him and find out.” Said Zander.”

“No I will go you stay here and cover my shift”

“Okay, fine”

I walked out of the cell and towards the guard rooms. I snuck in and sat in one of the empty lockers. I waited for the longest ten minutes in my life but it payed off. I saw Robert walk into the guard room.

“Stop” I heard a deep slow voice.

“Yes sir.” Robert replied.

I could not tell who the strange man was he was dressed in a suit with a long black detective cloak on the outside. He wore a detective hat, and carried a long black and silver cane with a dragon head at the top.

"Did you do what I told you" said the mysterious man in the cloak.

"Um yes sir the people that were causing you problems are not in the world anymore."

"Good"

Ting I heard a sound from across the room one of the guards walked out and pointed a gun at Robert and the Mystery man.

"Hands up said the guard."

Both of their hands were up, I caught a glimpse of the man's eyes; one was black and the other red I did not know who it was but his eyes were like the devil.

"I knew you were breaking the rules and committing crimes Robert, and who are you? The one the cloak."

"I am not of your concern but since you have seen me you must die good by."

I saw him click the side of his cane. Suddenly the mouth of the dragon opened on the cane and a spark sparked, suddenly fire sprayed out and completely covered and burned the guard he did not have a chance to scream he was dead to fast.

"What a pity he looked so kind."

"Remember what I said get rid of the three CIA agents who were assigned to you."

"Yes, sir."

"I made sure they were in prison so they would be easier to kill so do your job."

"Yes, sir."

But I knew that there was yet one more person in the room who was not supposed to be there it was Tomson the prison rat he had spied on everyone and he also was very smart I heard a small hissing sound from the back room, I knew what he did. He had loosened the pipe in the prison and let the flammable gas pour out. Clink he slipped up when the sound rung Robert pulled out his gun, found him, and grabbed him. Sir I found him holding him up.

"Step back Robert." He grabbed his cane and dropped it. "Listen you little rat do you really think that I am stupid? Why I heard the hissing from the pipe I know that there are flammable gasses in the prison system. You thought you outsmarted me but really you were

stupid." He lifted his arm flicked his wrist and suddenly a knife shot out
of the end of his sleeve. Rat had no time to run he was down in seconds.
Suddenly it came to me I knew who the mystery man was I have seen
him before once seven years ago. I remembered those two weapons the
cane and knife they were both made by him, Professor Demoriheala.

"Remember your job Robert."

Suddenly the mysterious professor disappeared into the shadows. I
saw Robert grab the dead bodies, and place him in a bag, zipped it up,
and shoved it into a locker, shut it and locked it. When he was gone
I snuck back into F block. This was bad, Professor Demoriheala was
dangerous and not to mention powerful. I did not know who he really
was but all I knew was that he was a weapons expert and that he was a
dangerous criminal who was unfortunately a genius.

When I got back to F block it was almost time for lunch.

"What happened?" Said Zander.

"We are dead, guess who put us here who framed us for those
murders, who is still trying to kill us. Professor Demoriheala. "

"Oh no we are dead."

"I know which means we have to get out of here now. How far are
we?"

"Well, we have the tools to cut through the bars. Um you told me
that the guardroom next door is gassed and flammable. So we can get
the alarm cover; and once the alarm goes off we cut through the bars
after we can shut the shades and pretend we are asleep. The spotlight
sweeps past the space in between us and the space in between the fence
every seventy seconds, so we will have enough time to get there. The
spotlight in between the fence and the wall is sixty meters and the
light will sweep past every one hundred seconds, so we can get the
contraption Jacob made working and we get over the fence. Once we
are out we head for the woods and to the storage and get our stuff and
head off to freedom."

I knew we had to leave now. It was time to go. Today was the day
we get our freedom. The equipment was in place. Everything was ready
it was time. The day continued so fast before I knew it I was in bed
pretending I was asleep. *Ding Ding Ding* My watch rung twelve. It was
time.

We grabbed our things and were ready. It began I cracked the hole in our cell and turned the blow torch, in seconds the fire alarm went off. RIIIIIING. It began.

"Saw Jacob Zander."

"We are trying okay"

"Okay"

The alarms were ringing so loud we were glad. The guards were yelling the running hectically around the sounds of screaming and gunfire was all we heard other than the alarm. The bars were harder to saw than we thought I decided to try burning them also so I heated them for a couple seconds and the went back to sawing after ten minutes the bars broke enough for us squeeze through. We all got through We walked out it was time to run to the fence but there was a problem that we did not think would happen there were 4 spotlights turned on there was no getting across without being seen. We were dead we could not go back and we could not move forward we were going to die.

"What are we going to do?" yelled Zander"

"I don't know." I replied.

"Come on, you are the smartest person in the world. You were the best CIA agent they ever had. You can do this."

"Let me think!"

"Okay."

It was too late the spotlight was ten seconds away from us. We would be caught. nine, eight I still could not think straight six, five, four, I figured it out, two I jumped up and ripped the power cords out the spotlight turned off and we ran like the wind. I grabbed the torch and burned the fence with no problem. We ran across the space in between the fence and the wall. Once we got in range we fired the contraption Jacob made. It grabbed on to upper part of the wall and it had a rope attached to it. I climbed first Zander second and Jacob Third. We all were over in no time. We cut the rope tied it to the wall and climbed down.

"Freedom!" Yelled Zander.

"We are not home free yet we still have to get out of here." I hollered back.

"Let's go." Jacob scolded at us both.

We ran on and on we heard the gunfire and the sounds of the dogs at our heals. They found out. We ran on and on until we got the storage

I picked the lock with a paper clip that I picked up back at the prison. I opened the door and inside was filled with stuff new clothes costumes a couple weapons and a car. We all got changed and my hair changed from a Black to a red. My eyes were now green. I had lighter color skin and I had a pair of glasses. The others changed Also they did not look like themselves at all. We all picked up our weapons I carried a P99 hand gun in my shoulder holster. I also had a Derringer attached to a contraption on my left arm the contraption would spring if i flicked my wrist, and the Derringer would pop out automatically. It would shoot at whatever I pointed it at when I flicked. Zander carried two Uzis one in the left holster one in the right. Jacob carried a Glock handgun and a briefcase that had an MP7 in side. Which was rigged with a trigger at the sop of the case so the case could fire. We were ready we all got in the car ad drove off.

As we entered the highway there were a group of cops at a road block. We stopped at the road block.

"Hello officer, how may I help you" I said in a British accent.

"Hi can I see your identification."

"Sure mate." I said maintaining the British voice. I handed him my driver license (fake).

"Okay he who are they."

"Well mate he is my brother he is my other brother and we all want go to see the tower in Chicago downtown."

"What is that under your coat?"

"What mate?"

"Your jacket, take it off."

"Sir I can't."

"Why"

"Um uh well you see, uh."

"He has a tumor that he does not want seen it looks bad." Said Jacob.

"Hm well okay, You can go."

We drove on past the road block and on to freedom. We drove on and on, we stopped by a holiday inn to stay the night we all stayed in one room. We all got some sleep but before dawn we left and were on the road again. I decided to call my friend who worked for the MI6.

He knew our situation so I wanted to see if we could get a job for the M16. He picked up.

"Hello"

"Hey Mac."

"Steven hello you got out of prison I knew you would."

"Hey I was wondering if you can help us get a job or something."

"No problem I am sending a jet right now you will be MI6 in no time.

"Seriously?"

"Yes my friend just tell me where you are."

"Not that I am not happy, nut why are you so nice."

"You are my friend and you saved my life twice I will help you."

"Okay thanks man."

"No problem mate."

We were in the U.K. and part of the MI6 In no time. We were took 6 months to train and do everything else but fate now was on our side. We had our first mission.

"Steven you and you brother along with Zander are hereby given your first mission. Your mission is to bring Professor Demoriheala to Justice do you got that."

"Yes sir." we all said.

"Steven, you are now 27X0, Jacob you are 27C0, Zander you are 21X0. You Know your mission go."

"Yes sir."

"And one more thing if you fail the whole of U.K. and U.S. will not be here anymore. So don't fail."

"Sir we will proudly do our duty for queen and country. I walked out the door.

Bang! Bang! Bang! "Steven get down." Yelled Zander.

"I know I know." I hollered back.

We were stuck behind two desks, we were in a shoot out in a insurance office. We had been chasing Professor Demoriheala For three weeks now and were running out of time but his goons were shooting at us from across the room and we were almost out of ammo.

"Jacob ware are you."

"I am downstairs and kind of preoccupied right now."

"Okay, but hurry up we are dying here."

"Okay I will try."

Bang! another shot came from the other end of this big room.

"We are going to die how many shots do you have left" He asked.

"Seven." I replied "You?"

"Two."

"Okay we are going to die but that does not matter now grab the bag of C4 and let's go."

We both made a dash for the door. Bang!

Escape from a Nightmare
By

Kai An Chee

"ARE THEY STILL BEHIND US?"

Carter kept his eyes straight ahead as he darted through the thick foliage. He glanced to the side, checking if anyone followed him. Carter's eyes teared up as the stinging wind blew towards him in a big gust, and his brown hair fell in front of his eyes. Nancy, Carter's sister, was out there in the forest somewhere. He wanted to call out to her, but didn't, for fear of being caught.

"He's over there! Get him!"

A tangle of angry voices echoed through the trees. Feet thundered towards Carter and crunched on the layers of leaves on the forest ground. Carter exhaled, his heart staring to pump faster and faster.

"Where's the little one?" The voices chorused again. Carter knew that "the little one" meant Nancy, his six-year-old sister. His breath caught in his throat as he thought of a million bad things that could happen if she were caught. He and Nancy had meant to stay together, but it was hard to do so in the middle of the thick forest surrounding the orphanage.

"Nancy!" Carter called out in a whisper, hoping that she would respond. "Nancy, where are you?"

"I haven't seen her," another voice said. Carter slowed to a stop and whipped around, searching to identify the speaker. His heart caught in his throat as another thousand bad possibilities exploded into his mind.

"Hi," a voice called. Carter breathed a sigh of relief; it was only Alice, a friend of his. Alice was one of the three people who Carter had run away from the orphanage with. Because they had grown up together, they were as close as biological siblings. There was also Alan, a sturdy, loyal boy who was fifteen, a year older than Carter, and Carter's younger sister Nancy. "Are you winded yet?" Alice asked.

Carter turned to Alice, frowning. "Don't do that. You scared me."

Alice smiled weakly, brushing the light hair out of her face. Although she smiled in a feeble attempt to show a positive attitude, Carter saw the strain that she tried to hide. Alice was Carter's closest friend. She was fourteen, the same age as Carter, with long dark hair and two big, dark eyes. She was slender, but not anywhere near skinny, and was constantly complaining about being too fat. "What do you want me to do? Call out my name when I come close to you?" Alice attempted another smile, which ended up looking like a grimace.

"That would be nice."

The sound of angry curses reminded Carter that they needed to go.

Carter started running; he knew that Alice would catch up. His heart sped up again as he remembered that this wasn't a normal day with his friends: today they were running away.

It had sounded like such a great idea to run away when the four of them were back at the orphanage. Carter, Alan, Alice, and Nancy had always been outcasts. They had been mistreated by bullies and caretakers alike, and had finally decided to run away after a particularly large boy had tried to break Nancy's arm after she had accidentally knocked over his cup of water. Life in the orphanage couldn't be any worse than life in the real world.

Carter spied a road through the trees and pointed to it, hoping that Alice could see it too. As they turned into the path, Carter's thoughts went to his sister. Would she be okay? Would she be able to find the little path? Carter tried hard to push the negative thoughts out of his head and dwell on the positive, but it was hard to do when his sister and best friend were gone. His breath came hard and fast as he stumbled on the rocks that littered the ground. It was very early in the morning, and the sun was staring to peek its head over the horizon. The sky shone brilliantly with a million different colors, pinks and purples and yellows and oranges in every hue. The round yolk of the sun shimmered in the distance, as if suspended by invisible cables. It was beautiful, and if Carter weren't running for his life, he would have stopped to appreciate it.

They wove through the trees without a backward glance. Carter ran fast and far; he was faster than Alice. Carter ran without slowing until his lungs burned and his legs screamed profanities in his ears. They had finally reached the little road that Carter had seen through the trees. It was a small, winding dirt path that looked untouched. Carter staggered back, catching his breath.

"Have we lost them?" he panted, staring back into the thick ring of forest that separated the orphanage from the outside world. Beside him, Alice sank down onto her knees and then onto her back. Beads of sweat trickled down her temple, and her hair stuck to her forehead. "I think so."

Carter stared back into the forest, his heart pumping again. Where were Nancy and Alan?

"Nancy!" Carter cried, running back into the forest. He cupped his hands around his mouth. "Nancy?" This time, Carter didn't care if the caretakers heard his voice and found him; it was better to be caught without Nancy and Alan than it was to go on not knowing what had happened to them.

Carter's heart beat in panic. He had lost both his best friend and his little sister so quickly! He dropped down onto his knees, a feeling of depression and fear creeping onto him. Carter felt utterly useless; he couldn't do anything right.

"Carter?" a voice called. Carter whipped around, nearly losing his balance and falling onto the damp moss. Behind him stood a little girl, about four feet and three inches tall, with messy brown hair and a smattering of freckles on her nose.

"Nancy!" Carter cried, running towards his sister and hugging her tightly. He took a deep breath, assuring himself that everything was okay. Then Carter noticed that Nancy was alone.

"Where's Alan?" he asked, his voice rising in pitch. He glanced back at Nancy, hoping for some good news.

Nancy hung her head. Her bottom lip quivered, making Carter feel something in the bottom of his stomach. "Oh no...Nancy, he's not..."

"They got him. They got Alan. He's back there now." Nancy buried her head in Carter's chest and cried.

Carter patted Nancy on the back, reeling in shock. Punishment at the orphanage was horrible. The caretakers beat disobedient children with wooden canes and leather belts, leaving welts and bruises that hurt for days. The sadistic caretakers enjoyed torturing the students: it gave them something entertaining to do. Whenever someone so much as stepped a toe out of line, he or she received agonizing punishment. The caretakers also specifically liked to punish Carter, Nancy, Alice, and Alan; Carter and Nancy were Unnaturals, and Alice and Alan were their friends.

Carter had discovered that he was an Unnatural when he learned he could make people do things for him. It was as if he had an Unnaturally high charisma so that people just had to do whatever he said. His ability was not invincible; people who were strong willed could avoid it. It was handy at times, but a curse at others. When the caretakers discovered this "power" of his, they became hell-bent on making life miserable for him and anyone who associated with him.

Six years ago, when Carter was eight-years-old, he had been smart enough to know that his sister would probably have what he had. Nancy developed the power to go into a person's head and look at the person's memories. She could also take the memories from someone by touching the person's temple and going inside of his or her head to weed out which memory she chose. When Nancy had surfed through a few of the boys' heads at the orphanage, they had ganged up on her and had beaten her up. This, along with the punishments from the caretakers, had turned Nancy into a depressed child.

Carter led Nancy back to where Alice sat. Alice's big eyes lit up, but her smile fell when she realized that Alan was missing.

"Did they get him?"

"Yeah. They got him." Carter hung his head, ashamed that he could not save his friend. His former feeling of uselessness returned quickly.

"Oh no," Alice moaned, putting her head in her hands. "What are we going to do?"

Carter didn't want to answer the question. Out of the selfishness of his own heart, he wanted to keep going. But Carter really did care about Alan, and going ahead would mean forgetting Alan and saving themselves. He glanced at Alice, who had put her head down on her knees. Her chest heaved with the intensity of her sobs, and tears dripped down onto the dirt. After a few moments, Alice lifted her head. She wiped her bloodshot eyes on her arm, and stood up.

"Alan would want us to go," Alice said softly but firmly. Carter remembered that there was a time that Alice and Alan had dated, but it hadn't lasted long when the caretakers had threatened to punish them for having something more than a friendly relationship. He knew that if anyone was to know Alan, it was Alice.

Carter nodded sadly. The decision was made. They stared back into the forest with a melancholy gaze. Alan was gone. The empty ache in Carter's chest wouldn't go away. Running away—or trying to run away—was the worst crime in the eyes of the caretakers. Alan would be severely punished.

They wandered down the dirt road. As Carter stared out into the trees that surrounded the path, he took a deep breath of chilly air. He glanced at Nancy, who stared dejectedly at the ground. Her eyes were red and bloodshot, and her bottom lip quivered nonstop. Alice looked lost in comparison to her usual bubbly attitude. Her eyes were foggy and disconnected as her feet moved over the ground. Carter concentrated on what they were going to do when they got there. But where was "there"? There was no set destination, which could be called "there." Not yet, at least. Carter frowned and rubbed his forehead.

The three of them kept walking, going deeper and deeper into the forest. It didn't matter to Carter that the forest would probably lead them to some random, probably dangerous place: at least they were away from the orphanage. Rain started to fall softly, pattering gently on the ground. The air had a mossy, earthy smell. They would have to find shelter soon.

"Look, a cave!" Carter called out. They were so far from the orphanage now that Carter couldn't see the high towers that rose above the main hall. The entrance to a cave stood twenty feet in front of them. It wasn't very large, but the space allowed them to squish inside.

They walked down the end of the road to the cave and climbed inside the large hole in the rock. Nancy stretched her legs out, and Carter leaned against the rock wall, wondering what they would do for the rest of their lives.

"Hey! Look at this!" Alice said, pointing to a rock that had shifted in the wall. Exposed was a large black hole. It was definitely not high enough for Carter to stand up and enter, but high enough so that they could crawl on their knees.

"Wow," Carter whispered, crawling closer to the hole. He plunged his hand into the darkness, searching for the walls. The walls of the tunnel were fairly close to each other, but wide enough for Carter's broad back to squeeze through. As Carter glanced closer, he could see a dim glow at the other side. "There's light," he said in disbelief.

"Maybe they have food," Alice said wistfully. "Light either means fire or electricity, which would probably mean food. Or warmth." She shivered in her wet t-shirt and threadbare jeans. "We should go check."

"How about Nancy?" Carter asked, motioning to his sister. She sat with her eyes closed, leaning against the wall. "She can't come with us! What if something dangerous happens?"

"We'll go by ourselves," Alice said, "Nancy doesn't mind. Do you, Nancy?"

Nancy opened her eyes and stared at Carter. He knew Nancy well enough to tell that she wanted to go. She frowned and closed her eyes. "Come back soon."

Carter sighed. "Fine. Let's go." He hugged Nancy, and then crawled into the hole right behind Alice. The hole smelled of rot and dirt, and the walls were slightly damp. Carter ducked, careful to keep his head down so that it wouldn't hit the ceiling of the tunnel. He took deep breaths as he moved forward, thinking about getting out of the tunnel instead of being in it. They moved in silence, concentrating on getting to the other side. The light at the other side grew brighter and bigger with every step that they took.

Finally, Carter emerged from the hole. Breathing a sigh of relief, he stretched and then peered back through the hole, hoping to catch a glimpse of Nancy. They were too far away; Nancy couldn't be seen at all. He hoped that she was okay.

"Carter! Come look!"

Carter whipped around at the sound of his name. Alice stood with her mouth open, pointing to a table laden with food. Fruits, meats, and various types of drinks covered every inch of the long wooden table. Carter inhaled, and the sweet smell of roast chicken nearly made him start drooling. Round, fat grapes shone in the light of the fire that flickered in the corner. A silver goblet sat in the middle of this feast, brimming with water.

The kids dug in without hesitation. Carter didn't care whose food it was, or if there was anything wrong with it. It was food. They hadn't eaten for several hours; food was like gold. Carter crunched grapes and slurped water. Alice feasted on a chicken thigh that she had torn directly off the body of the succulent roast chicken. Both kids licked and chewed until their faces were covered in sauces and their hands were sticky. Carter felt that everything was right when there was warm, good food in his stomach. He'd never eaten that well in his life.

Alice heaved a contented sigh. "That was a great meal. We should take some back for Nancy."

The voice that answered her was not Carter's. "You can eat like that all the time if you join me."

Both kids whipped around at the sound of the new voice. Behind them stood a tall, thin woman with pale blonde hair. She looked elegant and graceful, like a regal animal. Her high cheekbones pulled her white, pale skin taut. She was dressed in a long, light blue robe made of shimmering silk, with a shawl thrown over her shoulders. Her piercing blue eyes made Carter shudder when he made eye contact with her.

"W-who are you?" stammered Alice. Alice wiped her greasy hands on her jeans nervously.

The tall woman smiled cruelly. "My name is Leia. I'm just like you." she paused, "Well, one of you."

Carter felt stumped: how could this woman know that he was an Unnatural? She couldn't. He'd never met her before, and even if he had, Carter doubted that he would ever tell anyone his deepest, darkest secret. The only people who knew about his and Nancy's powers were Alice and Alan, and the caretakers at the orphanage.

"What do you mean?" Alice asked, breaking the tense silence. Carter glanced sideways at her, shooting her warning glares. He wasn't a mind reader, but Carter had the feeling that this woman was not one someone who would be messed with. "What do you mean "like you"?"

"I mean like your friend, dear," she said, smiling at Carter. "You must know about the power. The one that makes you…special?"

Carter trembled, not knowing how this woman knew and why she was asking him about it. "What are you talking about?" he lied feebly. "I don't have any powers!"

Leia only gave him a knowing glance. "Don't try to hide it."

Carter exhaled heavily, his heart thumping in his chest. There was no way out of this. "Fine. Yes. I'm an Unnatural. Are you happy, now? What do you want?" he demanded, almost shouting.

The tall, graceful woman moved across the room and sat down. She adjusted her shawl and robes, and then said, "I'm going to cut to the chase. I want you to join my army of…Unnaturals. For years now, I have been assembling an army of people like you and me," she glanced at Carter, "as well as people like you." Leia stopped to cast a glance at Alice, who was standing dumbfounded by the table laden with food.

"Well, I'm not really giving you a choice. You will join me, because I have a certain little friend of yours held hostage." As soon as the words left Leia's lips, a door to the side of the large room swung open. From the door came two men carrying a squirming, struggling sack. The sack was printed with the word NANCY in big, bold letters.

"Nancy!" Carter cried, running to the wriggling sack. Before he could get there or anywhere close, he was thrown against the wall. Carter slid down the wall and crumpled like a doll on the floor, pain surging through his bones. His head spun round and round as he tried to grasp the concept that there were more people like Nancy and himself.

"Leave my friend alone!" Alice cried. Carter watched from the ground level as she threw a punch at Leia but was stopped as if by an invisible man. Alice fell to the ground with a thump, right in front of Leia's feet. One of the men who held Nancy let out a loud guffaw. It had to be him who was making them fly against the walls. Carter exhaled as he pulled himself up and crawled over to where Alice lay.

Leia approached the two children, the smiling expression on her face now gone.

"Let me be very clear," she hissed, spittle flying from her mouth into Carter and Alice's faces, "you will join me in taking down the orphanage and, after that, anywhere else I tell you. If you agree, which you will, your precious Nancy will be freed. If you struggle, she dies. It's just that simple."

Carter's eyes closed as one of the older men came close to him and picked him up carelessly, tossing Carter onto his broad back and carrying him into another room. Carter didn't want to see what was happening anymore; it was too painful.

*   *   *

Carter woke up in a dank cell. An odorous smell made him gag and throw up onto the floor, heaving up his feast from earlier that day. He didn't know where he was for a second, until he remembered the entire Leia fiasco. What a horrible day! There wasn't anything that he could do. Carter felt useless.

As he sat contemplating, a series of coughs echoed through the room. Carter didn't know how large the room was because it was completely dark, but he was sure that it wasn't small.

"Water!" a raspy voice called out. "Water! I need water! Does anyone have water?"

Carter crawled backwards on his hands and feet, bumping into a wall. He took a wild gasp and pressed himself hard against the cold surface. How many people were there? Ten? Twenty? Carter opened his eyes wide, hoping that there would be some light or that his eyes would adjust to the darkness; they didn't. It was simply too dark. His heart beat fast in his chest, and Carter's head spun as he tried to reassure himself that everything would be okay.

As he listened closer, Carter could hear the faint sound of hands slapping against stone. He didn't know what was going on, but he didn't like it. Suddenly, there was a bright light. A door was opened, allowing rays of light to illuminate the room. Carter gasped when he saw dozens of thin, malnourished children. Their ages ranged from as young as Nancy to older than Carter. Giant, buggy eyes stared up at Carter out of gaunt faces. The children slapped their hands against the ground and moaned urgently. It was like a nightmare.

"All right, all right, you brats!" the man at the door said. He carried three plates of food and a tall pitcher of water. There were no cups or cutlery. As he entered the room, the children spread away, making a path. He walked to the middle of the room and set the food and water down. Carter felt his stomach growling, empty from when he had thrown up. Then he looked at all the kids; was this the only food that they were getting? There were so many of them! Carter sighed, knowing that he would probably become illiterate and malnourished like the other children, who were communicating via moans and yelps as if they were animals. Several of the children could still talk. They yelled profanities at the burly man who stood in the middle of the room.

"You!" the man said, pointing to Carter. "Come with me. Leia wants to meet with you."

Carter clambered to his feet hesitantly. He was afraid, but intrigued. Why did Leia want to meet with him specifically?

"Hurry up!" the man yelled. "Move aside, mongrels. Let the boy through."

Carter quickly walked through the crowd, who spread apart at the man's request. He emerged into the main room that he had been in before. The man led him into another room at the side, and then shut the door.

Leia sat on a purple upholstered chair in the middle of the room. Her expression was smooth and unreadable as she beckoned Carter closer with a wave of a finger. The room had a four-poster bed, which matched the purple chair, an old fashioned desk with a reading lamp, an elaborately carved chest, and several shelves of books. Carter looked around in amazement, having garnered a new appreciation for fancy things after being in that dank, smelly room. Only then did he realize that Nancy and Alice sat at Leia's feet as well.

"Nancy! Alice!" Carter cried, running forward to hug them. Alice gave him a warning glare, and Carter immediately bowed his head. He sat down on the only remaining empty stool there was. Nancy and Alice occupied the other two.

"Well, isn't this nice!" Leia said, clasping her hands together. "I'm finally with my two children again! And their little friend!"

Carter stopped her, "Excuse me, but what did you say? Your two children?"

Nancy nodded fervently, her head bobbing up and down. Carter saw that her filthy hair had been washed and now shined in two pigtails with bobbles attached to the edges. She looked clean and comfortable in a new yellow dress. Alice was showered, too, and wore a new blue shirt and white skirt. Her dark hair was shiny and carefully combed and was pinned up in a bun. "Leia is our mommy, Car! She told me that she didn't want to leave us, but she had to because she couldn't take care of us. She knew that one day we would come to her!" Nancy took Leia's hand as the older woman smiled at her endearingly.

"What?" Carter said, still not understanding. All his life, he had been told that he and Nancy had been dropped off at the orphanage when he was six and Nancy was just a few months old. Carter didn't remember anything before the orphanage and had accepted that he would never have parents or a family.

"It's true. I'm your real mother. How else would you think that you became Unnaturals? It's genetic, dear." Leia smiled in a very motherly way, and Carter almost found himself believing it.

"How about my dad?" he challenged.

"He died many years ago. His name was Howard. I miss him so much," Leia said, tears welling in her eyes. Her grip on Nancy's hand visibly tightened.

"What did you want to tell me?" Carter asked. "I still don't believe you and never will. Hurry up and get on with anything else you need to say so that I can get back to hell." He used his head to motion towards the dank cell. Leia sighed and let go of Nancy's hand. She stood and walked over to where Carter was and put a hand on his shoulder. Carter flinched at the feel of her hand but couldn't bring himself to push her away.

"Believe it or not, you are my child, Carter. And my children only have the best. I'm afraid that the house isn't big enough to give each one of you a room, so all three of you shall share. This is your home now; settle in!" With that, Leia clapped her hands and stood up. The man from before came in again and gruffly bowed to Leia. Then, he turned towards the kids and motioned for them to follow him. Dazed, Carter followed the man out of the purple room and back into the hall, where they wove down a corridor and into another room.

"I don't think that we can trust her," Carter whispered, hoping that Alice could hear him. They stopped at a room painted completely white, with three white beds and a white wicker chair. A bookcase that held a bunch of books stood tall against the wall, and a floor to ceiling mirror was parallel from the door, so that Carter could see his own stunned expression.

"If you need anything, just ring," the man said, pointing to a bell that was attached to the wall. "My name is Nathan. I hope that everything is suitable." He left quickly, closing the door behind him.

Carter sank down onto one of the beds, leaving grease and other dirt on the clean white duvet. Nancy was playing with two dolls with a content smile on her face. She looked happier than Carter had ever seen her. Alice had picked a book from the shelf and was idly flipping the pages as she lay on her bed. They were both acting as if everything was normal.

"How can you be so calm?" Carter shrieked, jumping off the bed. He didn't know how to handle their current situation. "Everything is going wrong!"

Alice looked up at him with a questioning look on her face. "How can you say that? Everything is going right! You found your birth mother, who was nice enough to take me into her home too. We have an actual room and food and toys! We've never been so fortunate, Carter. What more do you want?"

Anger bubbled inside of Carter, waiting to be unleashed. "We can't trust her! We don't even know who she is!"

Alice got up off her bed, and Nancy dropped the doll. Nancy frowned, giving her brother an angry stare before shouting, "Leia is our mommy, Car! I always wanted a mommy, and now I have one! You do too! Why can't you be happy?"

"Because we don't actually know if she's our mom, Nancy! We have to leave. Now!" Carter grabbed a backpack that was hanging on a hook and pulled the chest of drawers open, exposing neatly folded shirts and pants. He grabbed a handful and stuffed them into his backpack, eyes wide and crazed.

Alice ran over and pulled the bag out of his hands. Her angry and frustrated eyes told a story too complicated to say in words. "Carter, when something good happens to us, can't we just take it? You just have to go and question everything! Can't you see that maybe our luck is changing?" Alice stopped, panting. Her blazing eyes almost made Carter question his thinking process. "We are a team unit, Carter! It's all of us or none of us! And because we are a team, we are voting. It's not only your decision that matters. Mine does, and so does Nancy's. It's unfair that you're automatically taking charge as if you're our leader."

Carter was stumped. Alice always agreed with him, or told him gently if it got something wrong. She had never been so mean or rude to him! Couldn't they see that he was right? Carter bit down on his tongue, angry and frustrated.

"No. We're leaving!" he said determinedly, "I know what we need to do!" Carter looked Alice right in the eye, knowing that if Alice agreed with him, Nancy probably would too. "We are leaving. Leaving." Alice's eyes grew foggy for a second.

"Yeah. Leaving. Let's go, Nancy. He's right. This is stupid. We can't trust her," Alice said in a monotone. Nancy looked at her in disbelief, and then looked at Carter.

"No!" she yelled. The loud noise made Alice come out of her hazed state. Carter lost hold on her mind as Alice narrowed her eyes. "I can't believe you, Carter. Using compulsion on me! Ugh!" She threw her hands up and sat back on the bed. "I'm not leaving, Carter, and you can't make me. Not even using compulsion."

Carter sighed sadly. Clearly, they weren't going to follow him. He had to take drastic action. "Fine. Well, I'm leaving. You can come with me or can stay and rot here. I'll leave at nine tonight so that you have time to think." Carter glanced at the clock mounted on the wall. It said that it was seven o' clock in the evening. Two hours ought to be enough time to think.

Alice sighed and turned away from him. Carter stared at Nancy, begging his sister to follow him. He loved her a lot, but he couldn't live his life believing in a lie. Leia wasn't his mother, and he couldn't treat her as if she was. Tears started to dribble from Nancy's eyes, and she ran from the room angrily, slamming the door.

*   *   *

Nancy entered Leia's room with a loud sob. Leia turned around, smiling when she saw the little girl and then frowning when she saw the tears dribbling out of her eyes.

"He wants to leave, Mommy!" Nancy cried. "Carter wants to leave. He says that he's leaving at nine o' clock tonight! Make him stay!" Leia wrapped her arms around Nancy and cradled her.

"It'll be fine, Nancy, dear," she said, murmuring softly. Leia sighed in annoyance; this mothering business was more than she was cut out for. She preferred pets to children, which was why she kept all her Unnaturals locked up in the cell. However, she had made an exception for Nancy, Alice, and Carter. They were special—and crucial to her plan. Leia planned to use her Unnatural army to invade the orphanage that had mistreated her for the majority of her youth. The only reason why Carter and Nancy were not locked up in the cell was because they had powers which Leia had never seen before in her dozens of other Unnatural hostages. She had to be nice to them so that they would fight for her. That was why she had originally put Carter in the cell but let Nancy and Alice stay outside: he was the driving force behind the two girls. Without his drive, the two of them would stay.

The orphanage had been built on what was previously a circus freak-show town. On the outskirts of the town lived gypsies rumored to have "special powers". These powers were genetic, so the gypsies were careful not to have any children. When they did, the children were usually dropped off at the nearby orphanage. Leia's mother had been a gypsy.

"I'm so happy I found you, Mommy," Nancy said after she had cried it all out. "I love having a mom."

Leia smiled at the little girl and patted her on the head. "Go play now. I'll make everything better." Nancy smiled, and ran out of the room. As soon as she was gone, Leia leaned back in her chair. She couldn't let Carter get away. He was crucial to her plan to destroy the orphanage, and later, the gypsy towns outside. Carter was actually more powerful than his sister, Nancy. With the right training, he could the most powerful Unnatural of all. That was what Leia's power was: she was able to tell the potential and the skill of any Unnatural. That was how she had found Carter and his sister.

Suddenly, the door opened and Nancy popped her head back into the room. "I love you, Mama!"

Leia smiled sadly. Nancy was actually a sweet girl. If she really had been Leia's daughter, Leia truly would have loved her.

*   *   *

It was nine o' clock at night, and Carter was fully packed and ready to go. Neither Nancy nor Alice had spoken to him since his outburst. Carter wished that he could just be happy with Leia and her home, but he couldn't. Carter couldn't just be trusting with anyone, even if it meant having the food, room, and toys taken away.

"Are you honestly leaving?" Alice asked, speaking for the first time that evening. Her eyes were red-rimmed, but she hadn't said anything about changing her mind and going with Carter. "You're my best friend, you know..."

Carter gazed sadly at Alice. She had been his best friend and companion though his whole life. The thought of leaving her scared Carter a lot. He slung the backpack across his back and gave Alice a hug. She closed her eyes for a second, and then opened them.

"I'm going with you, Carter," she said, voice wavering. "I'd miss you too much if I didn't."

Carter felt like jumping for joy. Happy feelings bubbled inside of him. He wouldn't be alone! "Let's go. Quickly."

Alice stuffed some clothes in another backpack and put her shoes on quickly. Silently, the two of them snuck out of the room and into the hall.

"Hold it."

Leia stood in the middle of the room, flanked by Nathan and some other man which Carter didn't know. From behind Leia emerged Nancy, smiling at Carter sweetly.

"Nancy?" Carter said, voice cracking. His heart pounded quickly as he began to put the pieces together. Nancy had betrayed them. His sister had betrayed them. Carter felt like sinking to his knees and crying, but his expression stayed resolute. He would not show any signs of weakness.

"You're not going anywhere, Carter," Leia said, shaking her head. "Take one step, and something bad will happen."

Carter struggled to stay calm. His plan was falling to pieces, all because his sister had betrayed them. He should have known that this would happen; Nancy had practically worshipped Leia from the moment the older lady had proclaimed that she was their mother.

"Carter, don't leave!" Nancy cried. "Leia and I are trying to make you stay! Stay with us! You'll be happier here!"

Carter smiled sadly. He wished that he could be happy right now. Carter's beating heart blared in his ears. He could run. It was the only plan. If he ran and got caught, then he would die. Death seemed so welcome to Carter: maybe then would he find peace. Carter laughed bitterly: he was dying to be happy.

Carter made a snap decision and ran, moving his legs fast and darting in between Nathan and Leia. His heart thumped hard, beating so fast and loudly that he was sure that everyone could hear it. He had his eyes on the small tunnel in the wall that would lead him back outside, and he was almost there...

A high-pitched scream stopped Carter in his tracks. He turned around to find Nancy lying limp and pale white on the ground, there was no blood yet, but her horrible screams told Carter that she was in serious pain. Nathan stood a few feet away, holding a smoking gun. Nathan looked at the body on the ground, and his eyes widened. He seemed to be in shock at what he had just done. Nathan dropped the gun on the ground, his hands beginning to shake.

"No, no, Nancy!" Carter screamed, backtracking and running towards his sister. She struggled to a sitting position and clutched her shoulder as if she wanted to wrench it off. Carter grimaced as Nancy opened her mouth wide and let rip a wild, cannibalistic scream.

"I told you something bad would happen," Leia said nonchalantly, as if the fact that Nancy had been shot was no big deal. Carter screamed in rage, unspeakable feelings coursing through him. He bit down on his tongue to stop of noise, tasting saliva and bile and blood in his mouth as tears trickled down his cheeks. Grief and rage and anger at himself filled Carter's head to the point where he didn't know what to do.

Alice jumped on Nathan, who had picked the gun off the ground and was pointing it at Carter. Nathan had stopped shaking, and a predator-like look was in his eyes. Alice screamed a loud scream that echoed through the cave. Although she didn't manage to take Nathan down, Alice managed to knock the gun out of his hand. The small black device spun on the ground, stopping at Carter's feet. Carter acted on a whim and grabbed the gun. He pointed it at Leia and pulled the trigger, staggering back a few feet when the gun kicked back. As soon as the shot hit its target, Carter turned away. He had had his fair share of blood and gore for a lifetime.

"Alice, we're leaving," Carter cried in a desperate voice. He scooped Nancy's limp body up and ran towards the exit, Alice close behind him. They crawled through the hole quickly, never stopping to look back. Even after exiting the cave, they continued walking and walking, never looking back.

As they left the cave, Nancy continued screaming. Her screams were so loud that they made Carter shiver. Outside, rain fell heavily and water dripped off the branches of trees and onto the ground. Nancy still clutched her profusely bleeding shoulder.

"We need to find somewhere to go!" Carter yelled, trying to be heard over the pounding rain. He felt shocked at himself; he had shot somebody.

"Take a left and go to the fork in the road!" Alice cried, pointing. Carter nodded, and the three of them made their way to the fork. Carter's heart beat in panic; they would have to get Nancy to help or else something even worse would happen. Carter led the way, still holding Nancy's body tightly. His clothes were sticking to him, and his hair was plastered to his head. Carter was sure that they were never going to find anyone.

"What do we do, Carter?" Alice asked, turning to him with worry in her eyes. Carter felt like exploding.

"I don't know!" he screamed, "I don't know! Stop asking me! How am I supposed to know?"

"You—" Alice began, but was abruptly cut off when someone else's voice interrupted her.

"Excuse me? Are you okay?"

Both kids whipped around, expecting to see Leia standing out there in the rain. Nancy cried out in pain at the sudden movement. Carter saw a short woman, dressed in colorful scarves and robes. He could see the warm, friendly smile on her face.

"Who are you?" Carter asked, frowning. He was cautions, wary, ready to run away if the woman turned out to by psychotic like Leia. "What do you want?"

The woman's friendly smile faded a little bit. Carter felt bad that he was acting so rude towards this woman who seemed to have good intentions. "My name is Carter. Can you help us? Do you know where the nearest doctor is?" Anxiety and panic pounded through Carter's veins. This was his last resort. Bad intentions or good, the woman might be the only way to help Nancy.

"Oh, of course," the woman said, staring at Nancy worriedly. Blood was starting to seep through Nancy's shirt, making Carter feel like gagging. He was not good around blood. It made him nauseous. "Come this way. Quickly, quickly."

Alice stared at Carter with panic in her eyes, but he ducked his head. There was nothing else that they could do but follow the woman. Nancy needed help!

The woman pulled open a colorful tent door. The three kids stepped inside the warm space and their clothes dripped on the silk carpets lining the floor. The tent felt like safety and home.

"Set her down here," the woman said, "help is coming soon. My name is Zoya."

"Thank you, Zoya," Alice said gratefully. She smiled weakly and said, "My name is Alice. That's Nancy." Alice pointed to the small girl. "Nancy is Carter's sister. I'm their friend."

"Thank you so much, Zoya," Carter echoed. He hung his head, feeling strangely ashamed. He heard Zoya walking over to him, and felt her put a hand on his sopping head.

"Do you have a place to stay, Carter?"

Carter shrugged, and then shook his head. They did not have a place to stay. After help came, they would probably have nowhere to go.

"You can stay here as long as you want," Zoya said firmly. "I've always wanted children, but I could never have any. I can feel that you three are filled with goodness and pureness. You're just the type of children that I wish I could have had. Would it be okay with the three of you if I adopted you?"

The kids looked at each other in relief just as two other people burst into the tent and began cleaning the blood off Nancy.

"We would like that very much," Carter whispered, smiling slightly. "Pardon me for asking, but how did you know that we were filled with goodness?"

Zoya smiled mysteriously. "Being a gypsy, I was gifted with certain powers. I am able to tell a person's true nature by just looking at them."

Carter shared a knowing smile with Alice before turning to tell Zoya about how he and Nancy were Unnaturals. Somehow, he knew that their new life with Zoya would be safe and that they had finally found a home.

Expo Ransom

By

Frank Comey

THE SOFT HUM OF THE VAN LULLED THE REPRESENTATIVES TO SLEEP. The Expo committee members traveled back to the hotel to enjoy a relaxing night. Unknown to the committee, a parked sedan lay in wait for them, prepared to t-bone their unsuspecting victims. The van crossed the target area. The sedan sped up and smashed into the side of the van. Inside, drinks splashed and people lurched. The collision sent the loud noise of crunching metal through the until-then quiet night. A gang of masked men rushed the van. Grabbing the committee of Expo members, the gunmen escaped into the night.

"So that's your conclusion, huh?" Terrell Hazard stood at the crime scene next to a local inspector. The street was littered with car parts and smashed glass.

"Any leads about where these guys went?" Terrell questioned the Inspector.

"Bystanders said a white sedan appeared out of the alleyway and smashed into the committee's van. Then, another van pulled up and took the men away down Dong Xi Road. There are security tapes that show the gunmen in action, so some of my men are working on putting together a profile of these criminals."

Terrell turned around without thanking the inspector and walked back to his Ford GT. As the engine started, he whipped out his cell phone and dialed in a number.

"Hey, I'm coming by. We've got some new stuff to take care of. I'll tell you about it when I get there."

Flying through the Shanghai streets, Terrell Hazard was not your average person. At six feet four inches in height, Terrell was a tall African American. Years of hard work and training had earned him a chiseled appearance with standout athleticism. Wind whipped his face, but Terrell remained undaunted as his black and white convertible zoomed into the financial district of Lujiazui, Shanghai. A cold autumn wind blew through naked, leafless trees that were spread out among the gray buildings that surrounded them. Locals visiting the various pavilions packed the dusty Shanghai streets.

Unlike the locals, Terrell wasn't there to the visit. Terrell and his team of highly trained S.W.A.T. professionals were employed in the toughest situations. Essentially a private security organization, they were known across the world as Exterminate Insurgents and Retrieve Personnel, or E.I.A.R.P. This case was right in their field, and they were the best at what they did, retrieving hostages. Once the kidnapping of the Expo committee was reported, the scrambling local authorities called E.I.A.R.P.

Terrell strolled into the building from which E.I.A.R.P. operated. The headquarters were in Los Angeles, but this building served well as a temporary base of operations. Terrell's team sat waiting in the briefing room. His team consisted of other American law enforcement personnel, including Jay Dobbs, Hernandez, Alex Lee, Marcus Battle, and Jordan Russell. They were like a group of friends, but when a job came in, they were all business.

Hernandez, a Puerto Rican immigrant, grew up in an urban neighborhood, and eventually left the Los Angeles police department to join Terrell's team. Jay Dobbs hailed from Arizona. Once a Hell's Angel, he gave up his biker ways and went to LA in search of a job. He still carried around the Hell's Angels' favorite weapon, a sledgehammer. Marcus Battle, a boyhood friend, grew up in Terrell's neighborhood. Jordan Russell and Alex Lee originally worked in San Jose working as part of a S.W.A.T. team, but they also left to join Terrell's team.

At the core of the organization was Terrell Hazard. Born in Compton, California, Terrell grew up in an inner-city environment. Terrell thrived in the ghetto and was well on his way to becoming a young crime lord when his life changed. On his last day of high school, gunmen shot up his house in a drive-by shooting. While he partied with his friends, gang members brutally murdered his family. The heavy loss struck Terrell and led to soul-searching depression. More than once, Terrell had led such raids that ended in multiple shootings.

Seeing what he had become and what he was doing to the people in his community, he lit out of Compton and decided to spend his life stopping the people that were just like what he used to be, a criminal. Terrell enlisted in the United States Army and found refuge. Eventually going on to become a Navy Seal, Terrell served for ten years, working his way up to becoming a Lieutenant Colonel. Terrell eventually left the Army with an honorable discharge. He then started E.I.A.R.P. to keep his vow. And now he found himself on another high-stakes mission, just another day in the life of Terrell Hazard.

On the first day of the investigation, his team had made a good start. After meeting with local law enforcement to make vague profiles of the gunmen, they currently probed tediously through the security tapes, looking for a lead.

"Man, we've been looking through this tape for hours. I don't know about you guys, but I can't see anything," Jay complained.

"I'm telling you Jay, if you had a bit more tolerance for tedious work, you'd be unstoppable." Terrell still peered closely at the screen in front of them. "Look at the monitor. There." He pointed to a shadow coming from an alleyway near the parked sedan. "That's a silhouette. Someone else witnessed the kidnapping. He probably lit out when the kidnapping went down." True to Terrell's words, once the crash happened, a figure racing down the alleyway replaced the silhouette.

"Gotcha." The tape stopped with the image of the pedestrian racing down the alley.

"Poking around, don't we? Come on Terrell, that's grunt work!" Jay was not the type that enjoyed Q and A.

"You're learning already, man." Terrell laughed as he grabbed his jacket and headed for the door.

"Darn."

*　　　　*　　　　*

The day had been uneventful. After following the lead, they had searched through the local hutongs for anyone who had witnessed the crime. Nobody came forward. Silence held the community in a deadlock. As the team drove back to headquarters, a melancholy feeling drenched over them. They talked dully over their radios.

"Okay. That was a complete waste of time." Hernandez was in a poor mood after he had stepped in a puddle of unknown origins.

"Can't disagree with you there. That guy in the video sure can disappear at will. No doubt he's used to it," Terrell said. "Better luck tomorrow, eh?"

"I hope so. I want to get to the exciting part of this mission. Grunt work isn't my thing." Jay wasn't pleased with the day's exploits either.

The team pulled up to the headquarters. They saw a note pasted on the door. A message was written in scrawled Chinese characters.

"Yo, Lee!"

"What's up, guys?" Lee stepped out of his sleek, customized Nissan 350Z.

"What does this say? Since you're the only one that reads Chinese, you need to get over here." Lee strolled over to the rest of the team as they crowded around the small note.

"It reads, 'Come to Gong Qing Amusement Park at 4 PM, tomorrow. Make sure you aren't being tailed. If they find me, they will kill me.'"

"Man," Terrell exclaimed after Lee had translated the message. "This is getting serious. But as far as I'm concerned, this is the only lead that we've got. We've been waiting for something like this for five days. Following this is the best thing we can do right now. All the same, we better get strapped. Go with light arms. I want y'all up and ready right here at 8:00 AM sharp. Especially you, Lee."

*　　　　*　　　　*

The day promised to be a dreary one. A morning haze hung over the dusty Shanghai streets. Terrell and his team arrived at the slightly remote Gong Qing Amusement Park and paid their tolls.

"This is ridiculous," grumbled Terrell as he forked over twenty kuai. "Couldn't we have met somewhere that didn't rip you off?"

Terrell led his team through the gates of the Amusement Park. The Expo hogged the limelight, and people flocked there for entertainment. Gong Qing Amusement Park was barren compared to their usual attendance.

"Now what do we do?" Jordan said aloud.

"I guess we just wait," replied Marcus. "That dude wasn't very specific with his little note."

Not soon after the words had left his mouth, a man with a leather jacket and fake Nike's walked towards them.

"You are the special team, right?"

"Yes, we are," answered Lee. "You wrote us that note?"

"That was I. What I came to tell you was this. The men who kidnapped those Expo officials were Middle-Eastern. Their language sounded like Hebrew or some sort of Arabic," the man whispered uneasily.

"Wait. That's it?" Jordan asked plainly.

"Yes. I hope it will help you to save those people. What is this world coming to?" mumbled the man as he strolled away.

*   *   *

Back at headquarters, Terrell and his team diligently investigated every vague clue. A clock chimed ten times, indicating 10:00 PM. Terrell set his magnifying glass on top of a blurry photo and saw his team feverishly working to find any possible clue to the kidnapper's whereabouts.

"Honestly guys, I don't see how that guy helped us much. I don' t mean to be stereotypical, but aren't most terrorists these days from the Middle East?" Terrell questioned.

"You're right, Terrell, but most of those terrorists try to damage America. Why would they want to ransom some Expo officials? It just doesn't match their usual motives." Lee answered quickly. "Local help has been non-existent, and I think it's time we look for help on the international stage. Now, the man said that the kidnappers were Middle Eastern. We need to contact Middle-Eastern governments. Maybe they will know something about these men and if they have any connections back home."

"Okay, sounds like a plan," sighed Terrell. "I'm going to grab a coffee. Battle, I want you on the phone with the Israeli consulate. Tell them we need to contact someone about possible insurgents."

As Terrell crossed the threshold, Jordan caught up to him.

"Hold up, man, I'm coming with you. My eyelids are dropping like weights." Jordan was usually the one that nodded off during the late hours. He rushed up to the automatic doors and they started making their way to the closest cafe.

*   *   *

Once Terrell and Jordan returned from their quick coffee break, they got some good news from Marcus.

"We've got something. I talked to a government agent from Israel and they informed us of some deserters. They had issues with authority during their time in training, and unlike many other soldiers, these men were inhumane in their short stint on the battlefield. They had malice, unlike the other honest soldiers. It was clear that their intentions were not to serve the country. Unfortunately, before they could be detained, they lit out of the country. I guess the Israelis trained them pretty well because the men haven't been located yet. The Israeli secret service is sending over the files of the men. Most importantly, we've got to watch their leader. He's known as Ali K. I took one look at his picture, but that was all I needed. These guys are definitely trouble."

"Great, just what we needed. A bunch of crazy ex-soldiers who have a genuine sense of what they're doing," Jordan complained.

"They'll give us a run for our money, but it's not every day you see an Israeli in Shanghai. Besides, there are so many people on the streets that they've bound to be sighted somewhere. We just need to do some more poking around." Terrell announced confidently. "Let's all get some sleep. Who knows, maybe there will be some excitement tomorrow."

A solitary scoff came from Jay, already headed for the door.

*   *   *

The team of six men walked into the local bar. Eyes shifted towards them, then quickly away. Terrell realized that everyone inside knew that they were law enforcement of some kind. That was a risk they were going to have to take.

"I always liked to think that the local watering hole was the best place for street knowledge." Terrell spoke to Marcus.

"Yeah, but they ain't always the friendliest bunch if I get what I'm saying," came Marcus' grumbling reply as he returned the customers' glares with dirty looks of his own. The place was swarming with shady characters. "Lee, you better take this one."

"What do you have on draft?" inquired Lee as he walked up the beat-up bar table.

"Heineken and Qingdao. Whaddaya want?" came the sullen reply from the bartender.

"I'll have a Heineken. I was wondering if you could answer some questions."

The bartender's eyes widened. "Oh, no you don't. I'm not getting mixed up in any of this police business. I try my best to run an honest business and—"

Lee quickly cut off the nervous man. "Don't worry, sir. I just want to know if you've seen anyone out of place, maybe with a Middle-Eastern look to them. We're not going to be hauling anyone in today."

The barkeep loosened up. "Well, you should ask Dao about that one. He usually knows the word on the street better than me." The bartender scanned the room. "Hey Dao, come here!"

A man slowly crept towards the door, looking to be unnoticed.

"Sir!" Lee called out. Dao looked up with a sense of alarm and bona fide fear. He picked up a pint glass, threw it at Lee, and immediately raced out of the door. The glass narrowly missed Lee's head as it shattered harmlessly on the bar's back wall. The team was hot on his tail, hopping over tables to get to the door.

"This one's a runner," exclaimed Marcus, in an almost happy voice. "Get back here, punk!" Jay gave chase as well, although not quite as efficiently as his counterpart.

Terrell motioned for Jordan and Lee to hop into their cars. Luckily, they had all squeezed into two cars this time—Terrell's Ford GT and Lee's Nissan 350Z.

"Keep in touch." Terrell's voice crackled through the intercom system. The cars pulled out of the bar and raced down the road. Terrell and Lee scanned the road for Marcus and Jay. They saw them close on Dao's tail, about seventy meters down the road.

"I've nearly got this clown!" yelled Marcus' rough voice. Suddenly, Dao turned into a dimly-lit garage. A car door slammed. "Dang! He's got a ride! Hey, dude, get out of the car!" The sound of an engine turning over let the rest of the team know that Marcus had been beaten in the short foot race.

"Lee, pick up Marcus and Jay. I'm going after this nut-case."

"We don't know if he's guilty, man." Lee's reply came as Terrell sped down the streets.

"You should know my answer to that question, Lee. Guilty men never run." As soon as the words came out of his mouth, a dust-covered black Volkswagen Santana shot out of the garage in front of him, narrowly missing his car.

"That idiot almost smashed my ride! We've got to get this guy in handcuffs, and quick." Terrell immediately stepped on the gas and spun around, hot in pursuit of the runaway.

"You pick them up. I've got this one," Lee said confidently over the radio.

Terrell screeched to a halt. "For sure?"

"Yeah, this one's all mine. Drive back to headquarters and get Jay's Hummer. It's pretty close to here. Keep your ears open and your radio on. I'll find you someplace to ram him. He'll probably try to escape through the alleyways, so be ready." The tires squealed and Lee gave chase.

It was obvious that Dao had been in this situation before. He took the most dangerous routes through the winding alleyways, and nailed them perfectly. Lee had a better car, but he realized Dao was slowly pulling away. He needed a straight-away soon, or his prey would be out of his grasp.

On the road ahead, Lee spied a left hairpin turn.

"Oh, yeah." He gripped the emergency brake. "Now, for some real action." The whole team knew that Lee was the best driver. As he drew closer to the turn, he saw Dao somehow squeezing out the turn. Now Lee needed to do the same thing.

"Yeah, let's go!" Lee yanked on the emergency brake. His rear wheels squealed to a stop while the rest of his car kept moving. He pulled the wheel to the left. The car moved as part of him, graceful and reckless, yet under control. He manipulated the car like a piece of clay. Lee nailed the turn, and quickly got back on Dao's tail.

Lee chuckled, "Kid's stuff."

Dao looked into his rearview mirror and saw that Lee still trailed him. He knew he was in trouble.

"Terrell, where are you right now?" Lee asked as he clutched his built-in radio.

"I've gotten ahead of you, man. All that winding through those alleys gave me time to pull ahead."

"You ready to ram smash this punk?" Lee asked over radio.

"You bet I'm ready," Terrell answered. "I almost feel bad for this dude. I hear him coming up. You better slow down and get ready to rush his car."

Lee effortlessly completed a one-eighty degree turn and stopped. Dao looked back in confusion. That was the mistake that cost him.

Terrell executed his move perfectly. The front end of the Hummer H3 pulverized Dao's little Volkswagen. The deafening sound of burning rubber roared throughout the area. Dao's car spun uncontrollably for a few seconds and then skidded to a stop. The vehicle's tail had caved in on itself. To make a long story short, the car was totaled. Lee sprung out of his car with his Beretta M9 drawn. Terrell did the same but instead brandished one of his many Desert Eagles.

"You had enough?" Terrell asked impatiently as they pointed their firearms at Dao. He lay motionless in his trashed vehicle. "I may have done too much this time," Terrell sighed aloud.

"Let's hope not," gulped Lee, as they holstered their guns. "Come on, let's pry this lunatic out of there."

*   *   *

"How's that big, dumb head of yours feel? Not so good, huh?"

Dao awoke to a dark room and an unfriendly audience. All six of the E.I.A.R.P. members were staring coldly back at him. Waking up after hours of darkness with six guys staring back at you isn't very welcoming. Needless to say, they could be intimidating when they wanted to.

"Who are you?" Dao mumbled nervously.

"The question, my friend, is who are you?" Lee rebutted quickly. "And what do you know about the kidnapped Expo committee?"

"Oh no. You are the kidnappers, aren't you?" The poor guy was obviously still dazed from the crash. "Please don't hurt me. I haven't said a word to anybody, I swear on my life! I don't care if you keep me under house arrest, I just don't want to die! I'm only—" Jay cut off his rambling with a quick slap to the head.

"You didn't answer our question. Now, you seem like you've done your fair share of wrongs. But we aren't concerned about that right now. We aren't the police. But you also look like a guy who knows what's up. All we want from you is that you answer a few questions. That's all." Lee translated the lengthy speech.

Dao stared at them in a puzzled way. "Wait. You mean, I ran from you and got all banged up for nothing?"

"Yeah, you did. Why?" Lee asked in a humorous manner.

"Well, these past few days have been pretty crazy. When I saw that crash, I got totally paranoid. I've been kind of out of it, missing work and staying away from home. When I heard you guys were looking for me, I assumed the worst. For all I know, you could have been the kidnappers, looking to make sure that no one knew. I'm sorry about your car, man. No hard feelings, eh?"

"Yeah, it's okay," replied Jay, laughingly. "I'll get the government to replace it or something. The benefits we get are ridiculous."

"Okay. Well, to answer your question, I have heard some interesting information about these guys. What do you know?"

"That they're ex-Army Israelis. They deserted and kidnapped Expo VIP's for a ransom of ten million dollars," Lee responded quickly. "But that's not too important. What we need to know is where they're hiding, and if the hostages are still alive."

Dao had the look of a dog that had been kicked one too many times. "I can't say. I really want to, but if they found out, they wouldn't rest before I was six feet under. I don't want to live in fear for the rest of my life."

Jay slammed the table. "Listen to me, you selfish, paranoid hood. Those people's lives are at stake. All they've done is try to help the world share their discoveries. Now, they're being beaten, starved, harassed, and maybe murdered. I can tell you're usually a solo guy, but for once in your life, think about someone beside yourself. Tell us where the hostages are being held. We can help you. You're obviously not in the best state. From the looks of it, you're strung out on something, whether it be drugs or alcohol, and it's something you're used to. You need to kick that habit out the door. The drugs and the alcohol are tricking you. You won't have to live in fear! From what we know, there's about ten of them—not a whole army."

"Once this is all over, they'll be locked up for good. So either you're too boozed up to think straight, or you're just too scared to do what's right," Jay continued to stare daggers at Dao. "Now those people are in trouble. And I am fully prepared to do whatever I need to do to find out where they are. You feeling me?"

Dao finally broke. A crude mixture of sweat and tears ran down his face. "Okay. You're right. What am I worrying about?" He took a deep breath and then continued. He was definitely flustered. "From what I've heard, they're hiding out at this old warehouse. It hasn't been used for a couple years now, and all the import companies forgot about it. There's no guarantee that they're still there, but that's the latest news I've heard."

"Thank you, Dao. We appreciate it." Jay smiled. "I'm glad I didn't have to pull off your fingernails with my pliers."

Dao laughed nervously, "One more thing. Could I get these cuffs off?"

*   *   *

The end of the Expo was drawing nearer. People had enjoyed themselves, but the Expo had been scarred by the kidnapping of important Expo officials. Those poor people still hadn't been rescued. E.I.A.R.P. was working hard to save these people. They now knew where the hostages were being held. Ali K and his gang of deserters were about to get a big surprise.

The men of E.I.A.R.P. were gathered in their conference room. They had been looking for the kidnappers for weeks, and they now had the men in their grasp.

"Alright guys, listen up. Our plan to get those hostages out is our usual routine. Ali K and his associates have made it apparent that they aren't open for negotiation, so we're going to take it right to 'em. You guys have to remember that this mission is all about stealth. We'll be using silenced weapons as much as possible. If the kidnappers find that something's up too early, they'll most likely start killing hostages. We want to save the hostages and take out the kidnappers. Hopefully, the kidnappers will be the only casualties today."

"After doing a quick drive beside the abandoned warehouse, Lee and I have come up with a plan to storm the warehouse. From what we could see, there are two ways to enter the warehouse. One is right up the front. The main entrance is a closing metal door, a lot like a remote-controlled garage door. It's always open. Hernandez, Jay, and Jordan will enter through there. The other three—Lee, Battle, and I—will use a grappling hook to get onto the roof of the warehouse. There's an old air vent up there. After opening that up, we'll make your way down into the interior of the building. That will put us three closer to the hostages. A two-pronged attack will be more effective than an all-out bum-rush. Try not to pull a trigger until you hear "weapons free" from me. Once you hear that command and everyone is in position, take out the kidnappers swiftly and silently as possible. Any questions?"

* * *

The stage was set. Terrell and his team sat in a midnight black van as they drew nearer to the warehouse. Each man had his iPod on, getting mentally ready. The whole team knew that the mental preparation was just as important as any weapon check. Staring dauntingly ahead, each man breathed slowly and deeply. Jordan sat silently writing a letter to his girlfriend in LA. After all, this might be his last mission. Lee was at the wheel of the van, lip-syncing the words to "Break Stuff" by Limp Bizkit. Each man had his own way of preparing, but once they reached their destination, that all stopped.

Lee slowly eased the car to a stop about a block away from the warehouse. The men filed out and walked to the trunk of the van. Terrell pulled open the two back doors and revealed a plethora of weaponry. All kinds of grenades lined the doors. The inside walls held each team member's Kevlar and helmet. On the bed of the van lay each member's guns.

The entire team carried M4A1 Carbine's as their primary weapon. The men's side arms varied, Terrell's Desert Eagle's probably being the most exotic. They were all accustomed to getting their gear on, and in a matter of minutes, they were ready. Once everyone had strapped on their vests and gathered their equipment, Terrell called the team together.

"Okay, men. There are God knows how many hostages in there. We're getting them out. Remember the plan. Once we've secured the hostages, Lee and Battle will escort the hostages to safety. I'll then help eliminate the remaining kidnappers. Good luck."

*   *   *

Jordan, Jay and Hernandez crouched below the wall that bordered the warehouse's property. The warehouse was a dull gray and the once bright blue roof had grown dusty as well.

"You have to hand it to them, they picked a good place," Hernandez said nervously.

Jordan watched the solitary window for movement. After twenty seconds of anxiousness, he motioned for his team to move forward. The three men responsible for entering the front crouched low and moved quickly towards the door. Lee, Battle, and Terrell rushed to the wall of warehouse. Lee took a few steps back and flung up a grappling hook. It latched onto the edge of the roof. The men then grabbed onto the rope and started pulling themselves up. Down on the ground floor, Jordan, Jay, and Hernandez slowly made their way through the warehouse. The door led them onto an oil-stained dip that trucks had once backed into.

As the stepped out of the dip, they got a full view of the bottom floor. It was crowded with ramps and large shipping containers. They slowly stalked through the bottom floor. Then, they suddenly heard a distinct voice. It sounded like gibberish, but the team knew it was Hebrew. The door of a container lay wide open, and inside it the men could see a small table and two chairs. Two Israeli men sat playing cards, their AK-47's leaning against the wall.

"Enemies sighted," whispered Jordan over the intercom. "Two of them."

"Hold on," came the reply from Terrell. "We're not in position yet." Terrell and the two others had successfully hoisted themselves onto the roof of the building. Lee fiddled with the cover of the air vent and then bashed it in with the butt of his gun.

"Sometimes, brute strength is just the way to go." Lee chuckled to no one in particular. He placed the bashed up cover on the roof and stepped back. "After you, gentleman." Terrell went first, barely squeezing into the air vent. Next came Battle and Lee.

Terrell grumbled as he made his way down the tight air vent. He made a silent prayer of thanks when he saw the end of the vent. He reached the mouth of the vent and then stopped.

Jay and Jordan had their weapons trained on the Israelis. Completely oblivious to the danger, the criminals happily kept playing poker.

"We're in position. Weapons free." Terrell's voice came over radio.

A burst of silenced gunfire rang off as soon as the words came out of the Terrell's mouth. One burst was all they needed. The man with his back to the mouth of the container keeled back out of his chair, dead before he hit the ground. Jay and Jordan had worked the hard angle as best they could, but the other Israeli had a split second to react before being shot. Once he realized his accomplice had been shot, the Israeli lunged for his weapon. Just before reaching his AK, he was riddled with bullets. But he had gotten close enough. His falling momentum carried him to fall onto the gun. A burst of loud AK fire rung through the warehouse.

"Oh, dear," gulped Jay.

A shriek of Hebrew came from the upper floor.

Terrell, Battle, and Lee were out of the air vent and making their way along the cat-walk-like second floor. On the other side of the wide warehouse, there were three Israelis. They had hopped down to the bottom floor and began firing away at the other three team members. Terrell and his team were about to fire when they were met with a more immediate problem. As they entered the center room, they saw six Israelis crouched and facing the other direction. Without a flinch, they mowed down all six of the men.

Jordan, Jay, and Hernandez weren't so fortunate. They had gotten themselves in a tight position. Pinned down in the container, they had only one way out. Every time they tried to escape from the container, gunfire peppered the opening.

"We're pinned down in a shipping container. There are three enemies on the ground floor constantly firing at us. Little help?" Hernandez pleaded.

In a heartbeat, Terrell and his two team members made their way to a good position to fire at the ground level enemies. Once behind the enemies, they opened fire. Two of the Israelis were quickly felled, but one of them found some cover.

"We need to get the hostages. Can you handle this guy?" Terrell's voice crackled over the radio.

"Yeah, we've got this one," Jordan said as the three E.I.A.R.P. operatives on the ground floor moved steadily forward.

Terrell's team returned to the central room. As they entered the outer room, they heard movement from the inner room. Still wary of enemies, they were making their way into the inner room when they heard more movement and more Hebrew. It was coming closer. Terrell motioned for his team to get low. Terrell peaked around the corner and quickly swiveled his head back.

"One coming down the hall quick!" Terrell quipped. He moved his team back out of the outer room.

A mad yell echoed through the rooms as a killer came out of the hallway blazing. Lee and Battle fired at him, but Terrell had his back turned. A spray of gun fire whizzed over them, but a few bullets hit Terrell square in the back. He fell forward with a loud groan as the Israeli's dead body thumped to the floor.

"Terrell!" Battle slowly turned him over. Terrell's face appeared twisted with pain, but he was alive.

"Thank God for Kevlar. All the same, I'm definitely going to have a gigantic bruise in the morning." Terrell mumbled. As he stumbled up to his feet, more movement came from the inner room.

They had some good news over the intercom. "Enemy down," came Jay's voice. "We'll be up there soon to search for the hostages."

The team moved in this time, and saw an office setting. This was probably where the warehouse company's office once was. A few old, dusty cubicles lined the room. The hostages were nowhere in sight. Suddenly, gunfire came from their left. A man wearing a keffiyeh—a traditional Middle Eastern headdress—crouched at the side of a cubicle, firing at them. The team dove behind a cubicle, bullets narrowly missing Lee's legs.

"Would it be too sudden to guess that was Ali K?" Lee asked.

"No way," said Battle. "That's definitely him. Are you sure there are no hostages here?"

"Yeah, why?" inquired Terrell.

Battle's answer was the click of a fragmentation grenade pin. He gave it a high arching throw and it landed and the left side of the office. A loud bang sounded through the room seconds later.

A cry of agony came from the area of the explosion. No doubt Ali K had been shredded by the grenade. Marcus rose up to investigate.

Too late, Terrell yelled, "Marcus, don't!" Ali K's prone body appeared from the dark and he hurled a combat knife Marcus' way. It made a clean slicing noise as it imbedded itself in Marcus' calf.

"That sneaky..." Marcus sank behind a cubicle. "I'm alright," his voice came over the radio. "You guys are going to have to end this though, I can't move for my life."

Terrell's face tightened. Terrell had always had loyalty like a dog, and since Marcus was a close friend, he didn't take kindly to people messing up his close friend. Terrell tossed aside his M4 and pulled out his Desert Eagles. Shiny and chromed out, Terrell lifted them above his head. He moved to a different row of cubicles and slowly made his way towards Ali K. He peered over a cubicle and saw Ali K limping towards a door.

"These hostages will be dead in five minutes!" yelled Ali K in broken English. Terrell took his chance. Jogging towards Ali K with his guns brandished, he fired five shots. That was all he needed. The .50 caliber Action Express rounds made quick work of Ali K. His body slumped to the floor.

*   *   *

It was October 31, 2010. Halloween Night. The last day of the Expo. On the stage, for everyone to see, were the E.I.A.R.P. staff. They had successfully rescued all of the hostages. Besides a few bruises and cuts, the hostages had come out unscathed. Marcus was still on crunches from his leg wound, but everyone else was fine.

An important member of the Expo committee, also one of the hostages, came to the stand.

"By the grace of God, I stand here today free from captivity. I can tell you, these last few weeks have been the worst of my life, but thanks to these men, my colleagues and I have to suffer no longer. I can't fully express our deep gratitude towards the men of E.I.A.R.P. In honor of them, the Shanghai Municipal Government has decided to put up a large mural near the Nan Pu Bridge."

Resounding applause came from the crowd, and E.I.A.R.P. took their bows. They had done America proud in the past few days.

Later, in the reception after the closing ceremony, the team sat at a table stuffing their faces with cake.

"So, what are we going to do now, man?" Battle asked the team.

"Back to LA for me. Shanghai's great, but LA is still the only place for me," smiled Terrell.

"I hear you, man. I haven't had a good burger in months," laughed Jay. "We still get the usual week off after a major mission right?"

"I guess you're entitled to that," answered Terrell. "But after that, I want to see you all back at headquarters. Anyone who's late is cleaning and oiling all of our gear!"

To the Other Side

By

Zachary Estey

MURNEN ENDURED THE DARK GLANCES OF HIS FELLOW VILLAGERS AS he stepped into the low building. He had no reason to be here, but, he had felt the need to come into the village. Since his childhood, he had been known as a coward and hadn't had the courage to stand up for himself and his friends; so his friends had left him until he had only one left. His name was Carmalan, and he was the only one who believed in Murnen to the very end. But the end came sooner than either of them thought.

They had gone walking in the woods that surrounded the village that morning. They stopped, and Murnen prepared to make lunch. Carmalan had gone into a dense thicket of trees to look for firewood. Suddenly Murnen heard a cry, which seemed to have come from close to the place where Carmalan had entered the woods. Following his footprints he was lead to the edge of the swift flowing river that ran past the village. The footprints halted abruptly at the edge of a ten-meter drop to the fast moving water below.

He looked over the ledge and spied a body caught on the rocks below. Agony held Murnen, not only from terror but also from a will that would not let him attempt to rescue his friend. He realized with shame that he was too frightened to even help his friend. He watched powerless as water slowly swept his friend from the rocks and carried him downriver. As he stood stricken with grief, a good part of the edge gave way beneath him, and he jumped back an instant before it went crashing into the torrent beneath. He quickly looked over the edge again but the vision was gone, and there was nothing to be seen but the water rushing underneath.

Murnen collapsed in anguish, letting his tears join the running water that had carried his friend away and transformed his life.

He lay there the rest of the day and the following night. Weeping until he had no more to give, asking of God why this had to happen, and above all cursing that he had not enough courage to even help his only friend. Finally the next afternoon, wretched and fatigued, Murnen dragged himself back to his house wondering why this scourge ever had to be laid on him.

Murnen stayed locked in his room for most of the next month, sinking into depression and hopelessness. Carmalan's body was found two days after the accident at the next village down the river, and brought back. Murnen wanted to approach the body but he feared that in death Carmalan would scorn him for his failure. Eventually Murnen summoned himself the courage to look but; but it appeared to him as if Carmalan had died in great suffering. Murnen did not attend Carmalan's funeral but instead stayed by himself, haunted by images of their time together.

Even after recovering enough to leave his room and work about his house, Murnen was more withdrawn and made an effort to avoid everyone else, though this did not turn out to be hard as the other villagers attempted to avoid him as well.

That was twenty-five years ago and things had changed very little. He was still avoided, still unhappy, and still blamed for letting another person die. He had grown used to the contempt that was showed to him by the villagers. He now lived by himself on the outskirts of town farming his own food and only occasionally coming into the village to buy or sell. But now here he was, in one of the most crowded places in town, with no other reason or direction than a notion. Casting his hood over his face, Murnen sat down at a table, ordered a drink, and fell to musing over distant memories.

He waited for an hour at that table, not speaking other than to refill his cup. Eventually seeing that nothing was going to happen that night, he stood up and exited the building. Walking back through the town, his gaze promptly settled on a small sign advertising the need of an extra person in a treasure hunting expedition. Whether because too many drinks clouded his mind or the need to escape this small town and go to places where his place was not already set for him and to earn a small percent of redemption, or whether it was because of all these things he did not know, but what he did realize was that in his thought he had passed through the low door standing next to the sign.

He walked home, staggered by what he had done but also feeling a sense of fate that he had not felt since he was a child.

Murnen folded back the cloak that was wrapped about him. Looking at the tall pines towering over them he tried to recall the previous day's events. The company had been plagued by bad weather since they had set out. The group had set out in high spirits four days earlier but frequent thunderstorms, a biting cold wind from the North, as well as rough and muddy terrain had made everyone downcast.

The area they had been traveling through was fairly well populated and so they had been able to make their way from village to village. Food had not been a problem despite the weather and they had only been forced to sleep outside one of the days. But now they were drawing near to the desolate lands that stretched beyond the edges of the maps.

Soon the villages that they had been passing through along the way would start to dwindle and eventually fade altogether. Once they passed into that land they would have to resort to hunting and foraging to acquire their food instead of buying it at villages along the way. The terrain had been fairly level so far but the land had started to rise and had become quite rocky. Their going had been hindered by the increasing unevenness of the ground and so when they reached the river they bartered boats to ferry them down the long leagues. The weather had cleared last night and this morning was the first day of sunshine they had had.

"What time is it" Murnen called out.

"The second hour after the sunrise" answered a voice.

He looked up to see that it was Balkor.

Rising slowly so as not unbalance the boat, Murnen sat up and looked at the new surroundings. Tall trees marched up right to the riverbank on both sides throwing long shadows over the river. Sitting in his boat were Balkor and Torvan. The second boat on his left was occupied by Dronor, Ravon, and Gutlaf, and on his right were Anglorad and Darnamor. Their boats were sitting precariously low in the water because of the amount of supplies they were carrying. It was eerily quite and it seemed to the company that there could be someone watching them behind every tree and shadow.

"Have you ever been out this far out" asked Murnen with a vague wave of his hand.

"Once before but that was many years ago, but there is not much to recall from that story" Balkor responded.

Murnen looked uneasily at the water running past his face. Since the death of Carmalan he had not been able to approach any river without visions of his childhood coming to his head. Strangely he did not remember any such circumstance yesterday.

"I am forgetting him," he thought ruefully, remembering the very reason why he was here. "He would not have done the same."

Towards noon the rivers current began to slacken and they were forced to bring out paddles. It seemed that they were floating over glass broken only by their paddles. Their spirits had risen from the excellent weather and allowed them to chat merrily the whole day.

As the day wore on and afternoon passed into evening they began to search for a suitable area to land and make camp. This was found at an abandoned outpost along the river where landing bay had been made before it was overrun. Upon inspection it was found that the buildings were still standing and not in great disrepair, and it was decided to stay in one of them.

Looking out the door during the night; Murnen was able to see a fog drifting over them. It seemed that he sawed many pale wraiths; men heavily clad moving in a solemn procession through these deserted streets, but even these ghosts faded as sleep came upon him. The next day passed much the same as the first but a sense of unquiet and foreboding crept on them.

It had been planned that another team would be coming over land to meet them at an the outthrust of the mountains closest to the river where the north road passed in between. They would be bringing the extra supplies needed by both teams to cross the area after. Beyond that there was a vast wasteland forcing them to leave the river and trek over land. The details of what they were looking for would be discussed when they met. All that day the mountains had been looming on the horizon, slowly growing in size as they approached.

The light had almost faded when they espied a natural bay where they could land. Dragging their boats on shore they made camp under a red sky.

Dawn showed a very different world than Murnen had imagined. All his life he had lived on the flat plains but for the first time in his life mountains dominated his sight and even now they were clinging onto their foothills. Climbing over low hills they came upon the road.

A startled cry brought everyone in earshot running towards it. Soon they found the answer to the sound. Behind a large rock outcrop a single body was lying faced down. An arrow protruded from his back and another had pierced his hand, the head visible on the other side. Close by lay his sword.

As they crowded around Anglorad advanced on the body and turned it over. A murmur of astonishment ran through them as their spirits, lifted by the sunlight, fell to their feet. This man was known to be the organizer of the other team. Upon inspection of the surrounding area only one more body was found but it was clear to all that the rest had either been killed or taken prisoner along with all the supplies. Despair overtook them as they realized that they would not have enough food to last the next few days.

It was decided that they could not go back upstream because fighting against the current would prove longer than their food supplies would last. Going back overland would have taken even longer. The only course of action left to them was to continue their original journey and let fate run its course.

There was no complaint from any of them as they set out on their long trek. All were busy with their own thoughts and Murnen, like all of them, considered again why he had ever become embroiled in this stupid journey. The sun drew high as they walked past but the heat did not bring with it any warmth to warm their hearts.

Murnen stared up at the black roof that closed them in. They were sleeping in a low hall formed by the boughs of trees. Although there was room for all of them to stand up straight, Murnen still felt stifled in this breezeless space. The group was staying in the dense woods that lined the northern side of the mountains.

Game was very plentiful and they had been able to sustain themselves by hunting. They could still not return though, because they had not the means to carry enough food or water on foot overland. Their best hope at this point was to follow the wagon tracks that led away from the site of the attack. They speculated that whoever had attacked the other group had also captured their supplies and horses and trying to recapture some of these things would allow them to return. So they were trying to quickly make a gain on the attackers so as to ambush them before they returned to wherever they were taking the plunder. It seemed that the attackers feared no real danger and so were taking their time hopefully allowing them to catch up in time.

Turning on his side Murnen saw that Dronor was still awake.

"Do you believe that we will ever be able to get back" Murnen enquired.

"I don't like to think about those things" Dronor answered slowly. "If fate allows it, we will."

"But do you think that we will be able to get back?" he persisted.

"You know what I said!" the sharpness of his voice startling Murnen. "Why don't you just go to sleep so that maybe you will have enough strength to get back yourself!"

Late that night Murnen was startled to hear a lantern being uncovered in the gloom. He heard a rumble far off in the distance and wondered what it was. As the lantern wound its way around trees and past him. He rose, and followed it.

There was already a group of people as he approached. Even with the lantern light it was hard to discern their faces. A few of them, like him, had forgotten to put on jackets before venturing out of bed and were constantly shifting and rubbing their hands to try to stay warm. All were straining to hear and guess what the distant rumblings were. Though they did not know what it was, the low rumblings sounded like the sound a foul laughter. They stayed still for the next few minutes before quietly drifting back to their beds, leaving answers until the light of morning.

The morning did not reveal anything new as the cliffs on the south side of the forest, as well as the trees, blocked their view. They did not have to wait long though; they soon found the site of the sounds. There was a large area in their path that had been covered by rocks and boulders.

Wagons with crushed and bloodied bodies of horses still attached, just showed through the rocks. With this sign their brief hope that had been pushing them on, disappeared and each of them realized that they would never be able to return home unless by some chance they were rescued. There were no bodies among the rubble so they assumed that everyone had escaped but that they were now, like them, without supplies.

They quickly checked to make sure that the attackers were not in sight. Then they started to clear the rubble hoping to be able to salvage some supplies. It seemed to them that there were many more wagons there than what the second company would have brought not saying that there were probably many more buried in the rubble. What these extra wagons were for they could only guess. They had not been digging long before they heard a long low winded horn from the north. This was soon answered by one to the southeast.

They were trapped in between the two parties and the rubble with only a small swath of forest to the east to escape into. Before they could reach the trees one of the parties emerged over a crest, stopping when they were noticed. Not waiting to find out what the party's intent was they immediately began to attack. Arrows whizzed overhead, striking nearby trees, as the enemy archers tried to find a mark, but they were blinded by the sun beating down on them above.

Anglorad, Gutlaf, and Balkor turned and released arrows of their own allowing for the rest to escape. Running through the trees they were aware when one of the arrows found a mark by the scream that went up. Not knowing whether it was friend or foe who had been hit their fear spurred them into an even faster run as more cries erupted. When the cries of battle grew dim they slowed their pace allowing themselves time to regain their breath. They were soon joined by Balkor and Gutlaf who were breathing too heavily to speak, but a look of desperation and grief was on their faces. The others looked around expectantly for Anglorad but he could not be seen through the trees.

Finally after a minute Torvan blurted out, "what happened?"

Gutlaf being the first to recover answered him. "There were only ten in the opposing group and we were able to hold them off with arrows. Their aim was inaccurate as the sun was in their eyes and we were able to hit at least three."

Pausing to take a drink he continued. "When we deemed that you were far enough away we prepared to run but at that moment a stray arrow pierced Anglorad in the thigh preventing him from running. We faltered in our escape seeing his condition but he commanded and begged us to go on saying that we would all be killed or captured if we stayed and that also he would serve as a distraction to further put them behind our trail."

Seeing the wisdom in his words we left, leaving him there, and as he said these words a look of pain passed across his face and which soon was seen on the faces of others. "Whether he was killed or captured, I do not know."

Shocked by this new misfortune they did not hear the new sound until it was too late. Feet, they heard feet running through the undergrowth. Seeing that it was futile to flee, they quickly resorted to climing trees and hoping for the best. Seeing a tall tree with large outthrust boughs, Murnen instinctively ran towards it and was joined by Rovan and Torvan. Climbing as high up as the tree could support they hoped to not be seen by unfriendly eyes.

Soon they could hear the sound of voices as well speaking a foreign tongue. Soon the pursuers stopped speaking and silence reigned in their patch of wood. Their approach was not seen until they were almost directly under the trees that the company hid in. They noticed that all the pursuers were clothed in long, hooded cloaks colored a dark green to blend into the woods around them. The party tried to remain as still as possible; trying to control their breathing so they would not be heard.

The pursuers had fanned out to cover as much ground as possible. Only two men passed under their trees and but they were not noticed. They company waited patiently for the pursuers return. It was not long, soon they could hear them coming. They were still not talking but were not doing as much to soften their steps, coming back in groups of two or three. As the noises of feet faded and eventually disappeared the company let themselves down quietly from the trees, not willing to chance that a sharp-eared straggler might hear them.

The remaining company huddled around a tree and Gutlaf spoke first. "Our first priority is to formulate what we will do now. I advise to continue our same course of action, pursuing the people attacked our second company seems to be the only thing that we can do with hope to complete."

Several heads nodded in agreement.

"But how will that help us," Murnen asked.

"We cannot hope to turn back and head home without starving," Gutlaf answered. "We were originally pursuing the attackers to uncover our supplies and recapture horses. Even if we could dig out the supplies, the horses are dead and so we have no way to carry it with us. If anyone knows where to get food and water it is the raiders, and it seems that it is still our best option to follow them. Also supposing they captured Anglorad, then at least we have a hope of rescuing him if we follow them. I assume that they have a settlement close by here. It is essential that we can catch up to them before they get there so that we can hopefully set an ambush."

They waited for another few hours, allowing time for the raiders to set out before them so that they should not cross paths. In the meantime they refilled their water bottles and organized their supplies trying to keep themselves occupied but eventually they gave in to boredom. As it neared mid-afternoon they set out, walking warily through the woods hoping for the trees to give some concealment.

They set out and soon came back to the area of the rock slide. Anglorad was not there and they assumed that he had been captured. The raiders that had been injured were not present either, suggesting that they were still alive. The land rose as the followed the raiders deeper into the mountains. With the failing light it became increasingly difficult for the company to navigate through this difficult terrain. Though working through the rocks was an exhausting and time wasting they concluded that it was the only way to pass the raiders during the night as they would be traveling slowly because of their wounded. Since they set out they had not heard a single sound suggesting that the raiders were close. Even now in the dark the lit no fires or torches, just as they had done, not wanting to be seen.

The morning dawned bright and fair. They had not slept through the whole night, taking a long detour so that they would not meet the raiders during the night. Torvan and Rovan and set out at dawn to scout out the raider's location. They returned three hours later saying that they were encamped about six kilometers back. Because of their wounded they were relying rather on superior numbers and watchfulness to keep them safe. They would have at the most only two hours to prepare.

It was hoped that they could devise an ambush and they began looking for a suitable location that this could be carried out. They chose a long valley as their target. To the south the valley was walled by a short cliff, and to the north by a river surrounded by a dense wood. Going further eastward the cliffs veered to the north colliding with the forest and the river. There was ford in the river, the only place where it was narrow and shallow enough to be crossed. Past this the cliff straightened out and the river followed at its base until a mile further on the cliffs gave way and the river turned southward.

They posted Rovan and Balkor as archers on the cliff at the point where it curved to the north. Allowing for a a shooting spot that had a view of everything around and the sun would be behind it as the raiders approached making it nearly impossible for them to hit the two archers with the sun in their eyes. Torvan and Dronor would be posted by the fords to ensure that none came could get past if they escaped the rest of them. This left the remaining three, Murnen, Gutlaf, and Darnamor to set the initial ambush.

The rest of their time was spent readying their weapons and preparing for the coming battle. Trees from close to the river where chopped down and placed across the path through the valley, so as to hinder them when they got to the northward bend allowing easier targets for the archers. Any that abandoned the main way and tried to escape through the trees would be enclosed in by the river making their only option of escape at the fords.

After preparations they resigned themselves to waiting. Soon the raiders began to cautiously creep up the valley; realizing that it was a prime place for an ambush as well. Murnen, Gutlaf, and Darnomor hid at the skirts of the forest, making sure that the trees gave them some cover while firing. Murnen was shaking with fear and anticipation, he did not want to take part in this attack but something in him told him that if he did not, he would die today. Slowly letting the raiders pass their position they drew bows, aiming for the raiders backs.

At Gutlaf's sign they fired simultaneously, cries erupting seconds later. Hearing the commotion down below the three men on the ridge stood up and began firing into the group of raiders. Many shot wildly into the trees, but seeing this was futile they most of the raiders either charged into the forest or ran for the fords. As the charging raiders neared their position the men fired their last arrows and then drew swords.

Murnen remained rooted in fear as Gutlaf and Darnamor leapt at their opponents, taking the attackers by surprise. Terrified, he could only watch as his friends killed first one then another raider. But soon more raiders ran up and they became overpowered. Gutlaf and Darnamor were pushed deeper into the forest, closer to Murnen's position. With a cry Gutlaf tripped over a fallen log, as the raider's leader jumped above him preparing for the final stroke. But, faster than he could swing, Murnen darted out of the trees and drove his sword through the attacker, the point protruding from the other side.

The other raiders only took a second to recover but in that second Gutlaf jumped back up and renewed his attack, beheaded one of his opponents; the rest fled in terror. They quickly gathered their weapons and took off in pursuit. Bolting out of the forest the men found the wounded from the earlier attacks, abandoned by their comrades. All of them were dead; it appeared that they had cut their own wrists to avoid capture. They found Anglorad as well; he had been beheaded a short time before. Seeing their friend in this state, they were put in a state of fury and all of it directed towards the remaining raiders. Not wanting to leave him in this state they quickly lit a torch and set him, along with the fallen raiders, ablaze before quickly taking up their pursuit. At the fords Torvan and Dronor were facing the eight remaining raiders, trying to hold them at bay.

The enemy had almost won to the other side when Gulaf, Darnamor, and Murnen fell upon the from behind. In the resulting fray most of the raiders were killed but two escaped into the trees. The river ran red with the blood of their fallen opponents. In their surprise the raiders had not put up much resistance. Seeing that some of their opponents had escaped they followed madly in pursuit. Bursting out of the trees they saw the escapees running like mad across the plain, overcome with fear.

The company followed in equal wrath heedless to the many wounds they themselves had acquired.

As the cliffs receded the raiders turned onto them and run madly uphill straight towards a narrow ravine. Just as they were about to enter Balkor and Rovan emerged from a nearby tree letting arrows fly at the escaping raiders. One of them stumbled and did not rise again. The remaining raider entered the ravine with Balkor and Rovan close on his heels.

As the other main part of the company approached they heard noises coming from a gaping hole in the rock wall on the east side of the ravine. Upon closer inspection it was found to be a skillfully crafted and hidden door. Balkor and Rovan were found a short distance inside. The last remaining raider was on the ground, a large gash in his arm. They had been able to capture him because of his weakened state from blood loss.

"Where do these tunnels lead?" Rovan demanded.

He did not answer at first but in a labored voice he said, "to… the other side."

"And what is this other side?" Rovan asked.

Instead of a response they received only laughter, but amid this he uttered "they will come." His laughter slowly died until all was silent.

"I do not know what he means by the other side," Gutlaf said "But at this point we have no other choice than to brave these tunnels. Hurry!"

They ran down the passage as quickly as they could, heedless of the sound that they made. The tunnel was wide enough for three men to walk side by side. But soon their energy began to ebb and they were forced into a walk.

Torches lined the edges of the tunnel and they promptly lit some to carry with them. They did not see any other people along the whole way but as they worked their way deeper into the mountains they began to see opening in the side of the main way leading off into a darkness that even the torches failed to penetrate. They kept up this pace for two hours before resting for a halt. The tunnel seemed endless, but it did not falter from its course, keeping straight the whole time through.

They continued on like this for another three hours, the tunnel never deviating from its course. As the cold, monotonous hours passed each man began to wonder whether this tunnel even had an end, and if it did, whether they would ever get out. Each of them began to imagine, or half imagine slow scrapings and whispers coming from the extending tunnels.

An icy wind began to blow through the tunnel, its tendrils penetrating cloth and flesh. Chilled as they were the company suddenly realized that this was the first sign that had been given that they were nearing the end. Rushing forward with expectation they were not long before they reached a solid wall blocking their path. As the torchlight struck it, it seemed to be interwoven with shimmering veins. At first they stared at it trying to find a way to open it, but seeing a vertical crack down the middle, Torvan approached it and pushing with both hands, thrust the doors open. The night air was chill as they stepped out. All around them smoke rose, making a thick haze over the plain. Before them hundreds of fires burned. Warily the group rose and headed down the slope before them. They had not been walking more than ten minutes before a loud voice behind them demanded their surrender.

Turning around to face this new threat they found a group of men, not dressed in the cloaks of the raiders, but rather in the attire of the army. Stories were quickly exchanged by both groups, and after they had been searched it was revealed that the raiders had emptied their full force into the villages in the surrounding area, pillaging and burning as they went along. It had been expected that they would attack this area for a time and so the army had built a barracks close by. They had caught the raiders by surprise cutting them off from the mountains. In the resulting battle the raiding forces had been decimated by the horsed men that fought against them. They were now working to try to control the fires that blazed out of control.

From their descriptions the army was able to find a covert mining operation run by the raiders in the west of the desert. And so each remaining member of the company returned home with the fortune that they had at first embarked to find, as well as lifelong friendships. Murnen became a celebrated member of the land and soon thereafter moved into a large community with other members of the team. He lived out the rest of his year with wealth and mirth in abundance and, never again did he feel that he was a failure.

Collide

By

Fiona Ho

RED. PEOPLE DESCRIBED HER WITH THAT ONE SIMPLE WORD. EVERY moment people saw her in the room, with her neat (too neat) uniform, everything completely in place, and her expressionless face, they panic. The two seats on each side of her front window seat were generally empty. She liked it just like that.

An eighth grader, Alice Lee hated being in the middle of stupid classmates who couldn't do anything but talk. With her blazing red hair tied into two pigtails on the same side her eyes held a flame that couldn't be diminished, by normal people anyway.

But today, when she walked into the classroom clad in an invisible force field, she found someone sitting in her usual seat. Flatly ignoring the person sitting there, Alice took the seat behind the other person and sat down.

Facing Alice, a mass of brown, curly hair brushed against Alice's face. Waving it off, she leaned back and stared at the board, giving occasional warning glares at the owner of the hair. Jotting down notes, Alice's pencil movements got slower and slower until she dozed off; just as she fell asleep, she thought she heard a giggle.

The lesson ended just like how it began, with Alice's face touching brown curly hair. Funny fact? Alice touched it.

"Why would you even want curly hair?" The recipient to Alice's harsh question just smiled, holding back a chuckle. Alice stood up, annoyed that someone didn't bother to give her a reply, and stormed off.

As Alice reached her next class, she realized that, for the first time, she had talked during class. Shaking her head in disbelief, she walked out of the class and went to the nurse's office in deep thought. Seeing the entrance to the office door open, Alice let out a small unnoticeable smile and walked in.

"Something the matter, Ali?"

"Told you not to call me that." Alice sat on the comfy bench as the nurse gave her a cup of boiling hot tea.

"Why not? I've been calling you that since you were a young child."

"Because it's embarrassing..." Seeing the woman's grin grow wider, Alice shook her head and sighed. "Do whatever you want." Leaning back on the sofa, she took the tea and muttered, "...hate school."

"You kids all say the same things." The nurse gave Alice a light pat on the head. Retreating back to her chair she asked, "What's wrong?"

Alice sighed and leaned even further back.

The nurse burst out laughing. Her voice echoed through the room, and she quickly clasped her hands over her mouth in a futile attempt to stop laughing.

"Oh Alice, oh Alice. How you make me laugh." The phone rang, and the nurse picked up the phone. Within seconds her face turned sullen.

"I'm sorry Alice, but I need to take this call."

"Okay..."

Mumbling some incoherent words, the nurse's face turned into a frown as she crossed her brows. Slamming her palm onto the table she hung up.

The nurse turned to face Alice and said, "Leave."

"Why?"

"Just leave."

"Fine," she said. Picking up her stuff, Alice stumbled out of the office, confused and annoyed. Well, more annoyed than confused.

Taking a slow pace she walked back toward class, dreading every minute of her long walk. Reaching the door, she sighed and pushed it open.

"Stupid." She murmured, entering the classroom. The whole class fell silent. The teacher broke the silence. "Where have you been, Alice? You're fifteen minutes late."

"Nurse." Sitting down Alice closed her eyes and paid no attention to the lesson, until she felt something annoying on her face.

"What do you want?"

"A smile." Grinning, a pair of deep brown eyes twinkled.

"Good luck with that." Turning around, Alice brushed a stray strand of hair off her face and continued with her original plan; ignoring the lesson.

Giving a little humph, the pair of eyes closed and disappeared. Sleeping soundly, Alice awakened with a jolt. The teacher stood right in front of her desk. An evil grin turned up at the corner of her teacher's mouth.

"Had a comfortable nap?"

Nodding, Alice smirked. "It was so wonderful, I have to take another one." Closing her eyes she nodded off; right before that she saw her teacher flabbergasted, and she heard a loud chuckle.

"Hey, wake up." Someone gave Alice a good shake.

Blinking open an eye, Alice stared at the evil curly locks. "What?"

"Class is over, sleepyhead."

"Don't call me that."

"Just you try to stop me."

Annoyed and unsatisfied Alice flicked the person on the nose and stormed off once again. Going to her assigned locker, she opened the lock and took her stuff out, putting them neatly away in her white, stainless bag.

'Phone… Pencil ca—'

"You forgot this!"

Turning around, Alice saw the curly hair for the third time that morning. Seeing her pencil has in that person's hands, she grabbed it and muttered a quiet thanks before putting her bag on and walking off. She dimly noticed someone else standing there as well but didn't know who it was.

*   *   *

Standing there where Alice walked off, the owner of the curly hair laughed. "Look what she forgot, Ray."

Turning around, Ray looked at a small red bag labeled with Alice's name, and rolled his eyes. "What is wrong with you?"

"Nothing."

"You're a sadist."

"Sure I am."

"You are."

"I just agreed with you."

Rolling his eyes, Ray walked away as the other person just smirked, staring at the red bag an evil glint growing larger.

*   *   *

Alice sat on her bed staring at the imperfect ceiling. She saw cracks and holes that she hadn't seen before, and she frowned every time she saw another imperfection. Running downstairs she called out, "Mom. I'm painting the ceiling."

No reply came. Biting her bottom lip, Alice went back upstairs and sat down on her bed once more. 'What happened that made Auntie chase me out of her office anyway?' Alice thought.

Taking out her cell phone, she dialed her aunt's—the nurse's—phone number. After about ten seconds someone picked up.

"Yeah? Bridget here. I'd say you've reached the Lee household, but you didn't, so HA." Feeling slightly embarrassed because she had such a person such as her aunt in her family, Alice shuddered and made a mental face palm.

"Auntie?"

Alice heard someone scream and fall down, not even a second later someone hung up. She stood there in the same position, not moving, and blinked. Repeating the process several times, Alice realized how strange she acted and sighed. Shaking her head, she heard the phone ring and went over to pick it up.

"Auntie?"

"Alice darling? Sorry about earlier, I was surprised that you called. I was surprised you even had a phone."

Alice rolled her eyes and retorted, "Just because I never called you before, doesn't mean I don't have a phone."

"Guess so…what did you want?"

"Why were you so freaked out earlier?"

After a long pause, a reply came, "Sorry. I overreacted. You know how much of a drama queen I am."

"Right," said Alice, her voice dripping with sarcasm.

"Well…I got to go! See you darling." The phone hung up again.

Staring back up at the ceiling feeling more confused than ever, Alice sighed and shook her head. Getting up, she moved to her desk and began taking out some books from class. Turning on her lamp, she began doing homework; suddenly she saw a strange flash. Everything around her turned dark, and a vision came to her.

She saw herself as a man singing and dancing with a girl the complete opposite of her. The distinct features of the girl, curly brown hair and an elfin face, fit her well. Wanting to scream, she opened her mouth and did just that. The girl turned around and smiled at Alice.

"This is fate."

Switching back to her usual self, Alice stood there, in shock. Wondering what happened, she brushed it off as a dream and walked downstairs wondering why she didn't see her mom this morning. While she was walking down, she saw the curly brown hair again. Alice screamed, "What are you doing here?"

"Nothing." Turning around, the curly brown hair disappeared.

Feeling annoyed, Alice stormed upstairs, making her footsteps as loud as possible; in an attempt to get rid of the feelings of annoyance she felt at the moment. When she got to her room, instead of opening it like a normal person, she punched it, kicked it, and then opened the door and stormed into her room.

Jumping onto her bed, she forgot about her homework and closed her eyes. Alice gave a sigh of content as she finally cooled down. The fire inside her turned off. Smiling slightly, she fell asleep.

*   *   *

As the light streamed in through the white curtains, Alice's eyes were already open. The fire in her eyes had been on since a few hours ago, before the sun came up.

"Morning Sun. Guess I beat you again." Giggling to herself, Alice rolled off the bed and went directly to her laptop. Finishing up the homework she didn't do last night she yawned.

When she finished all her homework, she went into her closet to change. There, in her sight, lay all sorts of reds and blacks. Carefully, she took out her school blazer, a shirt, and a pair of pants. She then put them on and spun around once.

Alice then took a glance at her watch and saw that it said 6:45 AM. Somewhat in shock, she wondered where her mom could be. Her mom should've come to bring her breakfast but she never did. Giving a confused look, Alice just sighed and went downstairs. Grabbing a piece of bread and a box of milk, she sat down, ate, and drank it all up. Stretching and yawning, Alice pulled on her book bag and slipped on her shoes. She tied her shoelaces and opened the door, leaving behind a clean kitchen table and an illusion of sparkles.

"The place where I really don't want to go," sighed Alice as she strolled along the sidewalk. Suddenly, her vision became blurry, and the dancing pair came back. This time however the girl faced towards her with a panicked look.

"Don't make the same mistake I did," came a raspy voice. "Don't trust the wrong people."

"Wait," yelled Alice. "What do you mean? Who can I trust then?"

"Look…you…don't misunderstand…save you." The girl blurred and with that Alice's conscious came back to reality.

'What was that?' she questioned feeling more confused than ever. Alice sighed and looked up once more. 'This is all that curly hair's fault! Making me have illusions and other stuff I'd be better off without. Maybe it's that person who's messing with me.'

Alice looked straight up full of determination. Flipping her hair, Alice smirked and walked the rest of the way to school without any hindrances.

*   *   *

"That's it for today's lesson class. Enjoy your weekend," said the teacher knowing that no one paid him any attention. "Remember that your five-thousand-word story is due next week."

Packing up her stuff, Alice thought that she'd be able to go through one class without having to confront any curly hair, the odds pushed against her. The moment that she looked up, the mass of curly hair drifted there, ready to annoy her.

'That is it!'

Jabbing a finger at the brunette's chest, Alice looked with a fierce determination. "What do you want from me?"

The brunette replied with a grin and the words, "A smile."

Raising her right hand, she slapped the person's left cheek and glowered. "Don't mess with me."

Suddenly, right as Alice was about to storm off in fury, her vision blurred and went black.

"Hey! What's wrong?"

This time Alice didn't see herself as a man or the woman "she" danced with. Fumbling around in the dark, Alice cried out, "Where…" She bit her bottom lip. "Why do you keep doing this to me?"

The girl appeared before Alice.

"Do…trust…aunt," said the hard to understand voice.

"What? I should trust my aunt?"

"Not…trust…man."

"Are you trying to say that I should trust man and not my aunt or my aunt and not man?"

The image of the girl disappeared, and in her place came the image of herself as a man.

"You are Alice correct?" asked the man.

Shaking, Alice bit her lip. 'Why can he talk so clearly while that girl just now couldn't?' She nodded her head once. 'He scares me.'

"Ah, so you are Alice. It seems like our time is up though."

Alice's body starts turning transparent. "Wha-what's happening?"

"Do not fret. You are returning to your world."

Right as Alice started seeing light again, a voice said. "We'll meet again."

'What if I don't…' Alice regained conscious as she saw someone standing right in front of her. 'Want to see you again?' Looking at the person in front of her she sighed. 'Well I definitely didn't want to see that again.'

"Why don't you?"

Jumping back, Alice stared in shock covering her mouth. 'Who is this person?'

"I'm Princess." Gesturing to the person next to him, he said, "And this is Ray."

Princess gave off a grin that slightly titled towards one side. "Oh. And I'm your fiancé." The words echoed in Alice's mind. Over and over and over they echoed.

"WHAT DO YOU MEAN FIANCE?"

*   *   *

"So that's where you've been, Mom? Finding me a fiancé?" Alice's words were like venom to her mother's ears. She wouldn't let go of the topic even though her mom had begged her to stop hours ago.

"Why do I have to get a fiancé? Even more, why does it have to be him?" Slamming a palm onto Princess's chest, Alice's face started tinting red from anger. Just as she thought of it, it happened. Her vision turned black once more, and in a moment, Alice realized she came back to the dark, cold emptiness.

"Alice." This time her male self approached her. "I told you we would meet again, did I not?"

"Yeah…" Still unsure if her man self be trustworthy, Alice sighed and wondered where the girl stood. She knew she wouldn't trust herself, so why trust her man self? Biting her bottom lip, Alice gave herself a mental slap. "Why am I acting all defenseless and insecure? I'm not supposed to be like this."

"Where is the girl that was with you?" Alice asked, regaining composure.

"You mean Blanca?" questioned Alice's man self. "I'm afraid you won't be seeing her anymore."

Shaking his fingers, he said, "Getting too attached to people you barely even know is a bad thing."

"ALICE!"

Staggering back, Alice heard a sharp, clear voice call out her name. Rubbing her temples her vision started blurring.

"Wake up woman." This time, Alice identified the voice as Princess's and automatically she opened her eyes. Stunned by the brightness of the room, Alice covered her face with an arm before having it pulled away by Princess.

"Finally! It took you awhile woman."

Rubbing her eyes, Alice frowned. "Don't call me that, Princess."

He poked Alice's nose and chuckled when he saw Alice's look of utter despair and horror. "I won't stop if you're still frowning."

Princess pulled the sides of Alice's mouth into a wide smile, avoiding the death glares and occasional bites. He then gave her a light pat on the head, similar to the way a owner pats his lovable pet. Though from the looks she gave him, lovable pet wouldn't be a very good description of her.

"See! You look better when you smile."

"Pff!" retorted Alice. "And you look better when you're quiet and when I didn't know your name."

"Too bad then." He gave Alice a light peck on the cheek and stood up. "I got to go. Here's my phone number just in case." Princess winked and took Alice's cell phone, inserting his own number, and left the building.

Feeling a sudden rush of anger onto her face, she turned beet red and turned around to face her mom. "MOTHER," Alice exclaimed.

"And I'm out of here," Alice's mother said sheepishly. "I have to get to work. Night, sweetheart." As soon as she finished talking she ran out the door.

Alice fumbled in anger. "My family is messed up."

Taking her book bag off, Alice laid it down next to the table. Scratching her head, Alice took off for her room.

Reaching the door she recently injured, Alice smiled and she clenched her palm into a tight fist and got into a fighting stance. Punching and kicking the door, she gave it a light pat. "Thanks door."

Opening the door, a strong fragrance of oranges filled the air. As the cold, air-conditioned air blew against her face, Alice sighed a sigh of relief. She leaped onto her bed and smiled.

"This is the best after all."

Noticing that her clock read 7:30 PM, she turned around and

snuggled into her blanket. "It's a once in a lifetime chance for me to sleep early."

Making strange airplane noises, Alice finished off by saying, "And of course Alice will take the chance and go for it!"

After just a few minutes of silence Alice started drifting off. Her vision became blurry but she knew that the strange dream wouldn't come to her again this time. Somehow she just knew it couldn't. Feeling dozy, Alice thought, 'If only every moment of my day was as peaceful as now… What did I ever do wrong?' And with that she fell asleep.

*   *   *

Alice woke up thinking that she had to go to school so she went to her closet to change but realized she didn't have school. Looking outside her window she saw that once again she had beaten the sun in waking up. Plopping down on her chair, Alice wondered what she should do next. As she spun around an idea came to her. She would go and take a nice, crisp morning walk.

Changing into a loose t-shirt and baggy jeans, Alice brushed her hair, brushed her teeth, and washed her face before tying her hair up in a ponytail and grabbing her MP3 player. Walking downstairs, she slipped on her shoes and left the house without a second glance.

"Stupid Mother."

Putting her earphones on, Alice started playing a light, soft tune and hummed along as she stared at the sky. In only a few seconds, Alice fell to the ground vision blurring once more.

"Al…ice," came a voice.

Alice opened her eyes to see the girl again. She looked worried and breathless, her complexion looked absolutely dreadful and Alice wondered if she had any major illnesses going on. She didn't want to wind up catching something that could result in her death.

Mentally smacking her forehead, she called herself an idiot and focused back to the girl floating in front of her.

"Alice… I have to tell you. Be careful of the other you in your…" The voice cracked, and an invisible figure chained the girl onto the wall.

"Careful…Alice…fate," and with that Alice woke up.

Blinking a couple of times Alice felt annoyed. "Why does this happen to me? Maybe that stupid Princess knows something." Gathering up her stuff and pride, Alice took out her cell phone and dialed his number.

She didn't even have to wait for the second ring before someone said, "Hello?"

"Is this...Princess?" asked Alice.

"Depends. Who's talking?" Alice could hear laughter from the other side, followed by a fit of giggles.

"Alice." The laughter stopped. But she could picture Princess growing a smirk and ego bigger than his head.

"Is there something you wanted Alice?" asked Princess, his tone playful.

"Um. I was wondering..."

"Yeah?" Princess urged her on.

"Are you the one who's messing with me?"

Alice wounded up telling Princess everything, about the dream, the girl, the man, the awkward feeling, her aunt acting strangely, and many other things.

She gave a weak smile and hushed, "This is probably the only time we've spent talking to each other without me blowing a fuse or wanting to choke you to a nice slow death.

Alice smiled in relief as Princess told her that, with his special ability, he can pull her away from the trance-like state at will.

"Thanks Princess."

"You're welcome." Alice pressed the red button and hung up. And with that, her vision blurred up again as she fell to the ground.

*   *   *

"What is this?" Alice demanded. Looking at her surroundings she saw that she kneeled there, trapped in a cage above a body of water.

"What is the meaning of this?"

Her man self appeared from the darkness in front of her. "Just a little revenge. Figure it wasn't good enough to trap one generation, but that nurse lady was sure dumb. Why would I want an old lady when I could have you?"

"You don't have me."

"On the contrary. When you told Princess everything, I came in power. I took over you."

Biting down her lower lip, Alice curled into a ball and shivered. "You'll never get away with this…"

*   *   *

Alice stayed there in the darkness. She didn't know how much time had passed or what happened. Her current need; to forget everything that had happened. She now doesn't know why she was put there, who Princess was, and how her life was in major jeopardy.

At that moment the girl appeared next to the cage with a key. Opening the cage door she gestured towards Alice to follow her. Doing what the girl said, Alice copied her footsteps exactly not wanting to get lost or left behind.

Eventually they wound up in a room where a dim light glowed and a large bed sat. There, a figure sleeping quietly on the bed.

"Kill…" A slender finger pointed to the figure sleeping on the bed and then pointed at Alice. Handing her a dagger, she disappeared.

Alice took a step forward, before wanting to stagger back. Then without Alice willing it to, her body plunged forward and stabbed the dagger in the figure's heart. The light suddenly became bright and Alice realized she stabbed Princess.

"I knew it. People always go and trust the weak, pathetic girl." The girl came from behind the bed with a huge smirk.

"Now look. You've killed your only chance out of here. You've fallen into my trap."

"No… This can't be right. I…I can't possibly."

"On the contrary, you are."

Alice didn't speak a word.

"I know this may be a bit shocking, but it's the truth." The girl put a hand on Alice's shoulder. "I get to take your life in the outside world now. Have fun in this dark isolated place. Until you decide to steal away the next generation's outside life anyway." And with that the girl disappeared.

Running all over the dark place, Alice realized knew no one lived anywhere near her. In less than five minutes, she went crazy.

"After all, those who were stronger to begin with, when they crack, there is no going back."

*　　　　　*　　　　　*

A cute little girl with blonde hair tied into a large ribbon and a light blue dress walked around the park. She looked around, sniffing all the flowers. She saw her mom waving at her and started to run before suddenly falling down, her vision blurring up.

As her eyes opened and she saw a man with curly brown hair and a girl with blazing red hair dancing. The dancing girl stopped and turned around to face the other girl.

With a smile she said, "Hello Blanca...this is fate."

As Blanca disappeared, the dancing girl looked at a mirror reflecting Blanca's face. "I got you."

What Goes Around Comes Around

By

Kelsa Kazyak

DEATH. ONE WORD THAT WE USE SO CASUALLY THESE DAYS. I HEAR the word death as often as I hear the word hello. If death is really all that casual, then what's the big deal? Why do people spend so much money on funerals? If you really hated the person, then you should have just said something; you don't need to go and celebrate their nonexistence. And, even if you feel you need to pay your respects whatever you do, just don't go and get drunk at a funeral. That is just unforgivable. I assume, though, only my mother would do that.

To my mom, my uncle's death was like ordering Chinese food, a regular routine: 'Come on, dear; loosen up. It's not like your uncle dies every day. Have a few drinks. They'll take the edge off of his death.'

What a loser. What kind of person says something like that at a funeral? Not to mention a funeral for her brother. Well, I'll admit that my mom does have some logic. My uncle does not die every day, but many other people do. Come to think of it death really isn't that much of a big deal. The truth is that we really are dying. Every breath you take, every move you make, you get one step closer to death.

We spend our whole life just simply trying to do everything we possibly can. When are people going to realize that we are only on this world for a short time; what's the point? Every breath is a choice, so why not just stop it now.

Sam deeply inhaled. I will stop it now. She crouched down in her seat still, trying her best to stop breathing. Her damp, light auburn hair clung to the sides of her face. It left puddles right at the edge of her rib cage, where the sleekly wet hair ended. Her pale eyes peered out the window and watched as the rain came pattering on the car.

The truck made a screeching sound as it swerved to the side of the road. The swift motion forced Sam to exhale. As the truck tried to ease onto the road, another vehicle came whipping by. Her family's scratched red pickup trunk rammed into the passing car, and her head flung into the back of her mother's seat. Sam's eyes went fuzzy, and a black light soon enveloped her mind.

Sam awoke to a muttering of doctors and nurses. Although she didn't want to admit it, her first thought fell upon her mother. "Where is my, Mom," Sam burst out. The room fell to complete silence. The nurses' eyes shifted skittishly to the ground. A tense glance passed between the doctors. "Will someone please tell me what's going on?" Sam now spoke with irritation, and she made sure that she showed it.

A tall, attractive, and husky doctor stepped forward. Sam slid slowly down in the hospital bed. "Your mother has suffered a mild wrist injury. She is in medical testing right now, but you should be able to see her soon. Now please calm down. You have some cuts and bruises but nothing serious. Try to get so rest. I will be periodically checking in on you. Let me know if anything starts to hurt."

The doctor's sincere and placid voice echoed in the room. He placed his arm on Sam's shoulder and looked her straight in the eyes. He helped Sam got as comfortable as possible and then left. The nurses and other doctors followed behind. One female Nurse, Sandy, stayed back to talk with Sam. She helped Sam set up the television. Immediately after Sandy left, Sam fell asleep.

Sam awoke in a panic. She muffled to catch her breath. Sweat surrounded her face. "Hey, honey, you awake?" Sam heard the faint whisper of her mother's voice. Sam mentally dropped her jaw in awe. For a split second she felt connected to her mother.

Sam's quick temper soon controlled her mouth. "I am now! Thanks for waking me up 'Mom' you're so considerate." Sam noticed her mother grimace at her sarcasm. Sam questioned her angry response. She thought, That's weird? It's obvious I don't care for my mom, but I'm not normally the one to ruin a moment of connection. Mom usually can handle that on her own. Sam shrugged off the thought and focused back into reality.

"What's with the attitude?" Her mother questioned with a hint of fury.

"Attitude? Me? You're the one who was too lazy to look to see if another car was coming. You're the one who could have very likely got one us killed, if not both of us. You're the one who is too impatient that you can't even wait till I wake up to yell at me." Sam's temper flew loose.

"You know what! I am sick of you smarting off to me! I am your mother, and you will talk to me with respect!" Sam's mom said, furiously.

"I'll talk to you with respect when you talk to me with respect."

"I'm the adult, and you're the child!" Sam's mother paused and added more slowly, in a controlled voice. "You know, you're right. I'm sorry. I should have been more careful on the road, and I'll … I'll let you be alone now." What started out with a rage quickly turned into a tranquil expression.

Sam stared in awe. Her mother never let her win arguments. Sam wanted to apologize, but before she could collect the words to say, her mother kissed her forehead and walked out the door. Sam felt too comfortable to do anything else, so she turned on the TV to try to distract herself. If one thing about Sam never changed, it was the fact that she couldn't be alone with her own thoughts.

Sam, too exhausted to search for a good channel, settled on the first news station. "I'm Andrea Anderson, and I'm here in Japan, where 472 people just died because an unexpected volcanic eruption hit the Hiroshima area." Sam couldn't stand to listen to anything about death, so she flipped to the next channel.

"Twenty-eight people found dead and over fifty still missing when two airplanes collided with each other at the North Dakota airport runway." Sam crinkled her noise in slight irritation and flipped to the next channel.

"Forty-three people died in a terrorist attack in southern India. I'm here, right now, where it all took place." Sam flipped the channel as fast as possible.

Another news channel played on the screen. "Nine died yesterday here in Cuba when a school building collapsed. All are said to be children." Sam couldn't take it. She turned off the TV and threw the remote onto her mattress. She sat in her bed with an angry expression on her face. She thought about the numbers she had just heard, 552. Five hundred, fifty-two people left this earth within two days, and that's all that she heard from watching the news for five minutes. Five hundred and fifty-two. Sam thought about all the other reasons people died: hunger, war, car crashes. She never realized that death surrounded her. She drifted into a deep sleep with the number 552 in her mind. She couldn't think of anything else, just 552.

*   *   *

"Get your butt out of bed and go get ready for school!" Her mom screamed up to her.

"I'm up! I'm up!" Sam swung her five foot two inch body out of bed and quickly tossed on some clothes. Sam, not very big into fashion, normally just flung on some clean clothes. Sam looked in the long mirror hanging on the inside of her closet door. She flattened the edges of her red T-shirt and smiled her crooked smile. On the rare occasion that she smiled her lovely left dimple became clearly visible.

Through the mirror Sam saw her mother enter the room. "I love your dimples, I have ever since you were a baby."

The self-conscience thirteen-year-old quickly turned away from the mirror. "Well, I hate them!"

"Why? They are so cute," Sam's mom said.

"I gotta go to school, Mom." Sam flung her backpack over her shoulder and rushed down the stairs.

"Okay, whatever Sam, see you tonight. I'm ordering Chinese food." Sam's mom said excitedly, following her down the stairs.

"Hey, would you happen to maybe be doing your job as a mother and know where my winter coat is, its starting to get cold?"

"Uh…I'm not sure but I'll have it for you when you get home from school." Sam's mom, Judie, looked defeated.

"You don't know where it is…? Shocker!" Sam raced out the door before her mother could say anything.

Sam went through the day just like any other day. The day seemed like a blur until Andrew Flord, Sam's die-hard crush, asked her out. Ecstatic, Sam literally leaped for joy. "Today is the best day ever," she thought. The rest of the day Sam spent daydreaming, she even answered a question from the teacher, "You're so cute…" The female teacher caught her in the middle of a trance.

The day continued with happy thoughts until the lunch bell rang. The school's popular, dreamy, all American big mouth came over and told Sam that he simply just dared Andrew to ask her out. "Your lying!" Sam said as she threatened to beat him up if he spread that rumor.

"Ask him yourself if you don't believe me." Jake stated with a hint of fear in his voice.

Sam walked over to Andrew. "Was it just a dare? Answer the question, stop making excuses and just tell me if it's true!" She whipped the tears from her eyes. She felt angry and completely crushed all at the same time.

"All right, all right… it's true, it was a dare. Come on there is no reason I'd never date a creepy, stalker like you. Come on get real!"

Sam ran immediately to the bathroom with tears streaming down her edgy face. The rest of the day seemed to be very fuzzy. Her eyes felt red and puffy all day long.

*   *   *

Sam's long walk home gave her plenty of time to think of ways to pick a fight with her mom or think about what happened out school, but of course Sam couldn't stand to think about her feelings. Instead, she blasted her mp3 player the whole way home. She couldn't even tell which song she was listening to. The angry noise on the inside of her voice half cancelled the rock'n'roll music coming from her MP3 player. When Sam finally got home her annoying little brother stood waiting for her at the doorstep.

"Hey what took you so long? Mom didn't find your winter coat. Well, she did, but it's from four years ago. Good luck trying to fit into that thing. I did see your actual one, however. Do you wanna now where it is?"

Richie, Sam's brother talked with an annoying buzzing sound in his quick, smarty pants, nine-year-old voice. Sam loves Richie but, most of the time she doesn't really like him. Richie has a terrible complication that forces him to be unaware of the difference between reality and fantasy. He goes around jabbing light sabers into strangers, and he waves his "magic" wand.

Sam tries to be mature about his dilemma, but most of the time she gets angry for having to be super caring to him all the time. Although I wish he was "normal," I feel kinda bad for him. He even gets picked on at school. Oh well! Not my problem! Schizophrenia! That's it! I always forget what it's called! Schizophrenia! Richie has some type of Schizophrenia that causes him to go into delusions! It's some sort of mental impairment (Mom doesn't like it when I say mental disorder).

Sam nodded. She really did want to know where to find her winter coat. "It's in the basement, in a box with some of your old cloths. You wanna know how I know this? I'll tell you anyway, I know this because I'm doing this family tree project for school."

Quickly Sam responded, "Why would I care about any of this anyway? And why would you be looking in the basement?"

"You would care because I'm your brother..."

"Exactly, all the more reason not to care!"

"I'm going to pretend you didn't say that because I know you love me; even if you don't want to admit it. And I was in the basement because Mom said there might be some important stuff about our family history down there" Richie said the second sentence very speedily so that Sam couldn't interrupt.

"Whatever, Dork Mc Dorky!" Sam stepped up the front porch and almost entered the house.

"Oh, I wouldn't do that if I were you," Richie's voice sounded soft, but he seemed to be hiding something.

"Why is that?" Sam started to sweat even though she tried not to show it.

"Mom's watching her soaps again," exclaimed Richie.

"You mean her soap operas? Oh come on you are such a baby. Who cares if she cries and throws her chocolate at the TV?"

Sure enough, Sam's mom was watching a lame soap opera and crying. "Why are you leaving her? Oh don't do this to poor Lucy!"

Judie screamed and threw a chocolate at the television. Sam normally didn't mind when her mom watched TV. It only bothered Sam when she would pay more attention to the TV than her.

"Mom, I know I don't come talk to you about my day a lot. Actually I never do, but I had a really bad day and I kinda just need some support and love…" Sam hesitated on the word. She only remembers saying that to her uncle. "And I know you love me … and I love you too. I was hoping we could start to build a better relationship. I don't want to spend my walks home from school thinking of ways to pick a fight with you. What do you say Mom?"

"I must be going deaf! Did I just her you be pleasant to Mom and say you love her all in the same sentence? I must be hearing things!" Richie rudely butted into the conversation as his usual bothering self.

"Oh, shut up Richie, I'm not talking to you!" Sam ravaged with fury. "So Mom… have anything to say?"

"What? I love you too sweetie. Hey can we talk about this later? I'm kinda in the middle of something." Sam's mom continued to tune in on the TV.

"Yeah, I can see that! I can also see I made a big mistake! I just remembered why I don't love you!" Sam scurried to her room and slammed the door behind her. "I hate you!" Sam cried for hours. Sam cried about her uncle, she cried about her mom, and she cried about her horrible day at school. After the crying died down, Sam did her homework. Her mom came up several times to try to apologize. Sam had locked the door, and whenever her mother tried to talk through the door, Sam would blast music.

"Come on honey; I'm sorry! I just love concentrating on my soaps. I want to hear about your bad day. Maybe I can help," Her mom asked questioningly.

"You do NOT care about my day! You don't care about me, and there is NOTHING you can do. When you really want to help, learn to be a mother and then we'll talk." Sam expressed her anger in every word. Sam fingered her hair with fury. She did this whenever extremely angry.

Sam tried to sleep. She desperately wanted to shut her mind down, but she slept fitfully with anger. She could not get comfortable. Her head spun around and around. The room appeared silent, but Sam felt as if words choked her.

Her nuisance of a brother decided to annoy Sam. "That must stink. Mom didn't even pay attention to you. In addition, she waited until after her television show finished to come up and talk to you. You must be furious."

"Oh, just go away!" Sam squeezed her eyelids very hard together. She hoped that after a long second and when she opened her eyes he would be gone. Sam opened her eyes and of course Richie still peered into the room. "Well, it was worth a try," Sam muttered under her breath.

"Sam! I'm trying to help." Richie smiled with a devilish crooked smile that what make just about anyone question his intentions.

Sam, who quickly picked up on the fact that he was not trying to help, asked. "How could you help me? And, why would you help me?"

"Because I love you!" Richie definitely had something up his sleeve, and Sam hoped to find out what. "You should go get your winter coat before you forget. It's supposed to be very cold tomorrow."

"Okay… but, I know you're up to something. I'm going to find out what it is." Sam questioned her brother. She knew that she should go get her winter coat, but something smelled fishy.

Sam moped down the long staircase. She reached ground level, where her mom still sat watching television. Sam snuck behind the dining room and just made it down the basement stairs before her mom glanced over. Sam, not ready to listen to her mother's forty-minute argumentative speech about Sam getting angry with her for no reason, snuck down the stairs. They would go back and forth, arguing about nonsense. She was not in the mode, and, quite frankly, Sam always wanted to win at arguments, and she didn't have enough energy to fight and win.

Sam used her sly spy skills to sneak down to the basement. Her eyes were concentrating on her feet and only glanced up now and then. She reached the end of the long curving staircase and a mound of boxes enveloped her vision. Only stacks and stacks of brown cardboard boxes clouded her vision. Black scribbly words were written down the side of some of the boxes; words like "kitchen" and "master suite."

Sam, not at all interested in any of the unopened boxes, figured, if it wasn't important enough to open two months ago when we got here to take care of my uncle, then it's not important enough for me to go rummaging in now.

Sam tossed and threw and broke and tore all kinds of boxes. Her jacket seemed to be nowhere to be found. Sam spent over an hour digging through unlabeled boxes. Sam's eyelids grew heavy, and she began to blink very slowly. Before she knew it, she found herself in a resting slumber.

*   *   *

Her quick power nap brought Sam some much-needed energy. She fumbled over some boxes that she had been lying on and brought herself back to reality. Sam circled the thin path she had made, to get a clear view of all the boxes, several times.

Sam, just about out of hope, spotted out of the corner of her eye a box entitled "winter..." Sam couldn't make out the last word, but she had a good feeling about this box she needed. She unsealed the top from the clear plastic moving tape and tilted the box on its side against another box. This is it, she thought! Finally I can get my jacket and get out of this creepy basement. Why have I been looking so long? I can always wear two sweatshirts if it gets cold... Oh yeah! Richie! I'm not sure what you're up to, but I'm going to find out. He is just probably going to like try to scare me or something. Whatever!

Sam opened the box, and many old letters fell out. At first Sam paid little attention to all the old letters and brushed them aside. She continued to dig through the box only to find her coat missing.

Sam had not been paying any attention to the letters until her eyes happened to peer on the perfect spot to see the name of the sender. At first she didn't even comprehend what she had just seen. She passed over the name so quickly she thought she saw things, but then determined to clarify her mind that she had not just seen what she thought see saw. She assumed she misread the name. No way... "No way!" Sam said the words aloud. She looked like had seen a ghost; the ghost of haunted letters past.

*   *   *

"You knew about this? Have you been hiding this from me all along? How could you do something like that? What kind of mother would ever think of hiding letters? They were addressed to me! You can't just take my stuff! You had no right to do that!" Sam felt furious. She stumbled over every other word. She tried to say so much at a time that she practically choked on her own words.

"Calm down! Calm down!"

"CALM DOWN? I need to calm down! You are the one who has been lying to me for my whole life. You made me think my own grandparents didn't love me! What were you going to do? Just hide their letters until they die?" Sam went ballistic.

"No! I'm not that mean of a mother! I did this because it was the right thing to do." Sam's mom's voice trembled.

"It's the right thing to do? The right thing for who mom? The right thing for me or you? You had no right to do that. Forcing me to believe that my own grandparents didn't love me! The letters were addressed to me!" Sam hurled a small stack of letters at her mom's face.

"I understand you're upset, but you will treat me with respect. I am your mother!" Tension grew with each word. The two girls silently prepared what to say next as if a heated debate provoked.

"I'll treat you with respect when you decide to respect me!" Sam sobbed every syllable. "Were you just afraid that if I got to know them I might decide to live with them and love them better?" Sam didn't know it at first but that was the exact reason her mother had hid the letters. Whether Sam knew it or her mother showed it, Sam's mother really loved Sam. Sam imagined her mom afraid that she would get mad, leave to her grandparents' house, and hate her forever. Sam knew the she was right. If only Sam knew what was really in store for her.

In a flash, Sam grabbed a knife from the kitchen table, swung her jacket over her arms, rushed through the garage door, and Sam made a grand exit by slamming the door. Judie assumed that Sam just needed some time to cool off. Her thought never fell upon what Sam prepared to do.

*　　　　*　　　　*

I can do this! I can do this! I have to! There is no point in living now... If I don't do this Mom will think it's okay to just not love me. She's only going to realize what she's missing once it's gone! The hazy, brisk air made it perfect weather for what had to be down. Sam needed to take her own life. She couldn't bear to live another day with her mother. *This is not how I want my life to end but I have no other choice.*

Should I streak myself here? Sam motioned to her thigh. *It will probably be too hard to stick the blade through.* Sam squinted her eyes and examined the blade carefully. *What about my wrist? Or I could just stab it through my heart? Maybe my neck?*

She broke down into tears. Her eyes went blotchy and she flopped to the ground. After an hour of crying, she blotted tears from her face and noticed the hard rock in front of her, her uncle's grave. It was the first time she had really read the grave.

"A dear friend, a loved brother, a superb uncle, and a genuine human being."

That's my uncle! Wonder what mom will write on my grave. Tears came streaming down her face. *Come on Sam, You can do this, you can do this. Just think when this is all over you'll get to be with your uncle. Where ever he is...* Sam picked up the knife that had fallen to the ground at the beginning of her first cry session, with her right hand. She stretched her right arm out and angled the knife just perfectly. Sam took a deep breath and drew the knife closer to chest. A second felt like an eon and each centimeter the knife drew closer felt like a mile.

"NO! Stop Sam! Don't do it!" Sam's mother burst out of the car. Panting frantically as she ran over to Sam. "Please stop!"

Sam, startled by the sound of a voice, dropped the knife and turned around. "Mom?"

She picked the knife back up. *I have three choices: A) kill myself now, B) don't kill myself and let Mom be the hero, or C) wait until mom is about three feet away, scream 'I know you don't love me' and then kill myself.*

Sam quickly decided that "C" would be the most painful for her mother. Then out of nowhere it hit her like a big yellow school bus. The reason option "C" would hurt her mother the most was because she loved her. Sam placed the knife on the ground and turned around.

Sam got up and ran over to meet her mother as fast as she could.

The two meet about five yards away from the Sam's uncle's grave. The two immediately joined in a much-needed hug.

"I never thought I'd say this, but I know you love me and I..." Sam choked up on the next word, "And... I love you," tears of joy streamed down her face.

"I love you too!! So much! I wouldn't change a hair on your head!" Sam's mom said boastfully.

"That's a line from one of your soap operas!"

"It still doesn't change how much I love you!" The mother and daughter sat there laughing, crying with joy, and showing signs of affection. Sam had never felt happier in her whole life and her mom never felt closer to Sam.

After many minutes of peaceful silence, Sam spoke. "How did you find me here?"

"Richie said that he was playing in the backyard when he heard you mutter to yourself that you were going to kill yourself by your uncle's grave."

"Well, Richie isn't known for keeping secrets so that makes sense, but I guess I oughta thank that little twerp." Sam made a mental note to thank Richie for speaking up and poking into other people's business. Sam felt a raindrop so she peered up to the sky and saw that it started to drizzle.

Sam's mother must have felt a drop too because she said. "Come on dear, let's get home. It looks like it might start to pour."

Sam, not in the mood to get wet, picked herself up and the two began to slowly make their way over to the car.

"Wait up." Sam heard a faint voice from behind.

"Did you hear something?" Sam's mother also questioned the noise.

"Yeah I think it's coming from behind." The two girls glanced back and to their surprise found Richie.

"Oh, hey there Richie! How did you get here?" Sam's mother asked.

"By the way Richie, thanks for telling mom where I was. I probably wouldn't be alive if it wasn't for you." Sam tried to sound sincere.

"Oh I'm glad you're still alive." Richie exclaimed. "Let's go celebrate!"

"Celebrate? Where?" Sam's mother asked with much confusion.

"I don't know..." Richie pondered. "Ice cream! We can go to the Dairy King Hut down the street."

"That sounds good! Is that okay with you Sam?" Sam's mohter said.

"Yeah! That sounds great, but we shouldn't stay long because I have lots of letters to read," Sam said with a hint of complaint.

They all got in their truck and drove down the street. Richie and Sam jumped out of the truck immediately upon arriving. Richie, so exited for ice cream, ran across the street without even looking.

"Richie! Oh my gosh!" Sam ran after him. "You could have been killed!" Sam breathed heavily.

"Sam! Richie!" Sam's mother sprinted across the street.

Sam, hearing her mother's voice, turned at the exact moment her mother was hit by a bus.

"Mom! Mom! MOM!" The bus had stopped and there were people standing in a large circle. Sam ran to her mother. Sam's mom didn't move. Sam just lay there crying until the ambulance came and collected her mother. Time seemed to have stood still.

"Is Mom... alright?" Richie crept beside Sam.

"Mom's dead," Sam informed him.

"This is all my fault, isn't it?" Richie burst into a stream of tears.

Sam did the bravest thing she had ever done. She cuddled him in her arms. Sam rocked him back and forth as they lie crying. "It's not your fault!" Sam said sincerely even though she blamed him entirely. I can imagine how Richie felt. I know nothing good will come out at getting mad at him. I need to forgive him. They were in this world together and all alone now. They had to be there for each other.

*   *   *

I was right. She wasn't going to miss her until she was gone. I didn't realize I was talking about myself.

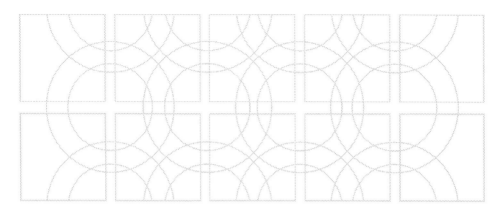

Finding Oneself

By

Laurence Lam

IN THE DARK AND NARROW, BUT LIVELY HALLWAY, MINORITY GROUPS huddled together to talk about their latest gossip. Here and there, people said, "Did you hear about the latest…?" The school seemed to be made of endless sporadic gossip. Anthony, a thirteen-year-old boy, had nowhere to go; a helpless wanderer lost in the forest. The local Chinese boy came to New Jersey to start a new life and attend an American public school. His dark brown hair and squinty eyes clearly expressed his Chinese ethnicity along with his slight chubbiness. Coming in at just sixty kilograms and five feet two inches, he looked like a fat dwarf compared to other students at his grade level.

Walking through the crowded hallways of Central New Jersey High School, Anthony Lee seemed like an object instead of a person. All the kids looked awkwardly at Anthony as though anticipating something. Anthony always acted shy and he didn't fit into the school environment. He just didn't fit.

When arriving at his first class, eighth grade science, Anthony placed his textbooks on the cold wooden desk. The dim lights flickered overhead. The overly decorated room had posters and science projects taped to the wall. Model airplanes hung from the wooden ceiling on short pieces of string. Anthony propped the chair against his sore back and took a deep breath, thinking, *how am I going to get through the day.*

When Mr. Sandberg, the science teacher, walked in, it relieved Anthony. Many of the kids threw paper planes through the air and sending curses across the room. The instant Mr. Sandberg stepped in, all the students rushed to their seats and just smiled. In Anthony's culture, disobedient behavior deserved punishment, but, here, the teacher sat down and smiled.

Mr. Sandberg pronounced, "Today we have a new student here with us. Anthony Lee joins our class, and I'd like all of you to welcome him."

At the back of the room, a few students snickered and made snorting noises, but the teacher rambled on. "Our class today will be focused on atoms and how they bond with other atoms…"

The discussion continued without any climax, and after two hours, snack time arrived.

The playground overflowed with happiness. Kids played on the swing-sets, and kids ran around on the pavement. Anthony found the new environment almost alien. *How could all these kids be having so much fun?* He thought to himself. Back in China, teachers did not like the idea of fun, and only enforced strict studying. In New Jersey, fun seemed to be the main learning experience for students. The new world truly baffled Anthony.

Unlike all the other kids, Anthony stayed by himself. No group accepted him. Constant doubts swirled around his head, and his vulnerability stood out. The bullies of the playground roamed around like lions. Each one carried a huge wad of money in their pockets, stealing from kids one by one until satisfied. The leader of the pack was Carter Benjani; a huge buff student who thought he controlled the school. Carter had light brown hair and a slight tan from his recent Hawaii holiday. Two of his recruits stood by his side, snickering and agreeing with Benjani every time he made a statement. They picked out vulnerable victims in the crowd and took lunch money for themselves.

Anthony, alone and susceptible to attack, walked around like a loner. As the bullies slowly advanced toward Anthony, sweat trickled down his white, plain school uniform. His hands clenched up in fright, and his eyes opened wide at the sight. The six-foot tall Carter towered over Anthony like David and Goliath.

Carter chuckled sinisterly, "Hey young boy. How's your first day at Central New Jersey High School. I hear you've made many new friends."

Tears filled Anthony's eyes.

Carter's companions started chortling in the background and gave each other high-fives. Carter then spoke, "Well, I'll give you a chance. Hand over your lunch money and we can be friends! Then things will be alright."

Anthony didn't know what to say. His poor English prevented a sophisticated answer, so he complied. Hands wobbling, he reached into his deep-blue trouser pockets and took out a five-dollar bill. Instantly, the smiles on the bullies' faces lit up, and they thanked Anthony for his kindness. Anthony knew that the gang lied about their promise, but didn't want to frustrate the gang more than he needed. No one back in China had ever committed robbery against him, and he started to doubt his life in America.

Anthony's unpleasant recess ended after twenty minutes, and he returned to the boring classroom. He didn't want any more hooligans messing around in the class again. The memories of the recess dilemma still lingered in his mind as he cautiously took a seat.

The social studies teacher Mrs. Crane walked into the room with a glum expression. As her feet hastily crossed the room, Anthony sensed another boring class.

The teacher started by placing her coffee mug on the hard metal table. She then picked up the humongous textbook lying on the table and told the class to flip to page 287. Anthony realized that many of the students at the back of the room, the troublemakers, started to stir up plans of disrupting class. Anthony didn't like this environment and decided to tell the teacher.

"Mrs. Crane," Anthony shouted, "the kids in the back of the room are annoying me."

The teacher quickly noticed the problem. Slamming her books on the table, she advanced toward the troublemakers. Glaring at Anthony, Carter and his gang pretended that nothing had happened and returned to their studies. The teacher saw that they acted their innocence and took quick note of it. She then turned around and walked back to her large metal desk. The teacher returned to her lecture about the effects of World War II.

The rest of the school day passed without incident, and once again, the hallways bustled with students chatting about their first day of school. Some had enjoyed their days more than others, but Anthony had the worst day of them all. Without saying a word, he carefully placed each school supply in his Winnie the Pooh backpack and headed back home. The urban setting bustled with businessman outside the school gates. After proceeding through the gates of Central New Jersey High School, Anthony hopped into his black Audi A6. An old Chinese man greeted him.

"How was your first day at school? How were the teachers? What was the school lunch like?" Anthony's father hastily asked.

Anthony didn't want to answer but remembered to be respectful. "My first day at school was great," he lied. "The teachers were amazing and I learned new things about atoms and their bonds. All the kids are very hard working and I fit in just right. The school lunch tasted amazing. I got a hot dog with potato salad." Anthony tried to pull out the widest grin possible.

Anthony's father responded pleasantly, "Well I hope you aren't having too much fun in school. Remember that learning is the most important aspect of school and ask questions if you don't understand."

The view of the Hudson River rushed past in the car windows as Anthony looked out. Massive buildings towered over the pier, each representing a part of New Jersey, each with a different personality. The sun began to set under the high-rise buildings. Although the view baffled Anthony, his current life reflected the exact opposite. In his life, many clouds covered the sun, and the water turned a murky grey. The seagulls that had swiftly tapped the water became ravens that cocked ferociously, searching for food to eat. The flowers wilted, and the tree's leaves began to crumble into ashes.

*   *   *

"Anthony, we're home." The mysterious voice woke Anthony up from his deep dream. Rubbing his eyes, Anthony looked up to see his home. The tall mansion rose above him and he hurriedly stepped out of the car.

The enormous mansion measured twice the size of the house he had in China. The stylish curves and details on the support pillars suggested a more classic style of housing. Inside, the ceiling rose high above Anthony's head and the chandelier dangled gracefully beneath. Anthony headed up the carpeted stairs to his massive room and slammed down his book bag. He then turned off the already lit lava lamp and jumped onto his bed. "I hate this stupid school," he screamed to the pillow. "All I'm ever going to be is a loner without a life."

Tears began to stream down his face and he clenched his teeth together. He released all his anger that he had previously kept in from his family. Using the brown school jacked he had bought at school, he wiped the tears off his eyes and blew his nose. Suddenly, sleep rolled in on him, and he closed his eyes. Almost instantly, Anthony's world became peaceful once again.

*   *   *

Anthony didn't know the time when his alarm rang. Outside his window, the sun rose over his neighbor's house. Chirping birds filled the oak tree in the front yard, and the sky the color of the ocean water. Immediately, one of his maids knocked on his door and entered. "Anthony! It's time to get up. It's already seven.

It took fifteen minutes to go from Anthony's house to school, but he had to prepare. Jumping out of bed, he felt the cold New Jersey wind surround him. After throwing on his white uniform and khakis, he proceeded out of his room, down the stairs, and into the kitchen. Five loaves of bread lay on the table and he took two. Rushing into his study-room, he shoved his school notebooks into a bag and set off in a sprint. On the way, Anthony took a glance at the clock and it read 7:30 AM. Happy with his late morning wake-up, Anthony steadily walked to the door and walked into the morning sunshine.

A white Lexus sat in front of the mansion, waiting for Anthony to enter the car. Anthony knew in all truth that he didn't want to go to school but his parents forced him. *Learning is essential to life,* echoed in his ears. As Anthony approached the car, a man with a white beard came out. He radiated happiness with sunglasses and a pair of white gloves, resembling a movie star. "Good morning Mr. Lee. I have prepared a cup of tea in the back seat. Please let me know if you need any more assistance."

"Thank you, Arnold but I'll be alright for now," Anthony said.

Anthony had always liked his driver. Upon entering the car, Anthony drifted off into a deep sleep.

"Anthony, we're here."

The words rang in Anthony's ears and he groaned as he exited the car. The familiar odor of fresh cut grass and the leaves of fall surrounded him. Kids wore jackets of numerous colors, which made the campus a lively array of taste. Only, Anthony wore a grey sweater, blue school pants, and a dull pair of Nike's. He looked like a black stone in the midst of flowers, a total misfit. As Anthony made his way through the school gates, he noticed a boy staring at him. Anthony had noticed him in class and he recalled his name to be Jarred.

"Hey Anthony! You're in my science class right? I thought I remembered you," exclaimed Jarred. "You want to hang out afterschool today. I can introduce you to my friends!"

Anthony, quite taken away by his friendliness, just smiled. "I'll try my best," he said in his best possible English.

The school day continued with no special circumstance. Just like the day before, Carter came by during recess to snatch money. Anthony had no choice but to go outside because the teachers encouraged *exercise*. No matter how angry he felt with Carter, he had no way out. Anthony didn't even consider standing up to Carter, so day after day, Carter robbed him.

The day he got back from school after being invited by Jarred, Anthony decided to give it a shot. He had never played much in China, let alone gone to a friend's house. Though not confident on the final outcome, Anthony trudged confidently into battle. When Anthony got back from school, he confronted his mother, Rachel, personally.

"Mom. I would really like to have some time with my friends after school. I know I haven't had this much in my life but I hope that this can change. I need to make some new friends."

Starting back from her newspaper, Anthony's mom replied, "You know the rule in this house! There is no playing but studying! Playing won't get you anywhere in life. How many times have we had this conversation? Go to your room and finish your homework. I still have ten worksheets for you in the living room."

Anthony had much to think about but stomped into his room obediently. First of all, his parents put a ban on playing in the house, but rather her mother had created the rule out of nowhere. Anthony had never bothered to ask his parents about playing because of an almost imminent turndown.

Why did I have to be born into this family? Anthony thought to himself.

He quickly changed into a blue sweater and jumped onto his comfy white chair. Not only did he need time to think, but his whole life had gone haywire. Anthony's attempt to make a living for himself had failed. *I guess I'll just have to tell Jarred tomorrow.*

*   *   *

The next morning, Anthony woke up to the buzz of his alarm clock. Anthony wiped his eyes and stood up. Last night, Anthony had formulated a plan to rebel against his parents and go on with his invitation.

Unlike the day before, rain poured down and the birds had disappeared from the oak tree. The Greek statues in the front yard looked darker from the rain, the pavement had turned an awful gray.

Well it seems even the weather has caught on with my attitude Anthony thought to himself. After racing down the stairs for a quick breakfast of tea and peanut butter, Anthony met his driver at the door. "Hello Mr. Lee. How are you today."

"I'm a bit tired, but I guess I'm OK," Anthony replied. "There's been a bit going on at school and home, so I'm quite busy now."

"Well that's OK. Everyone has to go through this teenage stage of life." Arnold gave Anthony at slight wink at the end of his sentence. Anthony worked so hard that he had no time to reflect on the past few days. All his planning had clouded his mind with ideas, but no results. *Maybe I should just keep it simple and give up on the plans* a voice rang out. However in the back of Anthony's mind, he still wanted to hang out with Jarred.

With his mind still running, Anthony entered the leather coated Lexus and traveled to the Central New Jersey High School. Upon arrival, he noticed a few students pointing at him awkwardly. Anthony barely made out the words; "He's…yeah…never talks…loser."

Although the last word stung the hardest, Anthony knew that he had to do something about the "never talks" portion. If he wanted friends, he needed to make an effort. Unloading his backpack onto his desk, Anthony cautiously approached a group of friendly students sitting at one of the desks. He heard Jarred conversing with his friends.

"Did you hear about Manchester United beating Man. City last week? Carling Cup Final baby!"

Anthony saw Jarred glance up. "Hey it's the new kid. Let him in the group and let's make new friends. We need reinforcements to counter those bullies. Anthony, how's it going?"

Anthony replied, "It's OK. Kind of tired." Anthony didn't look up from the table because everyone stared at him. After speaking, Anthony felt great. His previous nervousness during speaking turned into a happiness for being important.

"Well, all new students are like you, shy, tired, and most of the time quite kind." Jarred gave Anthony a quick smile and headed back to his seat. Class had just started.

Anthony entered his history class to find a packed room. He picked a seat next to Jarred and evenly spaced all his work on the desk. Carter and his gang of bullies took the back of the row, formulating plans for disrupting class once more. The danger of bullying lingered, especially following the past few days' events.

"HEY NEW KID!" A voice rang from the back of the classroom. "Maybe you should get yourself some protection because a storm's coming your way!"

Anthony nervously took in the words but kept quiet. His flabbergasted expression showed not only misery, but also a form of hatred toward Carter. Anthony never intended to disrupt their daily schedule; he intended to make the classroom a more peaceful place. Jarred and his friends had to be his way out. He just needed a solution to his parent's isolation problem.

*   *   *

Anthony knew that he had solidified his place in Jarred's friend's gatherings. During their common discussions about sports, Anthony had no input because of his lack of sporting knowledge. Other than a few games of volleyball back in China, he had never played a sport. Therefore, when Jarred and his friends started talking about Kobe Bryant, he became completely silent. He needed to talk to Jarred more about sports to gain some knowledge. Unfortunately, the "parent obstacle" constantly blocked his way.

After the morning class finished, Anthony went outside to the playground for break. He searched for bullies so in order to avoid them. He feared an attack from the gang. Something more serious than stealing money. His thoughts came true.

Jarred and his friends played basketball so he had no protection from the bullies. He had never played basketball and had suggested he not mess up one team's strategy. At the edge of his eyesight, he saw numerous large figures approaching him. Anthony tried to run, scream, and fight but nothing prevented the capturing.

"Hello little boy. It's good to see you again. I was just talking to my friends about…the incident during class a few days ago. I'd just like you to know that we don't receive that kind of behavior here." Carter reached into his pocket and took out a fragment of paper. He then started to pronounce the letter. "Dear Mr. Stevens (Carter's last name). I'd just like to inform you on your inappropriate behavior both in school and out of school. Your actions have bestowed many problems upon this prided school. For example, a student," Carter looked directly at Anthony and continued, "reported you stirring up the class."

At this, Carter folded the paper and gave Anthony a "you get the point?" look and stepped forward. All this time, Anthony cowered away and looked at the ground. He noticed that Carter and his friends had started to surround his exit pathways.

Once again, Anthony's teeth clenched and he tried to scrunch up his arms. Anthony always had nervous spurts when confronted by a danger. This time, however, the potential hazard rose. Carter's second man, Brant, picked up Anthony by his legs and dragged him to the garbage dumper. Anthony's cries of "Help! Help," faded and he cried softly under his breath.

The sky had turned a deathly brown and storm clouds boomed in the distance. A slight shower of rain fell upon event like background music. *How can I be going through this? This isn't what my life was supposed to be.* Carter continued to tow Anthony towards the huge green bin near the basketball courts. Amazingly, none of the other students even glimpsed at Anthony being abused. The teachers sat on a yellow bench scanning the playground but they didn't seem to care.

Anthony's world had turned silent and his sight had turned black and white. His nervous spout triggered his eyes to start swaying from side to side. His powerless arms and legs did nothing to stop the imminent. The grey pavement constantly lifted Anthony's uniform and scratched his back. Splinters of concrete poked into his skin, sending a sharp pain through his body. His arms felt like two worthless limbs, moving around on other's commands. The blood flow drained from his palms and a deathly white color followed.

The pain Anthony felt burned him physically and mentally. The abuse he faced terrified him. The pain suffered felt worse than his parents beating. At least the pain inflicted by the ruler stung for a while but left. The scratching of his body against the pavement never ended and he screamed in pain. "Stop! Stop! I'm sorry for everything I did! Stop!"

The bullies ignored Anthony and plowed on. The dark green bin came in sight. Anthony experienced weightlessness and the power of gravity when he landed in the bin. The bin sliced flesh off his right arm. The worst part of all came in the form of stench. The horrifying smell of rotten eggs, spoiled spaghetti, and molded broccoli drifted through the air.

When Anthony prepared to jump out, Carter pronounced, "I wouldn't do that if I were you. We're not done yet."

Instantly, two of his followers threw a metal lid over the bin and darkness fell upon Anthony.

"Hey guys, he's here."

A blinding light popped into the bin and Anthony made out Jarred and his friends. "We've been looking all over for you. When we heard about the bullies, we thought you'd be here." A slight grin from Jarred told Anthony that he might make it through.

*   *   *

After being rescued from the treacherous bin, Anthony called his parents and waited outside on the pavement. Anthony breathed a sigh of relief when he saw the white Lexus role into the empty parking lot. The images of being dragged along the concrete haunted Anthony's mind but he kept his composure. Anthony had requested both his parents to make the trip to school. He needed to explain a few events.

"Son, I think we need to talk. Get in the car," said Anthony's father.

Anthony bundled himself up and slid into the back seat. He didn't know what to expect from the talk, but he knew the final result. He just needed to try his best.

"So what happened, son?"

"I was just sitting outside when a group of bullies came up to me and grabbed me. I had caught them making plans to mess up class and they went ballistic mad. They dragged me across the concrete to the garbage bin and threw me in. They locked up the bin so I couldn't get out. I had to wait for someone to rescue me." Anthony had all intention of making his parents feel sorry for him. Anthony's only route towards having friends depended on the conversation.

"Well I'm sorry honey. Do you want to switch schools? There's a preppy high school just around the corner. You can study hard and get into good colleges…" Anthony's silence broke the happiness.

"Mom. It's not the school's problem but my problem." Anthony had to prove to his parents that friends depicted a real part of life. "I don't know about your high school life, but things have changed in the world. In order to have a successful school life, one must have friends. You two are restricting my urge to make new friends and that affects my academic life dramatically. I can't focus in class anymore because I'm scared someone's going to prank me. I can't walk outside the classroom knowing I'm safe from harm. All these things are part of my life and I hope you learn from this incident." Anthony wanted to lie down but the injuries from that day burned. Every time he lied back in his seat, a ferocious sting came spiraling up his back.

"Anthony. You know that we know what is best for you. We've made many decisions in our life that have impacted you in a good way, and I hope you realize that. However, this problem has brought a part of life we never experienced to the table. Back in our day, friends were plagues and studying, the cure."

The voice of Anthony's mother persuaded Anthony yet touched him but Anthony didn't show emotion on his face. "I know that things have changed since your father and I were married and I realize that people make friends now. I never knew this until now and I'll let you hang out once a week. Studies are still the most important part of your school but I'll allow you to see friends once in a while. I can speak for your father as well."

Tears of joy sprinkled out of Anthony's eyes and he knew he had won a hard-fought battle. He had persuaded his parents for once to do something he wanted to do himself. His constant persistence to fight off bullies and make friends had turned out with positive results and he felt great. Snuggling into a comfortable position, Anthony grinned as darkness overcame him once again.

*   *   *

"Let's go, go!" shouted Jarred from the stands. Anthony had stayed afterschool to play soccer with Jarred and his friends. The slight autumn breeze swept over him as he raced down the field to pressure the defender. Though a mystical sport to him, he set up for his first hang out experience.

"Pass left. Pass left." Anthony dribbled up to court with his teammates and coordinated a cross. He juked to the left and passed to the wing. Jarred skillfully put a one touch cross into the box for the header. As the ball swung in, the goalkeeper dove but completely fumbled and the ball bounced in front of goal. Anthony, totally clueless, jumped at the opportunity and slid in for the half volley. Defenders shot out from behind him but Anthony's quick reaction stunned them and he slid in for the goal. Fellow teammates jumped all around and tackled him to the ground.

Finally, Anthony began to come into the spotlight. He hid in the dark, but now he represented the star of the show. Anthony loved the feeling of everyone running around him. That day, Anthony's team ran out 1-0 winners and everyone cherished Anthony for his footy skills. Even some of the bullies backed off because of his popularity.

Through the intense few weeks of his Central New Jersey High School life, he had experienced much. His life had gone haywire, and he needed to cure it using help from friends and family. He knew the techniques, but he struggled to execute them. In the end, his perseverance paid off, and his life took another step towards joyfulness.

Sonya

By

Michelle Lou

"Play this."

Sonya's fingers flowed flawlessly over the worn-out ivory keys of the ancient piano as she played a complicated passage from Chopin, like her mother had instructed. The music swelled as it intensified, the notes twisting into a harmonious melody with perfect ease. Sonya's luxurious waist-length black hair fell over her face when she dipped her head to concentrate on the notes. Unfortunately, her pinky slipped off the black key, accidentally touching the white F before she could correct the mistake...

Smack. Sonya felt a stinging pain on her cheek. Surprised, she rocketed off the piano bench and put a hand to her hair-strewn face, feeling the throbbing under her palm. Her mother stood there with her hand raised, eyes blazing with fury and disappointment.

"Stop! Stop! Stop! What is wrong with you? Can't you see that this is an F sharp?" Mrs. Zheng yelled. She grabbed a red pen, circled the note in bright scarlet, and violently shook the sheet music in front of Sonya's eyes. "You are not resting until you can play this impromptu with every little technicality in place. You know you have a piano recital in about four weeks. You need to have this work of Chopin impeccably polished."

"But Mother!" Sonya protested. "I've already practiced for three hours! And I was really looking forward to going to Andrea's house for lunch today and hanging out with her..." The girl cringed under her mother's glare, and her voice faltered to a halt.

With piercing eyes, Mrs. Zheng frowned in disapproval and admonished her daughter, "Sonya, Andrea is a sophomore in high school who's nine years older than you. I don't want you to waste your precious time with that girl. You could be using it for doing much more productive things, such as practicing the piano or studying for the SATs. After all, we can't let your genius go to waste, Sonya."

"But—" Sonya hesitated. She bit her lips, holding back the profanities she wanted to hurl at the maternal, parental figure standing right before her. Secretly, she actually abhorred her mother. Dressed to perfection in a crisp white blouse and an immaculately ironed skirt, her mother had the mien of a flawless humane mother one sees on television shows. In reality, she was anything but. Internally, Sonya seethed and thought, "Just because I'm smarter than other girls doesn't mean that I would have to lose the freedom of having fun and hanging out with friends. If that were the case, then I wish that I didn't have the intelligence of a college student. I'd rather be an average girl who gets to spend her time relaxing instead of working all the time."

Mrs. Zheng maintained her stance and crossed her arms across her chest and glared at Sonya. "Don't 'but' me, young lady. Now, you either sit your behind back down onto that piano bench or go to your room until you get back into your practicing mode. I don't want to hear any nonsense about going over to Andrea's house this afternoon. Have I made myself clear?"

Sonya stared at her mother, and tears brimmed over in her aqua-grey eyes, dripping onto her eyelashes. Mrs. Zheng remained unmoved by her daughter's crying and raised an eyebrow, as if to say, "Well? What's your decision?"

Fuming, Sonya wiped away her tears with her sleeve and tried to keep her temper under control about the unfairness of the situation. "I think I'll go to my room," Sonya struggled to choke out. She then stomped out of the living room, raced up the stairs, and slammed the door to her quarters, with an audible bang.

She whirled around and gazed at her room. The gilded pure whiteness of the walls seemed to mock her, a deriding oxymoron at work. Sonya really did want to be an accomplished pianist; honestly she did. But the domineering control of her parents made music less and less appealing the more dominating they became. Sonya just couldn't TAKE it anymore.

She strode across her room and collapsed down onto her purple beanbag chair, sobbing so much now that all she could see in her field of vision were blurs of purple and white. A sudden flash of anger ripped through her. "How?" Sonya screamed. "How could they do this to me? I'm a good daughter. For the entire last week, I've practiced a total of twenty-three hours already. Why can't I take a little break?"

In her gust of frustration, Sonya picked up the closest object that came to hand and hurled it at the wall. A waterfall of pens and pencils cascaded down and scattered across the floor, leaving multiple scratches and marks on the once untainted wall. The wall seemed to represent how she felt inside, bruised and cut up from the words her mother had flung at her. A precious memory from two years ago flashed before her eyes.

A giggle. "Look Mommy! Look Daddy!" five-year-old Sonya pointed. "It's a purple beanbag chair! Oh please, oh please, oh please, can I have it?"

"But honey," Sonya's mother exclaimed, "your entire room is white! The lily patterned bedspread, the fuzzy rug on your floor, and the three bookcases you own are all the color of snow."

"And it wouldn't match, now would it?" Mr. Zheng interceded. He tweaked her nose as he teased her and then swung her up and twirled her around, right in the middle of the department store.

"It's okay!" Sonya proclaimed, as she shrieked with joy. "Anything will match with white! Please get me the beanbag? Please?"

Sonya's father chuckled and set Sonya back down in the shopping cart. "Anything for my little princess. After all, purple is the color of royalty. As you wish, my little girl."

Mrs. Zheng smiled in agreement, and added, "However, you have to promise that you'll practice the piano once we get home."

"Promise?" Mr. Zheng asked.

Sonya giggled again. "I promise!"

They bought it for her.

Sonya jerked back to reality, tears falling down her face faster than ever. She didn't feel very much like royalty right now. What had happened to her once loving and caring parents? All they did now was demand that she practice, practice, practice. There was never anything to look forward to. She felt an abrupt urge to physically express her feelings before she being forced to go back to the living room and practice again.

Sonya got up and stalked across the room, yanking five books off the top shelf of her first bookcase as she passed the midpoint of the wall. She heaved a hardcover copy of Pride and Prejudice at her bed that was pushed up against the other side of her room. It hit the backboard of the bed with a noisy, but dull, thump and slid onto her ivory pillow.

"Why?" she screamed as Black Beauty struck the bed's framework with a deafening crash.

"How could they?" Sonya screeched, as she chucked two more books at her bed.

"My cruel, unreasonable parents!" bawled the small, vulnerable seven-year-old. D. J., Machale's smiling face on the back cover of another novel, smashed against the wall.

Sonya collapsed onto the floor, her tiny body heaving as she sobbed. Tears streaked her pale, white face, and she felt spent after the sudden display of anger she had just shown. Her anger now dissipated, Sonya felt an overwhelming depression come over her. She kneeled on her carpet and cried.

*   *   *

Sonya wiped her tears on her sleeves and trudged out of her room toward the polished antique grand piano that dominated the living room. Honestly, she didn't want to play the piano just yet. However, there seemed to be some sort of unspoken agreement that Sonya had to resume practicing after she had finished expelling her emotions. It was almost as if she felt her mother's eyes boring into her back as she sat herself down on the firm piano bench. Sonya took a deep breath, poised her hands over the keys, and moved her fingers fluidly across the keyboard.

Sonya played even though she dreaded sitting at the piano. She played even though this was the farthest thing that she wanted to do right now. She played even though she felt that, at any minute, she could still break down in tears. She played because despite her antipathy toward practicing at the moment Sonya knew that she had to just suck up her emotions.

*   *   *

Weeks passed as little child prodigy Sonya worked and practiced all day, never stopping to rest. Her piano recital had gone infinitely well, not that her mother had actually acknowledged her achievement. Her mother now pressured her as she studied for the SAT exam scheduled only two weeks from today. Sonya would be the youngest child to take the exam. Sonya knew that her mother wanted her to use her genius to apply to the Julliard School of Music next year. Sonya didn't dare to rebel against her mother again, for the fear of being admonished. She was too frightened for that. Instead, Sonya buried her nose in her books all week and hoped that she would get a good enough score on the SATs to satisfy her parents.

Today, she decided that she wanted to take an online practice test and get it immediately scored so she could view her progress. She tiptoed into her father's study room so she could access his computer, carefully keeping quiet because it was almost midnight, and she didn't want to wake her parents.

"That's odd," she thought, as she approached the open door to her father's study room. "Father never leaves his door open."

Usually, Mr. and Mrs. Zheng were very careful about keeping things neat and in place. After all, they constantly scolded Sonya and told her to clean up her room. Maybe being a neat freak was one of the side effects of being a research scientist. However, tonight Sonya's parents must have forgotten to close the door before they went to sleep. Perhaps they had just been too tired and had forgotten to shut the door. It wasn't really that bizarre to find an open door, right?

Sonya had never used her parents' computer without their permission before now, but she thought that this would be an exception. The floorboard gently creaked as Sonya walked stealthily towards the sleek black Dell desktop computer that stood on the large oak desk. She sat down in the plush leather chair and turned on the computer, which made a small beep. The bright blue background glowed as Sonya typed in some commands. She accessed her mother's login account, using the hint available to guess that the password was her mother's birthday.

Sonya moved the mouse and was about to click the swirling E that represented Internet Explorer. However, a folder on the desktop caught her eye. Sonya's breath caught. Her hand, basked in the soft glow of the monitor, moved to click on the file named "High Priority Project S.O.N.Y.A." Sonya sucked in a deep breath and tried to open the folder.

"Darn," she muttered as a notification popped onto the screen. "The file is password protected." Intensely curious, she opened the application, Terminal, and typed in a few commands, searching for the encryption of the folder and trying to crack the password. She scrolled through pages of binary code, perusing the data carefully, until she saw the six-letter key to opening the folder.

Sonya typed in the code and felt her breath catch in her throat as document after document popped up onto the screen. Bright glaring words—S.O.N.Y.A. DNA ENCRYPTION, BEHAVIORAL OBSERVATION, DATA ANALYSIS—popped out at Sonya. Her eyes wide with shock, Sonya scrolled through an infinite string of numbers and multiple pages. Snatches of information popped out at her.

"Eye Color DNA Code: 10985327890987234612394651—"

"Specimen seems to flourish under supporting conditions, is intensely strained under extreme pressure—"

Tears welled up in Sonya's eyes. No... It can't be...

"Predict that it will perform better when standards are set higher—"

"Acts like teenage girl, intelligence level matured its personality overall—"

She couldn't breathe as her mind raced with traumatizing thoughts. "I'm an experiment. But how? I'm a person, here and in the flesh. I have feelings and thoughts. And I have parents! An experimental specimen doesn't have parents!

"Andrew Zheng and Rose Zheng in charge of experiment—"

"Pose as its parents, give it a normal upbringing—"

I'm not even referred to as a person! Sonya thought to herself with shock. I'm an "it!" The shock turned into woe. And my own parents probably don't even think of me as a daughter. They're just two scientists with an experiment to conduct and observe.

She gasped. "This is why they've been pushing me so much lately. It's all for the sake of this 'experiment' and to see how I would react under these different 'conditions.'"

Sonya couldn't bear to look at the screen anymore. It hurt her too much. On the verge of tears again, she completely shut down her feelings to avoid a complete mental breakdown. Sonya regained control of herself, and turning off the study room computer, she silently padded back to her room.

* * *

Sonya slapped a large manila folder onto the grand mahogany desk that nearly towered over her delicate three foot, six inch frame. A lanky, dark-haired young man, who barely seemed like a college student, sat directly across from her. Sonya read Mr. Sam Clayton's diploma that hung on the wall behind him, and she knew that he, a law graduate of Yale, was just about to take his first case. Mr. Clayton was young and nervous, eyes flitting back and forth between the little girl and the documents. Sonya observed the man as he wrung his hands. Mr. Clayton was obviously unsure of what to make of the young child that was here recruiting for the help of a lawyer. She realized that not only was it risky for him to side with a girl who was young enough to be in first grade, it would also be unnerving for him to have to work with a small kid.

Since it seemed like Mr. Clayton was not going to be the one to broach the topic first, Sonya forged ahead. "My name is Sonya Zheng," Sonya stated. She took a deep breath. "And I want to sue my parents for the rights to my own life."

Mr. Clayton stared at Sonya in shock. Sonya could imagine what he was thinking. "Why do you want to sue your own parents, Sonya? Did they not give you the cookie you wanted? Or did they take your toys away?"

Sonya glared at Mr. Clayton. "With all due respect, Mr. Clayton,

I know exactly what I'm doing. This has nothing to do with some trite problem like the lack of toys or sweets. I have an ample reason to sue my parents in court. In fact, if I'm lucky, I hope that I can get emancipated and be free to live by myself without any of their stifling control."

Mr. Clayton gaped at Sonya. "You don't seem like a typical six-year-old," he stated as he picked up Sonya's file and looked through it, noting her age.

"You have no idea," Sonya answered, a small sarcastic smirk playing on her face at the irony.

Mr. Clayton regained his composure. "However, do you know what it means to sue your very own parents? It would be internally heartbreaking, and the cost of this trial would be significantly large; I doubt you have the money to pay for this."

Tightlipped and defiant, Sonya reached into her knapsack and let an arrangement of coins and dollar bills fall from his palm and clatter onto the giant wooden desk. Mr. Clayton watched the waterfall of money drop onto his desk, and then turned away so he couldn't look. He observed the pattern of the large beige curtains in his office, watching the swirls and drops. Mr. Clayton turned his head away as Sonya poured all her life savings forward.

"This should be enough to pay for everything," Sonya remarked, keeping her voice even and level. She terribly wanted to leave her parents (Not parents. Scientists. Sonya reminded herself.) They were stifling, over-controlling, and too demanding. Not only that, but she found out that her entire life had been one big joke. She wasn't an actual person; she was an experiment. She was an experiment that was purposely genetically modified to be a super-genius. She was an experiment that could be played with and poked around by those biologists that Sonya used to call her parents without them feeling any empathy whatsoever. An experiment that just couldn't take the never-ending pressure to be the prodigy that she was created to be.

Sonya had wanted to get emancipated so badly that she had sold the necklace that her father (Scientist! Sonya chided herself) had gotten her on her fifth birthday at the pawn shop, getting only a quarter of the price that it was worth for the solid silver chain and the four-carat amethyst set in the center. However, the money still turned out to be quite a hefty sum, enough for Sonya to hire a lawyer.

The problem now was convincing the lawyer to actually take the case. Sonya carefully scrutinized Mr. Clayton facial expression, which remained surprisingly emotionless and flat. She suspected that this was probably a trick that he learned in law school so people wouldn't be able to tell what was going through his head. However, she could still tell that the gears were grinding in Mr. Clayton's head. Sonya anxiously waited for him to say something.

Mr. Clayton shook his head. He leaned forward in his chair and told Sonya, "Tell me why you want to sue your parents. Do it in detail and don't miss a single thing. I want to hear the entire story from the beginning to the end. There has to be an extremely good reason for you to want to be emancipated. If you don't, then don't even bother going to all this trouble."

Sonya looked at Mr. Clayton, and nodded. She took a deep breath and told him everything, from the pressure that was starting to build up on her, to the fact that she found out that she was a genetic experiment. Mr. Clayton listened intensely.

After Sonya finished with her story, he thoughtfully said, "We can try emancipating you…but it will be very risky. You are way too young to live by yourself. However, perhaps I can find some loopholes in this case, as you are a very exceptional girl." He nodded to himself and put Sonya's file into a cabinet that towered behind the mahogany desk.

Sonya let out a huge breath and sighed with relief. "Really?" she asked. "You'll represent me, Mr. Clayton?"

Mr. Clayton smiled broadly and offered out his hand. "Call me Sam," he replied.

* * *

Months passed as the papers for the court were filed. Meanwhile, Sonya stayed with her parents in their house—now a war zone. Her parents' voices, now guns, screamed deadly "word" bullets at her, and the house became a battlefield. Ever since they had received the notice of the court case, they tried all they could to make Sonya reconsider. Relief flowed through Sonya when the day of the trial finally came. Whenever she felt like she was going to fall apart, she thought of how, very soon, she wouldn't have to deal with all of this chaos anymore. Sonya spent much of her time avoiding her parents.

The day of the trial finally came. Sonya went to meet with Sam again right before the trial started. He went over the logistics of how Sonya was to behave in court, and he discussed what they were going to say. Sonya felt quite comfortable around Sam now. He acted as an older brother to her, offering her helpful and consolidating advice and being able to speak out for her in the legal world at the same time.

"I want you to stay silent Sonya unless they call you up onto the stand. I'll do most of the talking. Leave everything to me, kid." Sam affectionately ruffled her hair. He had taken to calling Sonya that after they started building up an almost sisterly/brotherly relationship. Their long sessions together had created a sort of bond between the two.

"The...the scientists," Sonya whispered. "They're extremely angry."

"You'll be fine. Just take deep breaths."

Sonya turned her head away, and her curtain of hair covered her face.

"The trial starts in five minutes," a blonde woman interrupted, her head peeking through the open doors, "so get ready." Sam nodded toward her direction and turned back towards Sonya.

"Are you okay?" Sam asked.

Sonya slowly looked up and nodded, fingers clutching each other nervously, the knuckles almost white. "Yeah, I am."

Sam looked at her with concern and smiled. "We're going to kick butt," he offered as advice.

Despite that fact that they were about to go to a trial that could decide the course of the rest of Sonya's life, his little joke lightened the tense atmosphere, and Sonya tentatively grinned back at him. They walked out the room and headed towards the courtroom.

The courtroom was amazingly intimidating. It had high dome ceilings and multiple rows of benches lining each side of the room. Towering over everything was a shiny, polished oak bench, where the judge would sit. Sonya and Sam slowly walked up the aisles between the rows of benches, trying to avoid drawing any attention. Sonya stared straight ahead to avoid the gazes of the jury and the guests.

Everybody else was already in place. At the defendants' table sat Mr. and Mrs. Zheng, looking angrier than ever. The audience watched curiously. The bailiff made them swear oaths before taking a seat.

"All rise for Judge Megate," boomed a loud voice, as a woman in black gowns glided into the courtroom and towards the bench. Sonya anxiously stood up and sat down. After going through the legal procedures before every trial, the judge finally banged her gavel and stated that court was in session.

"Your honor," Sam said as he stood up and strolled into the front of the room. "My client is pleading for emancipation from her parents."

Total chaos followed Sam's announcement, and a full-blown battle ensued.

*   *   *

"I rule in favor of Andrew and Rose Zheng, and deny the emancipation of Sonya from her parents," Judge Megate began. "Although the girl has every right to leave and live by herself, I'm afraid that Sonya just doesn't have the means to support herself until she reaches the legal age of eighteen. And, while Sonya may be on an intellectual level equal to or above most adults, she is still emotionally a little girl." Sonya's heart sank as the judge turned towards her and continued, "I'm sorry Sonya, but it just seems best this way. Case closed." The judge banged her gavel on the desk and left the room. Sonya sat there stunned and almost in tears. An entire waterfall of tears was cascading out of her eyes.

Sam stood there, obviously uncomfortable and having no idea what to say to Sonya to make her feel better. For a moment, he was at a loss of words. Sonya's parents marched over to where the two were standing, grabbed Sonya, and dragged her to the car. Mr. Zheng turned around and seemed like he was about to say something to Mr. Clayton, but then he closed his mouth, spun around, and headed towards the car. Sonya looked back at Sam watching them go. She tried to use her eyes to tell him goodbye. In an instant, Sonya decided against submitting to her parents. She broke free from her father's death grip on her arm and ran towards Sam.

"Don't let them take me! Please, Sam!" Sonya pleaded with an intense look in her eyes. "Take me with you," she said. "Take me with you."

As her father dragged her yet again to the car, Sonya thought she saw Sam give her a barely perceptible nod.

*   *   *

Days later, Sonya held her breath as she knocked on Sam's door. Through the glass, she could see him wondering curiously at whom it was, and he opened the door and poked his head through the crack and saw Sonya standing there on his doormat. "I...I ran away," she muttered. "I hope you'll let me stay here for a while." Grinning widely, Sam threw open the door and welcomed Sonya into the house. "Come on in," he said. "And luckily for you, I have a piano in my house."

Ecstatic, Sonya jumped for joy as she hopped onto the piano bench and played her heart out for Sam. Not once, did Sam interrupt her and criticize any of her playing. It soon became a tradition for them to sit around the piano in the evenings. Sam eventually appealed the case and won custody of Sonya. Once again, Sonya loved music and felt loved.

Vengeance

By

Kevin NA

FATHER! TIM SCREAMED IN HIS HEAD. TIM HAD A HORRIFIED LOOK ON his face as he saw his father facing against the truck full of German soldiers. He dared not go any closer than his current position, for he feared getting in trouble. Even though he could not hear much, he could see everything very clearly. As Tim saw his father getting slammed against the cold metal side of the truck. His father shouted out profanity. Tim did not know what to do, as he saw the Nazis take his father, his mother, and his sisters away. They were led into the back of the truck, were he saw other people from town.

Tim realized what was happening. He saw a German soldier take the necklace of the Jewish Star and slammed it against the ground. The necklace did not stand a chance against the stone pavement. The dust gathered on the road as the truck sped off. He was confused and in shock. What was happening? Tim thought to himself intently. His mind raced, adrenaline pumped through his body as he realized all the things that could have happened. Were his parents in trouble with the Germans? Were they ever coming back? Thousands of questions popped up in Tim's mind has he tried to figure out what was going on. He just could not bring himself to think what he would be like without his parents, without his family.

As the truck sped off into the distance, he saw families come out of hiding. He went next door to his neighbor's house, but no one was home. He knocked on other peoples house, but no one would open. Everyone had deserted him. No one would trust him.

If no one is going to help me, I am just going to have to help myself. Tim exclaimed into the empty streets. He first had to have to find out why his parents were taken away. He realized that if he were to start at the root of the problem, he would first have to find out what the problem was.

Tim walked back into his home, and went into his parents room to gather things. He was determined to find his family. As he looked at his parents things, he saw himself in the mirror. He questioned himself, interrogated would be a better word.

"What are you doing Tim? Look at yourself in the mirror. You have mud streaks across your face. You are only a kid, and you are up against the Nazi's. How are you going to do anything that would make a difference?" Tim looked at himself, a small child, only five feet in height. One might say he barely looked like the thirteen year old he was supposed to. He shook himself of the terrible thought has he looked around for clues.

He found his father's prayer cap, and all their religious things scattered across the floor. He was surprised, because many of these things he had not seen before. Planks were torn up in the ground as the ceiling looked as if it had fallen apart. He was scared as ever, to find that out in the backyard, the books of prayer and beliefs were being burned. He was desperate to find answers, and his family.

Tim lay in his bed, as he wept. For he knew that he would not see his family, in a long time. Tim thought about what he had to do. How would he survive without his parents, without money, without food? As he thought, his eyes focused on a piece of paper hanging under the dresser. As he got up, he crawled onto the floor and reached for it. He slowly took the piece of paper from the ledge, because he was scared what the piece of paper would say. As he unfolded the yellow page, he saw what had been hastily scrawled onto the paper.

My Dearest son,

If you are reading this paper, then we have already left. This is a very important that you tear this piece of paper up after you read it, so remember what I say carefully. You must have many questions right now, but I only have enough to time answer a few. The Germans have sent us to camps. We will probably die there so do not come looking for us. It will be a waste of time. I'm sorry to break it to you so suddenly.

If you take scissors and cut a hole in the mattress, there is about 300 dollars for you. Use this money to escape to Spain and do not come back. Spain will be the only place you are going to be welcomed, and be able to survive in.

Love forever,
Your family

Tears were streaming down his face as Tim read this out loud. A shadow was cast upon him as his tear drops dripped on the paper. He could not think, he was in too much shock. The only thing that could come to his mind was that, the Germans will pay.

Tim sluggishly trudged through the mud as rain poured down on his face. He was sad and confused at the same time. He could not understand why someone would take another person away just because of their religion. Tim had gone to school the next day to question his teacher about what had just happened to him and his family. His teacher, Mrs. White, had explained that, "Some people just don't like Jews."

With his possessions carried by a sling pack hung over his shoulder, he climbed onto his bicycle and started for the nearest general store. He needed to buy some items before setting off on a long trip to Spain. When he first got to the store, many of the people inside gave a loud gasp and then walked away quickly. He reached the cashier and presented the items he wanted to purchase. "One pocket knife, a flashlight, batteries, can of beans, and deck of cards will all be 12.50 cents please." Replied the cashier. Tim presented his bills and walked away quietly.

He set off on his bike for the docks. He was amazed at how many boats there were. There were so many different types of boats here!

There were fishing boats, ferries, cargo ships, even small houseboats. They were all decorated in many different colors. His eyes followed the horizon line to a dark part of the docks. There were black ships, armed with cannons and guns, that looked like ghost chariots that raced across the ocean. He shuddered to think who, or what, could possibly want to drive a ship like that. It was horror show of its own.

Tim raced himself to the ticket booth. "One ticket for spain please." He chirped. Tim was as nervous as a chicken in the pound. The cashier raised one of his eye brows and replied, "Sorry son, but we aren't allowing boats to go to Spain unless we give you a full background check."

"Why is that?" Tim questioned. The cashier looked at him real funny and pointed at the sign. If a Jew is spotted, please bring him to the German head quarters immediately, they will be handled as humanely as possible. The sign struck daggers into Tim's heart as he limped across the beach. He needed to get out of his town, France was unsettling for him right now.

He quickly paced around the lamppost. It all made sense to him now. His family was Jewish and were taken away by the Nazis. That is why everyone was avoiding him, no one ever made eye contact with him. It was like he was secluded from the entire world. He mind swirled as if a hurricane had struck him right in the stomach. Just because of my religion, what I believe in! This isn't fair. Why me? Why can't they choose another thing to pick on? Tim was a wreck.

He couldn't think straight, Should I go save my family, or do what they told me to and run off to Spain? He pondered this question as he walked the dirt road back to his house. If I do go to Spain, how will I ever get there? Everyone knows I am a Jew, and no one will let me leave the country. The dilemma had hit Tim right in the face, and he had no way to face it.

Dear family,
 I have worked five years in the camp. It is a terrible place to be. I am really thankful that you don't have to go through the same thing every day. This is going to be the end of me one day. I have been putting soles into shoes forever.
 Is this what I will be destined to do? Am I suppose to do

something else other than putting shoes together? I am only going through this for my family.

Why did I choose to not run away with my family. I am pretty sure that I could have done a better job if I had chosen to immigrate to a different country.

This camp destroys the soul so much that I barely remember what I came here for. The job is one fluid motion. You put the sole into the shoe, and you pass the shoe on to the person next to you.

I have been doing this motion for over five years and I think that I have repeated it over 50 million times.

This is my final goodbye and warning to you kids, leave your houses, and don't grow up to be like me.

Sincerely,
Your Father

Tim shocked himself when he found out that the little boy also had his family taken away and that he was alone now. He analyzed the little boy as he saw him tearing up. Tim thought, This boy must be very courageous and strong to go through such a shock at an age so young. Tim realized that this was probably happening to children all over the world and that he wasn't the only one that had to go through this tragic event. Children were losing their families all over the place just because they were Jewish. Then a thought struck Tim. When they find out that I am still here, the Germans will come for me too! Tim quickly grabbed the little boy and ran back to his house.

He was too horrified to find out what would actually happen to his own family. To his sisters and parents. He needed to save himself and his loved ones before they would be hurt, or ever worse, killed.

He grabbed what money he had and all the possessions he could carry, and started to look for a boat that would take him. As he pasted the docks again, he saw the horrifying boats that dwelled on the docks. He could not take his eyes off them. His eyes followed the horizon line to a dark part of the docks. There were black ships, armed with cannons and guns, that looked like ghost chariots that raced across the ocean.

He shuddered to think who, or what, could possibly want to drive a ship like that.

But Tim, being the curious boy that he was, he decided to venture upon one of these great black boats. He walked up, it was shaped like a sausage. Half of the boat was underwater, and the other half was on the surface. A small platform was at the end, protruding out of the water.

He tan on top of the platform, but making sure no one was around to see him. The ships were guarded by Patrolling soldiers. They were caring guns, black, and dangerous things that were slung around the backs of the soldier. Tim took his time finding a loop in their vision. There was none. The only way to get onto the ship without being spotted was from the water then.

Tim Jumped, headfirst into the ocean. He had been taught to swim by his grandparents, when they had the time to go fishing. He knew not to make much sound, so instead of free styling it to the ship, he breast stroked. Whoosh, Whoosh was the sound the water made. Tim felt his heart skip a beat when a soldier looked his way. He quickly dived into the ocean. The soldier stared, then grumbled, "Must have been some fish or something."

The boy then began to swim towards the ladder. It was wet, but it still flaked with pieces of orange rust. He jumped up and grabbed ahold of the railing. He then propelled himself down through the hatch.

It wasn't completely empty, there were still many guards on the ship. It was also very small compared to what he thought the size was, and could probably only be 50 feet long.

Tim started to walk towards the back of the ship, each step made his heart beat faster. He looked all around him, but nothing seemed familiar at all. He was lost in a giant maze like boat. He tried to open another door, but then the alarms started to wail. German Patrols started running towards him. He could hear the clanking of their metal boots on the ground. He started to run the other way.

"Schießen Sie den Eindringling!" The soldiers shouted. There was gunfire all around Tim. He could hear the bullets whiz past him. He started to bolt even faster towards the door. *He would make it,* Tim assured himself. He jumped over a railing, and the next.

Tim grabbed the ladder and start to scramble to the top. His hands were sweating so bad that he almost lost grip. The rust of the ladder was rubbing off onto his hands but he did not notice. His foot slipped as another slab of paint fell off the ladder. He could not think of what would happen if he fell down the ladder. He could only imagine the death and pain.

What bad luck was following him? Was this God's way of punishment? He did not know what to do. As he grabbed the last rail of the ladder he leaped and jumped into the water. The guards showed up on the top of the submarine a few moments later. Tim could feel his own heartbeat from his head. His head was pulsing. He could not think. He could only think of the horrible things that could have happened to his family, they would be forced to work, and his sister was only six. He had no choice, because the only way to get to his family, was to get caught.

As he dried off his clothes as he began looking for his backpack. His eyes widened as he realized that he could not find it. Three Hundred Dollars. Those three words echoed in his brain for hours. Three Hundred Dollars. His father's and mothers pay for a week. How could he have lost it?

Tim slowly walked towards the building with the red cape tossed across it. The swastika on the cape was like the symbol of death for him. Just looking at it sent shivers up his spine. But, Tim knew he had to do this, because he had to save his family. What little hope he had left would only be that they would be together, no matter what would happen to him.

"Hey, What are you doing?" The German guard yelled at him. The guard approached him, throwing away his cigarette.

"I have come here to present a Jew!" Tim cried out.

"Where is he? Jews are dangerous and children like you should not be with them!"

"I am the Jew"

Tim was shoved into a small room. "We will come and send you away in an hour." The ropes that were tied around his arms were cutting into his wrists. He could not do anything but hope that he would find his family after this. He looked at the walls of the small room. Many things had been itched in here. But he could not stand it. All the things that had happened to Tim suddenly came right down on him. He started to cry, bawling his eyes out. He laid on the cold stone floor, waiting for what was to come for him. His eyes got droopy, as he fell asleep, thinking of the misfortune that had been bestowed on him.

Tim was violently shook awake. The German soldier scolded at him for not being faster and dragged him from his feet. His arm was almost pulled out of his socket from the German's tug. This choice of his to go rescue his family seemed to be a bit crazy after a nights sleep on it. Many things and questions were circling around Tim's head as he tried to concentrate. "Move it!" The guard yelled as he jabbed Tim in the back with the butt of his gun. Tim could not focus or concentrate as he was led by the guard to the truck. Many other people were also here. The Germans then started to sort out the Jews. Women, men then children were each separately put into individual trucks.

Tim stared into the distance, as the truck sped off. He saw his own town fade into the mist surrounding the truck. This was going to be a long journey the thought to himself. As he then proceeded lean against the side of the truck. He thought for a while, the anxiety of all this happening to him was too much. He thought about how he could just end it right now if he jumped in front of another passing car. But then he thought about how he must be strong to rescue his family, how he would be the hero in the end. The rest of the world must have known about this, and other people would be trying to rescue his family. Not only his family, but his religion.

He looked around for a moment, as all the children were led aside. The Germans separated the families. Some fathers even tried to fight the Germans as they realized the families would be separated, maybe forever. A guard then shot the father on sight. He yelled out to the rest of the crowd, "This, is a warning. Anyone who tries to fight back, will be shot. You have, what, only your fists? We have guns, think before you act, or it maybe your last!" A guard told the children they were going for a quick shower. Lots of the children stared blankly at themselves, as they realized they were very dirty, ragged clothes. Tim could not wrap his mind around the concept of going for a shower? Weren't the Germans making the Jews go to work? Wouldn't they just have them shower after their work?

The guards marched around the small crowd of children. As they approached the shower area, Tim did not see anything suspicious. *It is actually a shower?* Tim thought.

As the children were led into the giant room, the giant door slammed shut. Then he thought about it, if it were just showers, why would they try so hard to keep them inside? This didn't add up. Tim looked around at the other children. The showers started to run, not with water, but this a yellow looking kind of gas.

"Run! Run for your lives, it's a trick!" Tim shouted out to the other children. Tim could not think of anything else as he watched the crowd of children suffocating in the gas.

"Try to break the shower heads, or cover them up with your shirt or something!" He shouted to the mob of children that were still standing.

He jumped and shimmied up the pole as he started to hit the showerhead. But it was solid, made out of reinforced steel. He could not help but realize that this was what they meant by shower. He stared at the pile of children.

His body started to heat up, as his insides started to burn. He fell down, his head hitting the hard cement. He then said a silent prayer that many others would repeat over the many years of massacre.

The Chip

By

Billy Radlein

ANGIE'S HEART WAS BEATING, THE WORLD WAS FADING, EVERYTHING around her was a big wreck. All she could hear was the faint calling of her sister, which awoke her, Jane. Angie dragged herself out of the wreckage, Angie saw their mangled car and felt her arm beating with throbbing pain and remembered about the car crash. Just then she realized her parents were still in the car, she screamed and rushed to the other side of the flipped car and looked into the passengers seat to find her mother and father sitting lifeless.

"Help!! Help!! Mom! Dad! wake up!!" yelled Angie. She felt tears gushing from her eyes and felt her world running into a screeching halt. Jane saw everything and rushed to hug her as she joined her crying with the horrible sight still in their view.

*   *   *

Buzzing is all Angie hears now her alarm clock, which jumps her out of bed. She glances down at her cast on her left arm with a sigh and starts putting on her clothes and fixing her tangled brown hair. She hears a knock on her door to find her big sister Jane to be there as she opens it. "Hey are you feeling alright?" Jane asked. "I'm feeling fine and my arm seems to feel like its getting better too." replied Angie. She heard footsteps thumping up the stairs to see their guardian, Joe. "Is everything all right girls?" said Joe. "Yeah we're just getting ready for today." The sun was shining with a nice cool breeze, the perfect weather outside. Somehow the bright sun and gentle breeze allowed Angie and Jane to forget for a moment about that devastating accident that stuck to their mind.

"Come, get in the car." said Joe.

"Coming" replied Angie as she took a few deep breaths when entering the back seat. Jane sat in the front seat. From the past accident Angie hated riding in cars especially the same spot where she was sitting during the accident. Jane as an older girl is learning to overcome it. The car shook lightly as it started, slowly is began backing out of the driveway.

"So what are some things you wanna go look for while we are shopping?"

"I'm fine I'm just gonna meet up with my friends." Said Angie.

"I'm not sure but I might need to pick a few things up." Said Jane. "Okay because we have to go to the Orlando Mall to pick a few things up." Said Joe. Despite the perfect, calming weather Angie hated riding in cars. As the car started speeding up to catch up with the speed limit. Angie clenched her fist and closed her eyes tightly.

*   *   *

Angie opens her eyes and looks around and sees her sister sitting next to her in the car and hears her say "Angie come on, wake up." she shook her. Angie looked around to see they arrived at the mall, then she wondered how she fell asleep so easily. She stretched and got out of the car and suddenly felt happy that she came out of the car alive and headed for the mall, she expected to meet her friends there.

She walked aside Jane as they walked to the entrance to the wide building with the sunlight shining warmly on her face and a small breeze hitting her back. They walked in and Joe said "Okay, Jane you and Angie have some money so you can go shopping for clothes that you need. I'll be just here for a few jeans and shoes. Angie call me when you are with your friends when you meet up with them so I know who you are with." Joe started walking the other direction as Jane and Angie headed to the second floor and got what they needed.

"Hey!" said a voice next to Angie, it was her best friend Hannah.

"Hey!" replied Angie as they hugged and two other friends joined, Marissa and Lauren.

"Hey Angie I haven't seen you in a month and your arm looks like it's getting better." said Hannah.

"Yeah thanks, it still isn't its best yet though." said Angie.

"Okay, I just called Joe and now I'm going to get some jeans so you have your phone so you can go with your friends." said Jane to Angie. Angie waved and walked away with her friends to continue with their day.

As Angie and Hannah and the rest of the group were walking along the side on their way to their favorite store 'Bang!' a deafening boom sounded the whole building. They heard screams as they instinctively ducked down for cover.

Confused and frightened at the same time, Angie and her friends stayed down as bits of debris fell from the ceiling and bells went off. After a few seconds, the girls got up and looked around. Terrified, they saw a sight of a worker a few yards away who was lying down...with nothing surrounding him but blood and the debris that had hit him. Two of the girls panicked, Angie tried to stay calm and turned her way from the horrible sight.

They could still hear screaming and alarms going off, Hannah quickly pulled her phone out and dialed 911.

Angie's pocket vibrated, it was Jane calling her on her phone. "Jane, I'm okay! where are you!?" said Angie. "I'm in Macy's, I don't know what is going on, ten seconds after the explosion there were these people walking through this entrance with guns. I can't even tell what kind of people they are they just rushed in. I hear people yelling and I'm not hurt and I'm in the clothes department.

Are you sure you are all okay?" said Jane in a very worried voice. "Yes, but nearby a worker got hit by falling debris and isn't breathing or anything. We called 911 and the ambulance should be coming." replied Angie. Suddenly a loud scream flies down the halls and Angie runs to the corner to look around and see the sight of guns being held in the hands of men jogging down the hall.

Angie wasn't sure what to do, "Follow me." said Angie as they swiftly but lightly went into the bathroom.

They heard the gunmen jog by the bathroom entrance, they then slowly and quietly came out and looked around the corner and saw the gunmen yelling out "Listen! We are looking for someone by the last name of Ozgard."

After Angie heard that she felt her heart jump. It was her last name.

She felt her head spin. She knew something was wrong so she quietly sneaked back around the corner and signaled the rest of the girls to follow. She and her friends quietly ran over to the Macy's to find Jane. "Angie!" yelled Jane.

Angie ran over to her sister. "Hey are you okay?" asked Angie. "I'm fine I'm just happy you aren't hurt."

Just then she remembered Joe. "Jane! Is Joe okay?" said Angie. "Oh my Gosh!" exclaimed Jane. She quickly pulled out her phone and dialed the number. Ringing. All she hears is ringing, no answer.

"Hello, this is Joe. I'm sorry but right now I can't reach the phone now. Please leave a message and I'll call you back when I can. Thank you." -Beep-

"Joe! where are you! Joe pick up! pick up! Joe pick up!" Jane started to worry. she hung up in a frustrated way. "We need to find him." said Angie.

"Okay, Lauren and Marissa, you guys stay here and hide down near the Macy's entrance and tell us what is happening. Me, Angie and Hannah are going to find Joe and see if we can get some keys for an easy way out." said Jane. "Okay." the other girls agreed. Jane led the way to the back staircase. They quietly went up to the staircase to avoid attention. They went up to the third floor to see nobody nearby. "There's the food court, maybe we can find something there.

They jogged over to the food court area, "Hannah, go behind the counters and back doors and see if you can find anything, keys, a phone, anything." said Angie.

"Okay." replied Hannah. She ran over to the counters and looked around for anything.

Jane spotted a police room. "Hey Angie over here." said Jane. They walked over to the police room and went in, nobody.

"Why are there no police or anyone here to help?" asked Angie.

"I don't know, I really don't know why any policemen are even in this mall." answered Jane.

Angie spotted a Taser gun, "Hey we can use this for defense in case we need it. How do you even use this thing though?" said Angie. She accidentally pulled the trigger which made the wires fly out right past Jane's face and stuck to the wall almost shocking Jane. "I'm so sorry!" said Angie.

"Please Angie just be very careful." said Jane. They walked out of the room.

"I've got them!" yelled Hannah as she jogged over to us with a ring of keys.

"Okay, anything else?" asked Angie.

"No I just found these keys and I'm sure they can unlock the back doors which are usually locked." said Hannah.

"Okay then." said Jane.

Angie could hear shouting coming from the first floor. Not screaming for help, but shouting. She dialed Lauren and called her with her phone. -Ring-

"Hey Angie I think somethings really up." said Lauren in a worried voice.

"What's going on?" asked Angie.

"Look over the railing to the first floor." answered Lauren.

Angie swiftly ran to the railing and looked over, she saw most of the gunmen there. Along with them were many civilians-hostages. "We are not leaving until we find the kids of the Ozgard family." "Oh my Gosh!" Angie gasped with fright.

Angie slowly backed away from the railing and ran back to the food court area. "Why is this happening? What do they want?" Angie said.

Jane saw a man far away down the hall laying there with a bit of blood around him. He looked familiar. Jane pointed him out to Angie and they ran to him.

Angie looked down to see that it was Joe. "Oh my Gosh! Joe!" Angie started shaking.

"Joe wake up! you have to wake up now! Wake up Joe!" Jane was saying that while shaking him repeatedly. He groaned, he could only move a little bit, he had a bit of consciousness in him. "Help pick him up." said Jane.

Jane, Hannah, and Angie all lifted him and brought him to the wall for him to sit up.

"I'll be right back." said Angie. She ran over back to the food court as fast as she could and grabbed cloths, she then retreated back to Joe. "We need to put pressure on his wound." said Angie. They wrapped the cloth around him and tried to get him back on his feet.

"Joe! Listen to me. Stay awake, do not fall asleep stay awake!" Jane yelled at him.

They all put their arms around him to help him walk down the back stairs. They met up with Lauren and Marissa.

"We're gonna get out of here." said Angie to all the girls. They went back to the back staircase and helped Joe go down to the first floor. Right in front of them was the back door that led outside. It was locked, Hannah took out the keys she found earlier and looked through them and tried them all out until she got the right key. They saw the light and the sun hit their faces as soon as the door opened. They quickly and quietly ran out while holding Joe. Closer and Closer to the car they got they kept up the pace. Once they made it to their car they carefully put Joe in the back next to Angie along with Marissa. Lauren sat in the front while Jane was driving.

"We need to get to the Hospital quick." said Angie. With a small sigh of relief they were happy they made it out of the mall and on their way out they saw many police cars headed to the mall.

"We need help! help!" Angie yelled as they entered the Emergency room entrance.

"Okay, we've got him." a lady said. Another doctor came in with a stretcher and we put him on it and they quickly rolled him around the corner into a room.

"I hope he's okay." said Lauren.

"Thanks, I do too." Angie said. The clock is ticking, slowly going by.

After an hour a doctor walks up to Angie. "He is going to live." he said.

"Oh, thank God" Jane said.

Relieved Angie let out a big breath that her guardian is alive, and that we would be re-united with who my dad called his best friend.

Six hours later another doctor came to Angie and Jane, "He is fine right now he is going to be out in a moment. He is hurt on his hip because that is where he was shot. Be careful because he is in a bit of pain but he'll be alright." said the doctor.

Just after he said that, Joe came in right behind him, walking.

"Joe!" said Jane.

Angie hugged him. "It's great that you are okay." said Angie.

"Why did that happen at the mall? Joe did you hear them asking for us? There's something they want from us but I don't know." said Angie.

"No, I was unconscious most of the time. I was worried so much about you two when that bomb went off, I'm just glad that you are all alive." replied Joe.

"We still need to know why these people are doing this and what they want. We don't have anything really important." said Jane.

"Joe, was there anything that our parents have left us?" asked Angie.

"Not anything I've heard of that may be really important." replied Joe.

Now it was kind of silent, the only thing she could hear was the curiosity going through everyone's minds. They are back in the car, Angie still frightened by the time the bomb blew up and saw the body of the worker on the ground lifeless, plus that she is sitting in the back of a car in the same spot during the time of the car crash. So many emotions were flying through her head right now. She was at least a bit happy she is going home, where she can relax and find out what is going on.

It was late at night when they arrived home, the stars above are hanging in the sky shining. Angie pulled out her cellphone when she got out of the car and dialed Marissa's number.

"Hello?" said Marissa.

"Hey Marissa, did you and Lauren get home safe?" asked Angie.

"Um, yes we did, both of our parents were extremely worried they practically cried when we got home, but I don't blame them. I'm very worried about the other civilians in the mall." said Marissa.

"Yeah me too. I'm gonna think and see if I can find out what is going on. So yeah, I just wanted to check up on you to make sure you were okay." said Angie.

"Yes well we are fine and thanks but my parents want me off the phone right now so I have to go. I'll talk to you later. Bye." said Marissa.

"Bye." said Angie. She hung up then headed for the front door of her traditional styled home.

The second she stepped into her house she had a weird sad but partially welcoming sensation. She fell onto the couch thinking about this whole day and what those horrible terrorists were up to. She got up and walked up to her room, "Goodnight Jane, I'll talk to you in the morning." said Angie.

"Goodnight." replied Jane.

Angie got undressed and jumped into her bed. The images and emotions of the horrible day kept flashing around in her mind. The good time with her friends, the explosion, the dead worker, hiding from the terrorists, finding Joe with blood around him, hearing her name being yelled out by the voices of the terrorists. She began to cry and felt tears run down. 'Are all of the other people in the mall alright? Did they make it out? Will those terrorists set off another bomb or keep trying to find us?' All of these questions which now remained unknown kept flowing through her head.

All of a sudden, a thought popped up right in her head. 'What if our parents had something that was really, really valuable to these terrorists? What if they knew something important and had it documented and we never knew about it?' She thought hard. Could it be true? Maybe, maybe not. She knew that if those terrorists where there to get her, then they would have to have had something important, the question is, what is it?

*   *   *

Buzz! Buzz! Buzz! Angie's alarm clock screaming in her ear. She felt very tired so she slowly and dreadfully got up like as if she were drunk. "Was that a dream?" Angie said to herself. "Maybe it was." she thought. She went to check on Joe, right when she saw him she saw the bandages and a big scar on his side.

"Yes, it was not a dream" she said to herself. As soon as she remembered the flashbacks of the other day: The bombing, the terrorists, her name being called by the terrorist, rushing Joe to the hospital. She remembered.

Angie rushed downstairs so fast almost tripped on her way downstairs. She went into the living room and turned on the TV. CNN came on the screen. 'Yesterday, it appears that there was a bombing terrorist attack at the Orlando Mall. Many people were hurt and five people including two workers were killed in the bombing. Many reports from people say that right after the bombing gunmen rushed into the building and hacked into the Police communication radio and shut everything down. After getting calls by 911 from civilians the ambulance and police came to the scene. Hurt civilians and workers were rushed to the hospital, two people didn't make it because of internal bleeding. After the police arrived to the Orlando Mall, the terrorists have escaped and they have lost track.'

After Angie heard that she laid down and held her head. "What do these people want!" Angie said to herself.

"Hey Angie." said Jane. "We need to see what is going on here with this attack and why they want us." she said.

"We need to maybe find something Mom and Dad had in which these people may want. We never really knew what Dad did when he was on business trips." said Angie. They searched the house. "I'm going to look in Dad's old office. You should look into the basement." said Angie.

"Okay." agreed Jane. Angie walked to the staircase and ascended up.

As she reached the hallway she looked at the door to the office that hasn't been touched in a while. 'Creeeeek' she heard as she slowly opened it and looked around to scan the setup of the office. There was a leather office chair set behind a medium sized dark wooden desk with the right side pushed against the wall facing a window with casual world style decorations sitting on the desk and a couple on a book shelf on the left side of the room filled with old books and a couple photo albums.

As the warm sunlight from the window shined in an area of the wooden floor she walked over to the bookshelf an pulled out a photo album. Some dust flew around as the book was slowly pulled out, Angie opened up the book and saw a big family picture of her, Jane, and her parents when she was five. Angie flipped the page and smiled when she saw a picture of her and her Mom making funny faces. She closed the book and walked over to the desk and sat down in the leather chair. She looked at a bronze reading lamp and switched it on. She felt the smooth wood of the desk and thought that the last person that was sitting in this spot was her father.

She opened up the drawers and they easily slid out and saw some files. She looked and rummaged through them and found nothing but what seemed to be just work papers. She let out a sigh then hardly pushed the drawer back in and suddenly 'Click' is what she heard. It sounded like something was unlocked.

She felt around the desk and put her hand under the bottom of the drawer and felt a small handle, she pulled it and saw a smaller unseen drawer automatically slowly slide out the bottom and inside was a big file filled with many papers. She took it out and saw stamps above the text saying 'Top Secret' and 'Government Only' and other ones. She gasped. "What is all of this?" she said to herself.

Then 'Knock knock' "Angie are you in there?" it was Joe's voice. She rapidly put the file back into the drawer and pushed it back in. She ran to the door and opened it.

"Yes I'm just looking at all of my Dad's old stuff." said Angie.

"Well. Okay. Are you alright right now?" said Joe. "Yes I just have a headache and my ears hurt from the explosion. The question is are you okay? You are recovering from a bullet wound." said Angie.

"Yes I'm fine it just hurts a bit." replied Joe. "Okay I'm going to be downstairs, you need to lie down Joe." said Angie.

"Okay." said Joe.

Angie walked downstairs and went to the basement door and opened it. She saw a light turned on at the bottom of the stairs so she knew Jane was still down there. She carefully step by step walked down and saw Jane looking for something useful for them to know.

"Jane." Angie said.

Jane jumped and turned around. "You scared me. Did you see anything?" said Jane.

"Yes I'll show you, it was all these secret information papers for the government and I think that there would be more so we need to keep looking." said Angie.

She placed her hand on the bar of a closed vice and she suddenly leaned into it. 'Clunk' made a noise and at the far end of the basement the wall went up and a small room with a hallway appeared. "Oh my Gosh." said Angie. Jane just stood in amazement.

They walked very slowly to the other side of the basement and looked into the hallway once Jane took her first step in rows of light flickered on and lit the whole room. they saw a metal vault at the end of the hallway.

"What do you think is in there?" asked Angie.

"I don't know but if its hidden like this it must be very important." said Jane. They walked over to the vault and looked at it. On the vault was a combination lock and an odd-shaped key hole on the side of the vault.

"Maybe that key is also hidden somewhere around this house." said Angie. "Maybe it is." said Jane.

They walked away from the big vault and headed back to the entrance. "I don't know if we should tell Joe about this, because he may get in the way or not believe us." said Angie.

"Yeah maybe we shouldn't." replied Jane. They walked out and two seconds after getting out the lights switched off, the vault area was blocked, the wall came back down then the vice lever went back up to where it was.

"Wow" said the girls simultaneously in amazement.

They both went upstairs. "Come on, I'll show you what I found." said Angie.

They ran up the stairs to the second floor. They walked up to the office door with Angie in front. They creeked the door open slowly and walked in and saw the big office chair and the dark wooden desk and the bookshelf.

"Over here." said Angie. She kneeled down and opened up the big drawer the slammed it shut and heard the click noise. She then stuck her hand underneath the drawer and found the handle and pulled it. The small drawer came out and they saw the file. "I found all the stuff in here." said Angie. They opened it and saw the Top Secret papers.

"Wow, what is all of this?" said Jane. They glanced and flipped through the papers and put them away.

"So, we do know what the terrorists are after." said Jane.

They walked down to the living room and sat down to take in the unbelievable things they saw. "Why do you think Mom and Dad wouldn't tell us?" asked Angie.

"I'm sure because it was just so important that they couldn't risk telling us and maybe having us tell other people." replied Jane.

"What about the terrorist, do you think they will attack again?" asked Angie. "Maybe, we just need to be ready and careful when leaving the house." said Jane.

Joe, after an hour came downstairs looking like he took a five hour sleep "Okay, anything you girls want to eat?" asked Joe.

"No we are making sandwiches. Joe you really do need to stay in bed and not walk around that much." said Jane.

"I'm fine. I'm just checking up on you. I'm going back into bed in a minute." said Joe. "Okay, just get well and tell us if you need anything." said Jane.

"What should we do about this?" said Angie.

"We should just hang tight and keep all of this stuff away from the terrorists. We should maybe look through mom and dad's stuff a bit more to see if we can find more information and what they were doing." said Jane.

They were very tired and needed to think about this whole life that their parents have had. 'Did one of my parents invent something that is in that vault that holds the most important information about the government or something? Do they have more things hidden that are very important?' Angie thought this through many many times as she laid down on the big couch in her living room.

Jane just sat and watched TV as she laid on the recliner. She felt like she was having a dream because of what she is seeing. The terrorist attack, finding files in her father's home office, finding a huge hidden vault in their basement. She can't believe any of it is happening. Angie was very tired and was laying down so she thought she might as well take a nap. She closed her eyes and felt weight gently press down her body and she drifted off to sleep.

'Crash!' Angie heard the moment she woke up from her nap. She thought something fell and broke. She looked at the clock and saw the numbers 6:28. It was dark outside. 'Crash!' Again she heard, and this time it sounded more like a window breaking.

"Jane?" said Angie. She went to the kitchen and grabbed a steel mallet. "Hello?" said Angie with a shaken voice. She slowly and quietly went upstairs where she heard the crash coming from. She got to the top of the stairs and crept around the right corner.

Walking down the hall she heard something making noise in her dad's office.

"Angie" she heard Jane whisper and pulled her down.

Angie shrieked with surprise.

"Shhh. Quiet." said Jane. "Somebody's in there we have to go in and find out." said Jane. "Okay, lets go." said Angie. They slowly stood up and crept towards the door and heard the rustling and fumbling sounds coming from the other side of the door. They slowly opened the door, Angie gripped the meat hammer in her hands tightly. 'Creeaak' went the door as they rushed in and saw a man with a ski mask looking through her dad's desk.

"Ahhhhhh!!" screamed Angie. "Joe!!! Help! Get out of here!" screamed Jane at the top of her voice. Joe ran over and saw the intruder and ran to get his pistol.

"Get out of here!" yelled Joe. Angie ran downstairs and flew over to the alarm system and rapidly pressed the Panic button and pressed the button that said Police. Sirens went off and ran upstairs and heard Joe's gun fired. She quickly went to the office and saw nothing but a bunch of papers on the floor and a broken glass window, no intruder in sight.

After four minutes the cops showed up. "Hey, you girls alright?" asked one big officer. "Yes, just a bit shocked." said Angie.

"Well okay." said the officer, he then walked away to talk to Joe.

"I'm sure that that person was after the files or something." said Angie to Jane. "Yes, he must have been after the files or something. Maybe one of the members of those terrorists." said Jane.

"It has to be." said Angie.

Next morning Angie woke up with a chilled feeling resting on her shoulders. She got up and walked into the office to find the broken window with a sheet over it to temporarily cover the opening. She saw Joe in the bedroom laying in his bed as if he had been up since three a.m.

"Jane. Jane wake up." said Angie as she was waking her sister lying in bed. Jane opened her eyes.

"Hey." she said.

"Girls we need to take a quick trip over to Bi-Lo and Lowe's for food and to get the windows fixed." said Joe. "It won't be long we just need to get a few things okay?" said Joe.

"Fine." said Angie. She got dressed and went out to wait for Joe and Jane.

"Okay come on." said Joe.

Jane was driving due to Joe being hurt and not being able to drive well. So she got into the driver's seat as Angie moved to the back.

"Let's go." said Angie in a low voice.

They backed out and headed to the Bi-Lo first. When they pulled into the big parking lot and found a spot near the entrance, Angie walked in and felt the cool air conditioning the second she stepped inside she felt very comfortable.

"Okay Angie, you go and find some milk with Jane, I'm going to find things at the deli and we need to get some chicken. Meet me over there when you get the milk." said Joe.

"Okay." said Jane.

Angie and Jane walked over to the back of the store where the milk usually is. They looked for the brand they needed and once they found it Angie reached for it.

"Okay lets move on." said Jane. They walked over to the deli and saw Joe there.

"Okay we got it." said Angie to Joe.

A tall thick yet small man in a black suit walked over to Angie and Joe. "Are you the children of the Ozgard family?" asked the man.

"Yes." replied Joe. "We need to talk with you." said the man.

They were directed to a room in the back of the store with a table and four chairs surrounding it. "Sit down please." said the man. Angie, Jane and Joe sat down.

"Is there something wrong?" asked Joe.

"Yes," said the man. "You remember the attack of the terrorists at the Orlando Mall a few says ago?" asked the man.

"Yes" replied Joe. "Well, it appears that those men were after you and want something really important which was involved in what Mr. and Mrs. Ozgard did for a job you may or may not have heard. They worked for the government. They held important information that has abilities such as tapping into the military missiles, which can launch into various countries. The information of this is put into a chip that may be locked away in your home. We have a key that we have recovered from Mr. Ozgard's pocket after the crash a few months ago. We believe that opens up the container of the chip." said the man.

'The vault in the basement.' Angie thought. "We must search your house or ask questions about any thing you have found that may lead us to it. This is very important, you remember the car accident, apparently that was not an accident. It was the terrorist who was at the mall a few days ago. They are after the information."

Angie felt a huge shut down on her legs, body and mind. 'It wasn't an accident.' She couldn't speak for a minute. Jane was also speechless.

"We need to immediately check your home." said the man. "Let me see some identification." said Joe. The man reached to his belt and pulled up a badge.

"Okay." said Joe.

They went back to the car and the man and other policemen followed them. They reached the house and pulled into the driveway. They went to the front door and Joe pulled out his key, it unlocked and they all walked in. Angie felt a weird feeling when she stepped into the home.

"We know where everything is." said Jane. Since Jane had already told them Angie just had to show them as well.

"Come up." said Angie. She led them into her dad's office and kneeled down at the drawer of the desk. She shut the drawer, reached down and yanked the handle and saw the smaller unseen drawer automatically come out. Joe watched in astonishment. Angie pulled out the file and handed it to the man.

"Great." said the man.

"Now come down here into the basement." said Angie. She lead them into the basement and saw the lever up she turned it. Nothing happened until she realized that she was supposed to turn it counter-clockwise, so she did so. A big noise sounded as the wall on the other side of the basement went up.

The man was happy Angie was able to help them find this so he just said "Good Job!"

They slowly walked into the hallway and the lights went off. Then 'Click!' but it wasn't the vault it was more like the sound of reloaded guns. Angie turned around and saw six of the terrorists behind everyone holding guns to their heads. Angie gasped with fear and Jane almost screamed. Six men with guns were pointing their weapons to the heads of Joe, the man, and four other policemen.

"What do you need?" asked the man.

"Give that girl the key." said the first one.

"Me?" Angie pointed to herself.

"Yes." replied the terrorist.

"Okay." said the man. He slowly reached into his pocket and pulled out an odd-looking key, not like a door key. He handed it to Angie and she carefully took it into her hand.

"Go! Unlock it now!" yelled the terrorist.

"Okay." said Angie. She tried to stay calm because panicking sometimes leads to no good. Her heart was pounding. She walked through the lit hallway and saw the vault door with a keyhole on the side of it. She approached the door and looked at the keyhole.

"Go! Hurry!" yelled the terrorist with anger.

Angie jumped with fright from his screaming and moved her hand with the key towards the hole. With trembling fingers she put it into the keyhole and turned it left. Then the sound of air pressure letting out sounded and the vault door slowly opened and a dim light inside appeared and got brighter and brighter in a few seconds. She looked inside and saw a small computer chip.

"Take it out!" yelled the terrorist. Angie's heart jumped, she reached in and grabbed the chip. She looked at the small chip. It had OZGRD C4*5 written on it. She walked back to the front of the hall.

"Give it!" said the terrorist with force.

Angie hesitated and carefully handed it to the terrorist. He yanked it from her hand.

"Excellent." said the terrorist with a deep greedy voice. The other terrorists put down their guns but still were ready for firing.

The man in the suit reached into his back pocket unnoticeably and rapidly pulled out a gun and aimed it.

"Hey! You think I won't shoot anyone? After bombing a mall? After killing their parents? You should just be smart and throw your gun down!" yelled the terrorist.

Then Angie saw a girl quietly come down the steps and peek in on them talking. All of a sudden she sees Lauren, with a small gun in her hand.

Lauren was looking around to see where she should shoot. She then spotted a water heater next to the terrorist speaking. She carefully aimed and fired. Hot water sprayed out of the tank into the terrorist's eyes.

"My eyes!" screeched the terrorist. He fell on the floor and the other terrorists looked up the staircase and saw Lauren at the top of the stairs. She ran and went around the corner just in time after the terrorists shot their guns. The man picked up the chip, which was dropped on the floor. The terrorist was still hurt and the man kicked his gun away.

"You are under arrest." he said to the terrorist.

"Oh my Gosh! Lauren!" yelled Angie after the men ran upstairs to catch her. Lauren ran outside with the five other terrorists out there surrounded by police in the driveway.

"Lauren!" Angie ran over to her friend and hugged her. "How did you do this?" asked Angie.

"Well I was coming over to visit you and I found out something was up because of the yelling of that terrorist because I recognized his voice so I called the Cops, and when I came inside Joe's gun was resting on the table, so I figured I should maybe get it to help." said Lauren.

"Thank you. You are an awesome friend." said Angie.

Jane helped Joe up and came running outside.

"Angie! Lauren!" she yelled and came up to hug them both relieved they are okay. Joe came out ran to Angie and hugged her.

"Where is the chip?" asked Angie. The man came to Angie.

"I've got it. We are going to take it in and keep it extra guarded in a government facility. "Great job girls." said the man. He pointed to Lauren. "If you haven't come in and called the cops or taken that shot, we would either be dead or the terrorists would be off with that chip in their possession." said the man.

Angie now had a good feeling. She had the feeling that her mom and dad were watching over her right now feeling so happy that she saved everyone from a devastating attack. So Angie felt her parents feeling pride in her, so she looked up and smiled.

New York, New York: November 2012

By

Joseph Schwalbach

THE SWORD FLEW TOWARDS MY FACE. I LEANED DOWN JUST IN TIME to avoid the blade's stinging bite. I lunged with my own blade towards the hooded attacker striking him right in the heart. I expected him to fall to the ground, but instead a light blinded me, and he disappeared.

"What the…?" *Who was that? Why was he attacking me? What was this mysterious blade that appeared in my hands?* Millions of questions rushed through my head. *I better get out of here before any more of those "things" attack me."*

I traveled toward safety as fast as my feet could carry me. There were buildings and alleyways all around me. I ran through the streets of New York with the blade still in my hand. I chose an alleyway to duck through, as an attempt to escape any pursuers. It didn't work. Suddenly three more of them trailed me.

Wow, those things sure are fast runners.

I saw a fire escape and decided that that was my best option. They went from being forty feet behind me to being ten feet behind me in a couple of seconds.

Almost to the fire escape.

They overtook me from behind and tackled me.

So close.

I tasted a mixture of my own blood and the pavement. The last thing I saw was the fading buildings and another blinding flash. Then another one. Then everything went black.

*　　　*　　　*

"He's waking up," an unfamiliar voice said. It had a weird accent I couldn't pinpoint. The blurry picture of three strange men in a tent filled my eyes. On the two other sides of me were two more beds like the one I was lying on. I suddenly felt cold.

"Can you hear me?" one of the strange voices said.

"Yes," I responded quickly, and regretted it immediately after. My face still stung from getting tackled by those weird hooded guys. I tried to open my eyes, to no avail.

"He is responsive," another strange voice said.

Who are these strange people? Seems I've been asking myself that question a lot lately.

"Hello John," said the third voice, but this one didn't have an accent.

This voice was calming, and I could've sworn I knew it from somewhere. I opened my eyes again, this time with success, and saw the fuzzy images of three people bending over me.

How did this man know my name? Where am I? Wait… where is that sword that appeared in my hand when the hooded thing, that I assumed was a man, attacked me?

"Who are you?" I asked wearily.

"I am Avan. We saved you from the Darkbearers, " The one with the soothing voice said.

"What is a Darkbearer?" I ran my hand through my medium length, dark hair. I sat up and got a better look at the three men. But one of them wasn't technically a man. He looked the same age as me but taller with blonde hair.

"A Darkbearer, my boy is a worker of evil."

"I'm James," the one that was my age said.

"How old are you?" I asked.

"Fourteen," he responded.

I knew it.

When I looked at the other two, I could immediately tell which one was Avan. Avan was tall with gray hair and a beard. He wore really strange clothes. I took a closer look and noticed that all three of the men wore strange clothes. The last one, the one with the accent, was twenty or maybe thirty and was medium height with black hair.

"Uh... Where am I?" I asked inquisitively. *Why hadn't I asked that earlier?*

The one that had black hair said, "You are in Gawe, but this will be explained later. First we must..."

"Wait," I butted in. "What is Gawe? How far from New York City is it?" My statement brought about a fit of laughter.

After it was over Avan explained, "Gawe is a world that mirrors your own, they are the exact same other than the fact that it is upside down. Our worlds are connected as well. You see, our worlds share a link. If this link is destroyed, both of our worlds will die. Our worlds feed off of each other; if one of our worlds were to be cut off of that link both would perish. You see John, the Mayans knew about this. That is why they foretold the end of the world, they knew about us and about Gawe. They predicted the end of the world, and they will be right unless you save it."

"*Yeah, I believe you, If the Mayans were so smart why didn't they predict their own death?*" I said sarcastically.

"John, we are serious," said James.

"Okay, let's pretend that the Mayans were right. Even so, what does your *Gawe* have to do with me?" I asked, getting bored of their charade. *All of this was just too much. Their fake world, their fake link, it was all fake. I was probably just asleep. This was all just a dream. The hooded men, the blinding lights, the weird people. This all must be a dream. Walking home from school I took a nap on the sidewalk.* I remembered the incredible pain. No dream, no matter how realistic, could produce that kind of pain.

After a minute of silence James blurted out, "You're the chosen one! Now stop treating this as if it is a game or as if it's not real! The fate of both of our worlds rests in your hands!"

"Uh... can I go home?" I asked a little bit frightened, and a little bit confused.

"You can, if you wish for both of our worlds to cease to exist," Avan said, in a calm, soothing voice. I thoroughly thought about it for a while. I arrived at a conclusion; I would do whatever they needed me to do.

"I'll do it, but… what exactly am I supposed to do?" I asked, wondering if it was anything too insane. I've seen enough insanity in, what I assumed to be twenty-four hours, to last a lifetime.

"What you have to do won't be easy," said the man who I still hadn't gotten a name from. "You will have to defeat the evil Amose, or he will destroy the link between our worlds."

*   *   *

Ah great, how am I going to do this? They want me to kill a man! First off, how will I be able to do it? Second off, how will I have the heart to do it? I won't be able to kill him.

"Who is this *Amose* person?" I asked anyone who wished to answer.

"He is not the kind of guy you would want to meet after school." Avan said.

Wow, an attempt at humor. I didn't think that Avan was the kind of person that could crack a joke.

"A thousand years ago he tried to enslave the Citizens of Gawe. He almost did, but the elders cast a spell casting him into stone. Now he has escaped, and is trying to destroy the world that destroyed him,"

I wondered if they had school in Gawe, and if James attended it. Back in New York, I was a freshman in high school. I looked at James and saw that he looked a lot like my best friend Paul Hawkins. Paul was a nice kid, but mischievous as well. One time we egged the house of Ronald Wattle, the school bully, and he caught us, so he wanted to fight. The next day at school we went back to back and beat him and his band of bullies up.

I really wish Paul were here to help me out here.

"We will bring your friend here if you will convince him to help you fight Amose," Avan said. *Can he read my mind?*

"Yes John, I can read your mind. And yes, John, we will grant you your wish of having your friend here," As his mention of this I was immediately excited. Having Paul here would make it so much better. Paul would help me fight this "Amose" person. I wondered if Amose was a regular person, or something freakier. I didn't want to guess at that very moment so I just dismissed it from my mind. There was a blinding flash that was all too familiar, and on the bed next to me appeared Paul in his Gym Clothes.

Wait, had I been knocked out for a day? It was 4:00 in the afternoon when I was walking home, and gym was the second class of the day for both Paul and me.

Zach started screaming upon the sight of the two men and one teen. I attempted to calm him down.

"Zach," I said to calm him down. He kept screaming. "Zach," He still screamed. "Zach!" He then noticed me and calmed down, but the look on his face still told me that he was scared out of his mind. "Zach, it's okay. I asked if you could come here, I need help," I said gently.

"Uh, ask if I could come where?" Zach asked, and I realized that he didn't know where he was. I proceeded to explain to him my situation. Zach looked amazed, and I wasn't sure how he would respond. "Oh man! That's so cool! Dude, thanks for choosing me to come help! We can kick this evil dude's..." he looked around and saw Amose. "... butt,"

"Zach," Avan said. "It will not be as simple as you think. You will have to undergo training to use a sword,"

I butted in. "Wait, we have to use a sword? Couldn't we just use like, a gun or something?"

"Yes, John," He said sarcastically. "We are going to go out and buy a gun in the middle of an alternate world. Of course you will learn how to use your sword. That is what we are for." He pointed at himself, James, and the man whose name I still hadn't learned. Avan said to Zach, "Zach, you will learn how to use the bow and arrow," Oh, and both of you, there is something I forgot to tell you about. Amose has an army of Darkbearers," *Oh Great.* I felt like running, just running until I couldn't run any farther. I just wanted to go home. Amose spoke again. "The end is near, and only you have the power to stop it. Are you up for the task?"

"Yes," I stated simply.

"Then get up," Avan said. "You two should get some sleep,"

Zach and I stood up, I almost fell, my legs had fallen asleep. Avan caught me and stood me back up. I saw on the trays on the sides of the beds some of the most medieval tools I had ever seen in my life. The scalpel was rusty, and the knives were the largest I had ever seen. The beds were stained with red, I didn't even want to know where that came from. My guess was that this was the hospital tent.

I realized that it was cold outside and started shivering. I heard a strong gust of wind outside and realized that it was freezing. I stepped out of the tent and saw that it was snowing heavily in the darkness. I saw a whole village full of people that were dressed the same as the three men we had met. There was a gigantic fire that sat in the middle of a circle of tents. That was probably where they cooked. Fatigue dulled the cold from snow that was blowing against my legs, certainly not clothes for cold weather.

"Avan," I said. "What time is it here?"

"Time for you to get a watch."

Another attempt at humor.

"It is 11:30 at night. You should rest if you are to defeat Amose. Let us hurry,"

We quickly walked to the tent that Zach and I would be sleeping in. It was on the outer most part of the circle of tents. Inside there were two beds. I hopped on the one on the left, and Zach hopped on the one on the right.

"We shall make warriors out of you two wimps," said the man whom I did not know the name of. I knew then that he didn't like me. I would find out later that he hated me. A lot.

*   *   *

"John! Hurry! Wake up!" Screamed a voice that I soon recognized to be James's. *It's really dark outside. Why would I be getting up?* My eyes quickly adjusted to the darkness as I saw James standing next to me. "Darkbearers! Darkbearers are attacking!"

My mind snapped to fight or flight mode. But then the strangest thing happened, my *iPhone* beeped. I pulled it out of my pocket. I had gotten a text message. I opened the message and saw that it said to look straight down. I saw on the ground the large blade that I had used to kill the Darkbearer.

"Wait, where is Zach?" I asked James.

"They already took him." My heart sank into my shoes.

"Okay then, we have to go get him!"

We ran out of the tent and saw the village all around us. Then we saw the Darkbearers running toward us. *Still hadn't seen what these freaks looked like under their hoods. I want to know, but I don't want to get close enough to find out.* The fire dimly lit the snow filled area and the tents were silhouetted. Then I saw them. Their red eyes shone like rubies in the darkness. About ten Darkbearers charged towards James and I. And what was worse was that one of them had a bag that I swore I heard Zach's screams from.

"Run!" James screamed.

"No. We are going to save him,"

"Don't be a hero John." I ignored James and charged towards the freaks, sword in hand. The cold stung my face as I ran the fastest I had ever ran in my entire life. As I neared the full-fledged army of Darkbearers, I swung my blade hitting three of them right in the neck. Then the three Darkbearers I had hit burst into flame. An arrow flew by me and hit one of them in the heart. I looked at James and noticed that he had a bow in his hand. He gave me a thumbs up. The one he hit also burst into flame.

Wow, what are these things made of?

Then one of them held out his hand and a floating fireball formed on top of it.

Wow again.

I knew I wasn't going to last among these things by myself. I attacked the one that had Zach in a bag, unsuccessfully. Then I was mad. I used all of my strength to lunge at the freak that had Zach. It hit him straight in the heart. He burst into flame, and I quickly grabbed the bag that held Zach. I sliced the top open and Zach jumped out gasping for air.

"Hurry!" I screamed. "Let's run! We can't take 'em all!" We ran as fast as our feet could carry us to where James was, then continued following him until we got to safety. There we met up with Avan and weird black haired guy.

"It is worse than I feared," Avan stated simply. "His army is already growing extremely strong and the more of them there are, the harder it will be to defeat Amose. We must act quickly if we still want to save our worlds. We must train you as soon as we can. In fact, we can start in the morning, because it is only 12:00 midnight your time,"

We ended up in the front of a huge snow covered mountain. At the very front there was a vast dark cavern. We walked inside the huge cave that looked like it went on forever.

"Get some sleep, or you will never be able to save the worlds," Weird dude who I still hadn't gotten the name of. That reminded me.

"Hey," I said. "What is your name?"

"Martin," He said.

Wow, such a normal name for such a weird guy.

Martin and James went out for some firewood while we sat in the damp cave.

Avan offered me his extra coat. I used it as a blanket.

When Martin and James returned from getting the firewood, Zach had already fallen asleep. Avan was pacing up and down and, I could have sworn, that when he was deep in thought fire would momentarily form above his palm.

"I'll arrange the firewood," James said. "Avan will light it." I wondered what that strange statement could have meant.

James delicately placed the firewood in a neat pile. Then Avan held his hand up, palm facing the roof of the cave, and a ball of fire formed above it. He threw the fire at the pile of wood. A flurry of flame lit up the cave momentarily, but calmed down after a second. Zach woke up with a start as the fire crackled the typical crackle. I was amazed that Avan, such an old man, could possess such strong powers. I wonder if I would be anywhere as cool as Avan. It was hard to fall asleep on the hard rocky surface. The fire made it warmer in the cave, and that put some ease into falling asleep.

*   *   *

I woke up to Martin and Avan having a hushed discussion.

"I don't think he will be ready," whispered Martin.

"With the proper training he will be able to do it. He just has to learn. I will train him today." Avan snapped back. I decided to butt in.

"You guys are talking about me; aren't you?"

"Oh, John… Good morning," Avan said in a cheerful voice.

I had a dream about my parents. That reminded me how much I

missed my normal life. *I would kill to be in school right now.* How many people do you know that'll say that?

" We must start training immediately if we are to make…"

"But I don't want to kill a man, no matter how evil he is. I could hold of Darkbearers while you kill him, but I won't kill a human being," I butted in.

"Only you can kill him John. Just think. Is the cost of one evil man one billion good people?" Avan said in a cool voice.

I thought about it, and he was right. I wouldn't one stupid man take the lives of billions of innocent people. I had an answer for Avan.

"Fine, I'll do it. But only because of all of the people he would kill,"

Thoughts swirled around in my head for a really long time. I was thinking about all that had happened since that one stupid Darkbearer had attacked me. *Why did this have to happen to me? Why couldn't this have happened to Ronald Wattle? He deserved to have this happen to him.*

The sound of Zach's obnoxious snoring woke me from my muse.

"Let's go, I want to learn what powers I have," I said quickly. I picked up my sword and walked towards Avan.

"First we must find out what your power is," Avan stated firmly. *Wait, power?* We walked out of the cave and into the snow. We were really far away by the time Avan said something else. "Martin, get over here," Avan almost shouted. No he was directing his words towards me. "You see my boy, Martin's power is seeing other people's powers."

Wow, what a useless power!

"But my boy, it is not useless. He can know what to expect from his enemies," he had read my mind again.

Martin reached us and he put his hand onto my forehead. He had a blank expression for a while, then his face turned almost into shock. He motioned silently for Avan to follow him. When they got out of my earshot Martin started speaking. Avan kept a calm cool face but I could see what he was thinking. Shock.

Oh My Gosh! My power sucks, or maybe I have no power. That would have been disappointing. As they came closer I decided that I would not care if I didn't have a power. I could kill him without powers. Avan was the first to speak.

"John, you just become even more important. You have the most rare power in Gawe. You can wield lightning,"

I almost jumped out of my skin. *Yes! The coolest power ever!*

"Now," Avan said, "we must begin training. We will start small and then work our way up. First off, try to make a spark on your fingertips. You must concentrate harder than you have ever concentrated before. Think about lightning and it will come,"

I thought about lightning, thinking about how easy it would be to take down Amose with lightning. I felt powerful, and my hands started feeling really weird. Then there was a crackling sound. Then I saw it, coming out of my right hand fingertips were sparks. Some of them lasted a long time, but some of them were short. I put my left hand in front of my right hand, and the sparks ran up through my hand, up my body, and stopped on my head. It felt weird, like what happens when you do a backflip, you get the tickling feeling in your stomach. And, believe it or not, the sparks didn't hurt.

Apparently Zach had woken up, and knew where we were because he appeared next to me.

"Don't sneak up on me like that!" I yelled to Zach. He had always had a knack for not alerting people to his position. *That would be really useful someday.*

"Sorry," he muttered. "Did you find out your powers? Is it cool? What is mine? When will I learn? How long will it take to learn?" He bombarded me with a barrage of questions, only a few of which I had an answer to.

"Hello Zach," Avan said. "Did you know that you snore like an animal?"

"No," He replied. "What kind of animal?"

"A pig, but that doesn't matter now." Avan said politely.

"I will see what your power is." Said Martin to Zach. Martin did the same thing he had done for me, except he did not looked shocked. *Wow, considering the circumstances "shocked" is a really bad pun.*

"You have the power of water," Martin said to Zach. Zach looked really disappointed.

"There isn't even any water around here, it is all frozen or covered with snow,"

"Zach," I said, "What is snow made out of?"

"Oh!" Zach exclaimed. "Does it work like that?" He inquired.

"Fortunately for you, it does work like that," Said James out of the blue. He had walked up behind us while we were talking. "I also have that power," said James.

"Okay, I will train John," Avan said. "And James will train Zach. But be hurried, we don't have much time before the Darkbearers find us,"

"John," Zach asked, "what is your power?"

"Lightning," I replied quickly. Zach started to laugh.

"Lucky," He stated. James and Zach went off to the other side of the opening in the forest. Within a couple of minutes I saw Zach pick up a huge chunk of snow. *He is much better than me at using his powers.*

Avan told me that I needed to focus more on the lightning, and not so much on what I was going to do with it. He wanted me to throw a bolt of lightning at a tree. I focused on it, but nothing happened. I realized that both of my arms were at my side, and that I would never be able to do it like that. I pointed my right arm towards the tree. I then saw the coolest thing ever. A lightning bolt left my hand and flew right towards that tree. Electricity ran up the tree causing burn marks.

Suddenly, I heard James and Zach screaming. I turned to see James and Paul being dragged away by a group of Darkbearesrs.

Wow! Why can't they defend themselves?

I saw Martin behind them.

"Martin, save them!" I screamed.

"I'm afraid I can't do that," And he held a sword near Zach's neck. "Come any closer and I will cut his throat. If you get in the way of Amose's plans again I will kill both of them," After he said that he opened a portal and ran through it, and Avan and me stood there.

"Don't worry John, he will be okay," Avan said. I was mad and channeled my anger towards Avan.

"If you can read minds, why didn't you see this coming?" I shouted.

"Because his power was not only to see powers, but to be able to block mind readers. "John, we must run, we have to save them,"

We ran for a couple of minutes in the snow, Avan led the way. I was soaking wet from the falling snow. Avan stopped running.

"I can't run any longer. I am an old man. But I do have a way to get us there even more quickly." He snapped his fingers together, and I heard galloping coming towards us. Two horses appeared out of the forest and neighed when they saw us. Avan immediately hopped on the brown one, and I hopped onto the white one. I had never ridden a horse before, and I was scared that it would throw me off of it. But this horse was extremely well trained because it followed Avan with intense focus. We rode for hours until I saw an opening in the forest.

I saw a bunch of Darkbearers guarding tents. I hid behind the final tree in the forest, and Avan threw a ball of snow to the right of the Darkbearers. They turned their weird hooded heads towards the sound, while me and Avan ran past them. We ducked into the first tent and heard the muffled cries of James and Zach. Luckily they were in the tent that we had just walked into. I used my sword to cut the rope that they were tied up in, and Avan pulled the tape off of their mouths.

I motioned for Zach and James to sneak out the back while Avan and me took out the Darkbearers. I ran out of the tent screaming and swinging my blade. I hit three of them in a couple of seconds and Avan took out the other five. Martin must have heard my screaming, because he ran out of one of the last tents in the row and took out his bow and arrow. I began rushing towards him, when I saw Zach pick up a huge mound of snow and throw it at him. It struck him right in the chest, and he flew towards the mountain that I had just noticed. I heard a man scream and then saw a lot more Darkbearers appear out of the air.

Then 'he' ran out of a tent. By he I meant Amose. He was the most disgusting person I had ever seen. He had looked normal at first glance, but when you took a closer look you saw that he was disturbing. He had black eyes. And not just black pupils, black irises, and the part that was supposed to be white was even black. And he had sharp teeth like an animal.

He pulled out a blood red sword. He disappeared for a second and then reappeared right next to Avan and stabbed right in the heart. I screamed and ran toward Avan. It all went silent until James screamed, "John!"

I looked up and saw an arrow whizzing towards me. It struck me right in the shoulder and I felt the most excruciating pain I had ever felt in my life. The arrow hit my shoulder bone so it stayed in my arm but I continued running towards Avan. I bent down next to him and saw that he was still alive, but just barely.

"Kill Amose, John," Were his final words.

I will fulfill your wishes Avan.

I charged towards the ugly man and slashed my blade but he teleported right before I could hit him. I charged towards him again, controlled by my emotions. He grabbed me and the next thing I knew I was on the top of the Berj Khalifa. It was the night there, and there was an intense thunderstorm, and I looked over the side. *Oh my God.* We must be at least half a mile high in the air. I looked around for Amose.

"You will never defeat me, John," he shouted. He appeared on the other side of the insanely tall tower. I charged towards him, but he teleported out of the way again. I heard thunder booming, and got so angry. The cloud's got darker. He appeared right next to me but an instant later he was gone, only to appear across from me. I heard thunder, and saw a bright light. I took this opportunity to run and stab him in the heart. When the light disappeared I saw Amose lying on the ground. He grabbed my leg and teleported back to Gawe.

I ran away from the dead man, right before he burst into flame. James rushed towards me and took a look at the arrow in my shoulder. I reached to pull it out.

"Don't! If you pull it out you'll die from blood loss. You have to get to a hospital." He threw me onto the white horse. The last thing I saw before I blacked out was the forest rushing by.

*   *   *

I woke up in the hospital bed of my hometown of New York, New York.

"Thank God you're okay!" My mom screamed. I wondered if my dad was here.

"Hey sport!"

Now I knew that he was.

"What happened?" I asked my parents.

"You didn't come home from school Monday, so we asked the police to look for you. They found you in an alley on Tuesday screaming about someone named Avan. You must have been mugged and shot, because there was a gaping hole in your right shoulder. We were so worried! We are so lucky that it wasn't worse. And Zach must have been with you because they found him right next to you, but he was okay," My dad explained.

"Come on, let's go home," my mom said.

I heard my phone beep. I looked at the messages. One from Mary Tembler, the girl I have had a crush on since sixth grade. The message said: *Hey John, u doing okay? Txt me when you get better.* I sent her back a message saying: *I'm feeling better. Hey, do u wanna go out this Friday?* It was the second hardest thing I had ever done. Almost instantly I heard the text message beep. *Yeah, that would be cool.* It read.

I stood up and we walked out of the hospital. I felt like a million bucks. Other than the hole in my shoulder, but that didn't matter now. I put my phone back in my pocket, and found a piece of paper. I looked at it and it read:

Dear John, Thank you for saving Gawe. We are eternally grateful. Come back and visit anytime. – James.

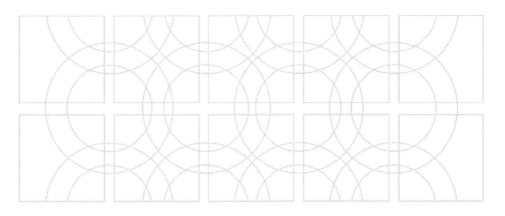

A Fat Boy's Success

By

Matthew Sung

"Hans, WAKE UP!" The shouting broke Hans' dream into millions of pieces.

"I hate this! I can get up whenever I want to!" thought Hans. Then he shouted, "I'm still tired! And I don't care about getting up! I'm sleeping!" Pushing his fat and bulky body off the bed was hard for Hans. It was almost summer vacation, and Hans hoped to have fun during summer.

Hans was a fifteen-year-old freshman who lived in a rich family in San Francisco. His mother couldn't give birth to children anymore after giving birth to Hans. So Hans was the only child, and his parents were willing to get anything for Hans. As Hans grew older and older, he increasingly got into trouble at school, home, and other public areas. He never did his homework and had been caught cheating on final exams, smoking, drinking, fighting, stealing, and so on. His parents weren't very happy these days because there businesses were not going very well. And with Hans' annoying problems, they began to think about sending Hans away to a strict boarding school.

Things went all wrong for Hans one night at the dinner table. "Hans," said Mom, who tried to look anguished. "Dad and I are going to send you to a boarding school next week, and you are going to stay there for a year. In that case, you wouldn't have to..."

"You guys cannot just throw me into a camp for one year and enjoy yourselves at home! What did I do wrong to make you guys hate me so much? There's no way..."

"ENOUGH, HANS!" Mom shouted. The whining of Hans irritated her. She took a sip of her juice, calmed down a little, and said in a stern voice to Hans. "Hans, did you know what you had been doing the past few years? I guess you don't know because you think that everything you do is correct. But apparently not, smoking, cheating, drinking, fighting, and stealing. You have done so many bad things, so we decided to send you to Reality Camp..."

"Reality Camp." These words just flashed through Hans' heart like thunder and broke it heartlessly. Hans stayed in his for the next couple of days. Didn't want to see the real world. He never thought that his parents would do this to him. He always bragged about how much his parents obeyed him, thinking how different he was compared to others. Now, he descended into the world of average people. He cried himself to sleep at night. Hans was seriously afraid.

It was a school with nothing much in the middle of the desert in Arizona. And Hans was the kind of kid that lived in big house, air-conditioned rooms, and everything he liked was around him. Hans just didn't seem to fit there, and that was one of the main reasons he was going the school. There used to be a lake in the land, but it just dried up twenty years ago. That made the school even hotter. The highest temperature in summer reached around ninety-six degrees in shade. Well, there was already not much shade at the school. With a dried lake, there were only like three or four trees. In addition, scorpions and rattlesnakes filled the desert. For spoiled kids like Hans, surviving in this camp seemed impossible.

Of course, Hans didn't have fun for the rest of the summer. Spent his summer mostly in his spacious and dark room.

Sitting in the back row of the bus, there was nobody else on the bus. Hans' parents stood outside, looked at him, wished that Hans can understand and forgive them. Hans turned his back towards his parents; he didn't want to look at them. "I'll never forgive them. I'll never forget what they had put me through now. And I'll make them regret for sending me away!" thought Hans, with anger and hatred deep inside his heart.

Then the driver started the engine."Errn, errn, errn…" the bus began to move. Hans quickly took a last peek at his parents, he grasped his fist very tight, and whispered, "I'll be back home soon…"

A hot wind blew across Hans' face. Huge sweat drops dripped down his chin onto the hot and cracked ground at the end of the roadway. Far in the front, Hans saw a camp with a few wooden cabins in the middle and four old oak trees in front of the cabins, creating a huge shaded area.

"Okay, Hans, let's beginning walking, or you will get really thirsty in a little time under this hot sun." Paul said. He was one of the counselors at the school that was responsible for picking up kids coming to attend the school.

"Then let's go. Before the stupid sun kills both of us," mumbled Hans in a bad humor.

As Hans got closer to the school, the clearer he could observe the school. On the right of the cabins, Hans saw some boys running around on a cleaned field playing soccer; some boys played basketball on an old and beat up basketball court. And on the left of the cabins, stood five big tents, the shower area, and the toilets.

"Ha, ha," Hans thought, "The basketball court is not even as good as mine back home, and what kind of dirty tents are those, I'm not going to sleep in them! I hate it!"

Paul seemed to read Hans' mind and said, "You are going to sleep in the tent that has a huge D in the front. Don't worry. It's not that bad, fifteen boys a tent, so it won't be too crowded."

Hans couldn't stand the way Paul say these things calmly, and shouted,

"Fifteen people! My room is not much smaller than the tent, and I slept in it myself! Are you serious? I will die one night because of suffocation!"

"Relax, Hans. You will get used to the environment in a very short time," said Paul in a gentle manner, trying to comfort Hans.

But Hans didn't care much, and yelled at Paul.

"How can I relax? I came here because my parents didn't want me anymore! They said they will come and pick me up in one year's time, but they didn't want me anymore! They are not even going to come and pick me. They must have already adopted a new child after I left, and now they are spoiling that little KID!"

"You mustn't think like that…"

"Whatever, forget it. Let's walk faster. I need water," said Hans.

"Okay, everybody, stop what you are doing and gather round," said Paul as he and Hans walked through the gate of the campsite. Soon, all the campers were around Paul and Hans. "Okay guys, this is Hans. And he will be here for one year. Treat him good. Make him miss this place when he's gone. Have fun, buddy," said Paul. He patted Hans' left shoulder and went away.

The boys around Hans hadn't gone away yet. Then a tall and tough guy in front of Hans began to speak,

"Hey, nice name you have here, Ha-a-a-a-ans. Ha ha ha ha ha ha ha ha…" and many other laughs came everywhere towards Hans.

"Oh great, this is just a great start for me," thought Hans, being sarcastic.

*   *   *

Lying in his bed, feeling lonely, Hans felt unprotected in his new surroundings, like a mouse trapped in a cage, didn't know where it is. After being laughed at the gate, the crowds faded away soon. And people didn't really care about Hans for the rest of the day. He sat under the tree by himself and did nothing for the afternoon. Sometimes some kids came to Hans and teased him, insulted him, and bullied him. And three of the boys chased Hans out of the shade. Hans hated them.

"Hey! So you are the new kid, huh? Do you have any idea where you are sitting in?" said the kid, with a manner full of pride and arrogance. The tall kid looked strong and had a much larger head than the other kids. And behind him were two other boys, one was a little chubby and had a medium height. The other was short and thin, and both of them had big heads, just like their boss in the front.

"Jack, the camp is going to waste more resources on this kid! We've had enough of this kind of losers. What's wrong with these instructors? They should choose more elites like us!" said the chubby kid.

"I know, Jason. These losers should be outside in the sun working instead of sitting in the shade like a lazy bum!" laughed Jack, "Okay, Hans. You seriously don't know where you are sitting in?"

Hans tried to act tough, and said, "Do you guys have a problem with where I'm sitting in? Can't you guys see that I'm sitting in the shade?"

"Ha, ha, ha, ha, trying to be tough, huh? Let me tell you something," Jack gave out an evil laugh, walked closer to Hans, and began to use his feet to dig up some dirt. "This is the JJJ brothers' shade! It's our shade! And you are sitting in our shade! You better get up and walk away, or I'm going to make you look really bad in front of everybody!" the shouting of Jack slowly gathered kids around the JJJ brothers and Hans.

"Since when this was your shade? This public property! If somebody really owns this shade, the owner would be more like me! Not you and your fat brains brothers!" said Hans, felt his hands shaking. He knew they would beat him up really bad if he keeps on pushing it.

"Whoa, whoa, whoa! You better get out of here soon, or we will make you go away." said Jackson, the thin and short guy always with an evil grin on his face. "Don't push it, Hans."

"Fine, I'll go!" said Hans, who was afraid to fight them. He slowly used his hands to push himself up. But Jack quickly pushed Hans back onto the ground, and said,

"After you said these insulting words to us, you think you can just walk away like this! What you said were offensive against our reputation, you need to pay for this foolish mistake you had made." Then Jack picked up some dirt from the pile he dug and sprinkled on Hans. "I know this is just a small punishment for you, but next time, it won't be the same again."

Laughing and walking away, the JJJ brothers left Hans, who was dirty and sweaty. Hans slowly got up and walked away from the teasing and laughter of the other boys...

Not wanting to think of anything anymore, Hans closed his eyes and fell asleep, trying to forget everything happened today.

*　　　　*　　　　*

"Get up! Everybody get up!" John shouted, who was one of the instructors at the camp. He didn't like him that much because John looked really mean and got along with the JJJ pretty well. It was five o'clock in the morning, Hans was still in his dream. Then John came and shook Hans, "Wake up! This is not your home, it's a school!"

"So what about a school." said Hans, who was still not awake, and didn't know what he was saying. "It is just a junkyard in the middle of the desert. Hot and filled with poor and annoying kids, including the instructors who are trying to act nice, but actually, they are not!"

"Okay, that's it! You are going to the King! Zero, help Hans to find it's way to the King. And you, buddy. Get dressed quickly and good luck," said John angrily then he walked out of the tent perking his head very high.

"You are a dead man now," Zero said to Hans as they were on their way to the King's cabin.

"Why be afraid? It is just a simple punishment in the King's cabin. He cannot kill me, or I can sue him!" said Hans, without a single fear of the King, because he got punished so many times before in school for cheating on tests, smoking, and so on.

"Being a dead man doesn't mean being killed; it means getting a punishment. According to what you had done, the punishment you are getting will be really bad, as bad as being dead. There was one time that a student did similar things like you, he almost had a nervous breakdown," said Zero, sounding like there were no hopes for Hans.

Hans began to feel hot and didn't really care about anything. "Whatever, Zero. I've already don't know what to do with my life, there seems to be no hope for me. My parents threw me in this stupid boarding school, and said they would pick me up after a year. These were all lies to comfort me! So I don't really care about anything now."

Zero didn't say anything after that. In front of the King's cabin, stood a big oak tree. "Ring the doorbell and wait for any orders," said Zero, who waited for the King after Hans went into the King's cabin.

*   *   *

Sitting in a comfortable chair in the King's cabin. He looked around while the King was talking to Zero outside. The outside of the cabin was wooden, so was the inside of it. Being in the desert, the cabin felt like a sauna, Hans was already sweating after he sat down in the chair.

"So, Hans. I just heard Zero said that you have lots of complaints about our school here, in the middle of the desert. Is that true?" asked the King, with a little smile on his face.

"Yeah it is true, but I was telling the truth back in the room. It is like a junkyard comparing to my old home! My parents dumped me here! In the middle of no…"

"Don't yell at me!" the King interrupted, Hans cowered in his chair a little, was scared of the angry instructor. "It is really disrespectful to yell at an instructor. And…Oh, I almost forgot to introduce myself to you. My name is Ken, as you already knew, people call me the King. I'm in charge of this school, so if you need any help, just find me. I will always be around. I will let you go this time, but don't do it again, or you will get punished badly. I trust you, Hans. I really do just don't let me lose the trust on you."

Still cowered in the chair and feeling a power of the word TRUST waking up every lazy nerve in his body. Hans was happy for what he had heard just now, since he began to remember things, nobody had said such word to him. After waking up from the paradise of the word TRUST, Hans faced to Ken and said, "I won't disappoint you again, Ken. Sorry about the trouble I made this time." Hans walked straight out of the cabin's door.

"Looks like Hans is already under control now," thought Ken, with a little grin on his face.

After coming back from Ken's cabin. It was already seven o'clock. Just as Hans walked into the canteen, John shouted, "Okay, guys. Breakfast time's over! Clean up and go to the supply room!" When John turned his head back, he saw Hans, who didn't look happy.

"Where's my breakfast?" asked Hans, who didn't want to starve in the morning.

"Sorry, Hans. You are too late for breakfast. Early birds catches the worms," said John, with a grin on his face.

"I don't care whether I'm late or not, I just want to eat my breakfast." said Hans, who was trying to keep his voice low, because he needed a better reason to get sent to Ken's cabin again.

"Second time today! In one morning! Do you really think that you can get away again from the King? You got away because it was your first time, and I knew that was going to happen. But it won't be like last time again for this time, so I'm warning you that I'm giving you a chance." said John, looking down at Hans, having a expression full of pride. Hans could feel that the flame of anger is hovering in his whole body, and exclaimed,

"Don't use those stupid punishments to scare me! They are useless! Teachers in school have been punishing me since the first day I walked in my kindergarten! Punishments are useless for me, USELESS! I know you didn't like me since I walked in that school gate yesterday!" the exploded words went right through John, and enraged him.

"Alright, impressive speech, Hans, really impressive. It's hard to believe that student can talk to a teacher like that, isn't it? I think we have a major misunderstanding between us. So why don't we just go to the King and resolve the developing conflict between us? Let's go!" said John, who was trying to act like Mr. Nice.

"Sure, bring it on, John. I'm not as easy as a usual kid is to deal with," thought Hans with an evil grin hanging on his face.

*   *   *

"Hans! I heard that you got sent to the King's cabin again! Is that true? Man, your just too cool for not staying out." said Zero, who sat down in front of Hans during dinner, and was really impressed by the first day of Hans. "Did you get punished?"

"Yeah, but it was nothing at all. Just standing in the cabin for the whole afternoon reflecting on what I said to John." Hans said, looked like he didn't really care about anything, began to eat his dinner.

"Oh, okay. I wish that won't happen to you again," said Zero.

"Oh! Nasty food this is! Sorry what's your name?" exclaimed Hans.

"Zero," Zero mumbled.

"Zero, don't tell me this is the food you guys eat every day! What a disgusting taste it has!" complained Hans; spitting all the food he had just put in his mouth.

"I'm afraid you are going to eat this kind of food for the rest of the year, Hans," mumbled Zero.

"This is just great. I got sent to Ken's cabin for the second time just because John didn't let me eat this nasty food! And the worst part is, I'm going to eat this kind of food for the rest of the year!" shouted Hans, being annoyed by how bad things are going on for him.

"Complaining again, fat boy?" said Jason and slapped Hans in the head, trying to provoke a fight.

"Always complaining doesn't bring you good health, you know that, Hans?" teased Jackson.

"You Fat brains can just shut up and get out of my eyesight. Or..." Hans suddenly couldn't think of anything he could boast about to scare them off.

"Or what? Fight us?" asked Jack sarcastically.

"No, or I will tell Ken you guys were bullying me!" said Hans, immediately realized that he said the wrong thing. First the fat brains giggled a little, then they burst into laughter,

"Ha, ha, ha, ha, ha, ha! You two heard that? What a loser! I thought you might say something big, but that was all you wanted to say? Ha ha...You are making me laughing really hard... Ha ha... Ha ha..."

Suddenly Ken's appeared to the Fat brains, and said gently, "Come on, you three. He is new here, be nice to make him feel better. Laughing at others and trying to provoke a fight between one another are now cool things to do. Now go do whatever you guys need to do."

"Yes, sir..." Jack, Jason, and Jackson mumbled. When Jack passed Hans, he whispered to Hans, "You lucked out this time, but not next time, fat boy."

"Thanks, Ken. We appreciate your help at this awkward time. I promise I will stop this kind of conflicts next time," said Zero, with a relief.

"Lame, whatever..." mumbled Hans, who stood up and began to walk away.

Ken turned to Zero with a wide smile, and said, "Keep it up, Zero. It is not going to take too much time." Zero nodded and shouted,

"Wait up, Hans! Let's go play cards!"

"No, I want to sleep now. I need to be able to get up at five o'clock tomorrow. So, no, I'm not playing." Hans turned his head back and said.

"Fine then. I guess I'll see you tomorrow then. Bye!"

Hans just kept on walking, didn't say a word.

*   *   *

Running up a little desert hill, the sweat drops were the symbols of every single step that Hans made, it was hot and tiring.

"I…can't take it anymore…it's too tired for me…How many pounds are in this backpack?" said Hans, who was soaked with his sweat, and couldn't help himself with his own breath.

"Well, Hans. I'm afraid it's going to be like this every day. However, when you get a healthy body, you will appreciate this," said Zero.

Everybody was running miles with backpacks after breakfast. After running one mile, Hans couldn't take it anymore. Hans had never done this kind of thing in his life before. Many kids ran laughing past Hans. Hans didn't care. But when a familiar voice appeared, Hans felt that something would go wrong for him.

"Ha, ha, Hans. How is it going? Running your fat belly off? ha ha ha ha!"

Hans stopped and pulled Zero beside him breathing really hard, and said, "Why… don't you… just shut… up!"

"I agree that I should shut up, but how are you going to make me shut up? Fight me? Race me?"

"I'm going to race you. I'll smoke you so bad!" said Hans, who didn't realized what he had just said. And Jack was extremely surprised to hear that a fat boy wanted to race the fastest guy in the school.

"Guys, all of you, come over here. The new kid here wanted to race me! Will the fat boy win me? I'm really getting exciting and nervous!"

Jack's sarcastic tone deeply enraged Hans. Unable to hold his anger anymore, he roared, "I'll smoke you so bad that you will never dare to lift your head up again! This afternoon during break time, we'll race!" Hans was pushed by his anger, and sped his way back down the hill to the school.

"You should have calm down and ignore Jack," said Zero loudly, Hans was surprised because Zero have never talked like that before. "He is the boss in this camp! Boys, follows him all the time, not only because he can talk, but also because that he almost has everything physically. The last person who raced him was two years ago, and he got smoked badly. Wanted to smoke is a joke for you, Hans. I'm not here trying to discourage you, but I'm telling the truth. Telling you what you should do now is not going to work, just wait until the race end," said Zero, who was really angry with Hans for such foolish things Hans just did.

"I can beat him, I can finish fifty meters in twelve seconds! I'm very fast! You will have nothing to say when I smoke him from the top to the bottom. Ha ha ha…" said Hans unconfidently, who tried to cover the dumbest mistake in the world.

Zero sighed and walked away, leaving Hans lost in his deep thoughts.

"What am I going to do! I'm so doomed, how am I going to win? There are no ways for me anymore. Now everybody's going to think I'm the dumbest loser who likes to make himself vaunted! I must think of a method to make this situation better for me immediately."

*　　　*　　　*

"Where is that fatboy? I'm so going to smoke him!" shouted Jack in a teasing tone. Almost everybody in the camp came to the basketball court. Jack and Hans were going to compete on one hundred meters.

"He must be hiding somewhere in this school! That coward! Without guts and braveness!" chuckled Jason. "Yeah! Coward! No guts!" the surrounding crowd shouted after Jason. Zero didn't know what to do it was pretty embarrassing for him, too, because he hung around with Hans a lot. But Zero stepped out, and said,

"Hans is not like that! He is not a coward! He had guts to declare a race on Jack this morning then he has the guts to come and face what he had done. He is a little slow, so he might be late. Trust me, we just have to wait for a little more time!"

"Wow, there is actually a guy that willing to embarrass himself for Hans! Okay, we will wait for five more minutes," said Jack, who was impressed by Zero sacrifice for Hans.

"There he comes!" a guy at the outer circle of the crowd suddenly shouted. "Hans is here! A plaudits for Hans for keeping his promise!" whistles, screams, and shouting came down like a storm.

"Hans, I knew I didn't get you wrong! Come on, let the race begin!" shouted Jack, who didn't look as happy as he sounded. The crowds turned down the volume of them, and began to wait for the race to begin.

Hans and Jack stood in ready position, bent down, and looking straight forward. It could have been a really good photo with the contrast of the faces; one filled with complicated kind of thoughts and stress, the other filled with relaxation that gave people an impression of belittling the opponent.

"Ready, set, GO!" Jackson shouted. Leaving a cloud of dust, there sprinted out a cheetah and a wild hog. Hans just saw that Jack easily pass him with several steps, and the distance of Jack and him went longer and longer. Then the next thing Hans knew was that Jack won all the plaudits, he won all the insults and teases, and Zero took him out of the place.

*   *   *

Another day has passed since Hans lost the race. Although Hans hated his parents fro sending him here, but he began to miss home. Hans didn't know what it was missing in his life, but he knew it was something really familiar and played a big art of his life. After losing the race badly, Hans learned to hold anger and think carefully before speaking something stupid out again. Hans bore days full of insults and teases, he bore really hard that sometimes he thought that he doesn't enough room for angers anymore in his heart, and he found the stress on him was increasing a little every day, he thought everything in his life were despair until one day...

Hans just finish eating his lunch and was walking towards the basketball field. When Hans passed Ken's cabin, he found there were two familiar adults sitting in front of Ken, then Hans realized they were his parents. The sight of his parents shocked Hans. "Why are parents here? What did I do wrong this time? I had been a really good kid these days. What did I do?" As Hans' parents' face flash through Hans' brain, Hans suddenly realized what he was missing in his life, it were his parents. Hans didn't go to play basketball. Instead, he went back to his tent and began to write a letter to his parents.

> *Dear Mom and Dad,*
>
> *How are you guys doing? Although I'm not having fun in this camp, but I'm learning a lot in this camp. Thank you for sending me to this camp.*
>
> *I'm sorry for disappointing you guys, and I have regretted for*

what I have done. I know for you guys that making a decision of sending me to this camp was a pain in the heart. I am sorry for the misunderstanding of mine on you guys' best decision for me. Living at the lowest point in my life since I was born, life was hard, being looked down by the others is miserable. I have always felt that there was not enough room in my heart for me for more anger. I need go work now, write later.
    Love,
    Hans

Hans folded the letter happily and took it to the mailbox at the gate of the school. Then he went to the wood shop to learn carpentering. Hans' stress took off a little, after knowing that his parents still cared a lot for him. But the insults and teases from John and other kids filled up the empty room again.

*   *   *

"The letters are here! Letters! The letters are here!" John shouted after getting merely one letter from the mailman in the early morning before running miles.

The letter was Hans', Hans was really happy to hear there was a letter for him. He rushed to John and got the envelope. Hans quickly tore open the envelope and took out the letter. The letter said:

Dear Hans,
    Mom and Dad were glad to hear from you. You still have a lot to learn. A person bearing too many angers is dangerous. I'm not saying that bearing angers are bad it is just that a person cannot bear too many angers or at a certain point the person will blow up and make a huge mess. So you have to neutralize the angers in your heart. Look around and find things that are good and makes you happy.
    Love,
    Mom and Dad

Hans looked around, nothing changed better. Then he stepped in front of a mirror and looked at himself. He found that he had been a lot thinner, taller, and muscular than before, he was actually kind of handsome now!

Then during the mile running, he found that he doesn't feel tired anymore and he was so much faster than before. Despite the insults and teases, Hans felt joy after discovering the extreme benefits on him. He felt like that he could run faster than Jack.

After talking to Zero, Hans surprised Zero with his extreme changes. It was true. It was true that Hans is fit now. News spread out really fast, and soon the whole camp realized the changes of Hans. Ken called Hans to his office.

"Congratulation on your success, Hans," said Ken.

"Thanks for your camp program, that really changed me a lot. Not only physical, but also in my heart. And I understand my parents now," said Hans, with a tone of confidence.

"I saw you that day. Actually I let Zero came to be your first friend to help you out, you did change, but that wasn't enough. So I called your parents to come and talk about you. Your parents agreed and came. We found that you have much potential that was buried by many sorts of reasons. I was going to let you communicate with parents for a bit. But then you wrote a letter and clarified everything that happened. I was really impressed by what you did, Hans, you will be a very successful man in the future." said Ken, giving Hans a huge smile. "What are you going to do about the JJJ brothers? What if they kept on picking on you?"

"Actually, I don't know. How should I deal with them?" asked Hans, who seemed interested in this topic.

"Why don't you and Jack just compete running, since you lost so badly last time? Sprinting one hundred meters, you are taller than him now, you should be able to smoke him." said Ken with a little evil grin, encouraging Hans to take back the glory of the other kids, who was being bullied by the JJJ brothers in the school.

"That's a good idea, I'll declare the race on him today, and I'll race him tomorrow! The whole thing will be over, and I hope they will learn something," said Hans, who approved the plan.

"Good, I wish you luck, Hans!" said Ken as Hans was walking out of the door of the cabin.

*　　　*　　　*

"Race tomorrow night! Race tomorrow night! Race between Hans and Jack! Race between Hans and Jack!" not long after Hans declared race on Jack, the whole began to be lively again.

"Are you sure, Jack? Are you sure you can smoke him again? Hans had seriously changed a lot!" whispered Jason.

"Of course I'm sure! I will always win! No matter how it is," said Jack evilly. "Jackson and Jason! Go and dig a small hole on the basketball court, and prepare a string hidden in the dirt. Make it neatly done."

"Ha, ha, we are going to win! Win, win, win, win." sang Jason and Jackson, and walked to the basketball court.

*　　　*　　　*

"Are the strings and the hole ready?" asked Jack quietly.

"Yes, they are neatly done, just stand on the right of the running lane and jump over the tripping string," said Jason and Jackson.

The race was about to begin, not only the students came to see the race, even the instructors came. Many people were cheering for Jack, and many people were cheering for Hans.

"Hey, Jack, let's get ready and race," said Hans.

"Sure, I'm really looking forward to the result of this race. Of course, I'm going to win again," said Jack arrogantly.

"A lot has changed, Jack. I will not lose again," said Hans.

"Then win! If you can win, just win! Now lets begin the race," said Jack.

Standing side by side, Hans could still hear and feel the heavy heartbeat he must win this one for the other kids, who were treated unfairly.

"Ready, set, GO!" shouted Zero. This time, leaving a brown sea behind, two cheetahs flew out and ran. Jack was faster at first, but Hans soon caught up and was passing Jack. "Ha ha, it's near the hole fall in and make me your boss! Hans!" thought Jack. And Hans didn't fall in, Jack was mad. Now Hans was about half a meter in front of Jack, people were amazed by the speed of Hans. Jack didn't seem to care because there was still a string in the front waiting to trip Hans. Jack suddenly jumped and landed, leaving the tripped Hans on the ground back behind with a wicked laughter. Hans didn't care about the wounds on his body he got up and kept running. Despite the other's attention, Jason, Jackson, and John cheered for Jack when he passed the finish line.

When Hans ran pass the finish line exhausted and wounded, everybody cheered for him. Everybody saw the trick that the JJJ Brothers played on Hans, but Hans didn't say anything, he just got up and kept on running. In theory, Jack won the race. But everybody knew that Hans had already smoked Jack before the race.

Everybody praised Hans. But when he saw the JJJ Brothers standing aside looked lost, he walked over there and stood in front of them. They looked up and were terrified.

"Please leave us alone! We are sorry for what we had did to you before. Just please leave us alone!"

"You guys have to chill. I'm not here to take revenge just to tell you guys my personal experience, everybody can make to their admired placements, and there are no difference between two children, just because on is richer and the other is poorer. Come on, lets go have fun together!" handing both of his hands to the three of them, Hans picked them up. It was hot out there.

*   *   *

"Hans' parents, Hans will surprise you by his amazing progress. How come you guys are not?" asked Paul happily, who was the instructor that took Hans in.

"We knew he would make it, and he did. Here he is, a brand new person," said Hans' parents proudly.

It had been a year since Hans got in the school, and that meant it was time for Hans to go home.

"Just like you said, Paul they have made me miss this place already. It's a turning point in my life," said Hans, filled with gratitude.

"We will miss you, too, Hans," said Paul. "You changed this place."

Hans nodded with a big smile on his face, turned to his parents with a wide smile, and said, "Now I can have fun for my summer vacation."

The Story of Adrianne Campos

By

Ingrid Yao

"Mom! Mom! Wake up! Talk to me! MOM!"

Those were the only words that came out of Aaron's mouth, the only words he could make out at the moment. Adrianne stared at her mom in awe. Then she looked over to the other side where her father lay in a small pool of blood. Minutes ago, Adrianne's parents left for a school auction event that night. Then just down the block, the speeding car went out of control. It hit against a curb. The vehicle flipped. Adrianne and her brother witnessed the whole thing.

"Adrianne! Hurry! Tell Mrs. Parker to call an ambulance!" Aaron cried out.

How could this have happened? Adrianne thought, as she ran over to Mrs. Parker's house, with tears swelling up in her eyes. Reaching the front door, she held her finger on the bell, listening to its continual ringing and desperately praying for a speedy response.

Mrs. Parker came to answer the door.

"My dear! What is the matter? Are you alright?"

"Mrs. Parker! You must help us! Please come out," Adrianne begged, sniffing back tears.

"Honey, what's the matter?" Mrs. Parker asked, allowing Adrianne to pull her out to the street. "Oh! My heavens!"

Mrs. Parker ran down the rocky, gray pavement to the wrecked car. Families, friends, and just plain passersby stopped and looked at what happened. Mrs. Parker dropped down on her knees and cried mournfully. "Oh my gosh! Anne! Tom! Anne! Wake up! Answer, Anne!" She took out her phone and frantically dialed for an ambulance.

A short time later an ambulance arrived. The sound of the vehicle's sirens were the only sounds heard. Adrianne couldn't think properly. Adrianne and her brother couldn't walk properly. Adrianne couldn't do anything properly after what she just witnessed. Firemen helped carry Adrianne's unconscious parents into the ambulance. Both children got into the ambulance with Mrs. Parker, who held their hands the whole way to the hospital.

Immediately upon arrival, nurses wheeled their parents into the emergency room. Mrs. Parker held onto both Adrianne and Aaron's hands as they sat in silence in the hallway. Suddenly, the "operation in progress" light went off, and all three of them jumped in unison.

"How are my parents?" asked Adrianne's brother asked first.

"Did they make it?" asked Adrianne with tears streaming from her blue eyes.

Mrs. Parker asked, "How are Mrs. Thompson and Mr. Thompson?"

"Sorry, we tried our best. They lost a lot of blood. I'm really sorry for what happened, but can you help me contact their relatives, so they can come sign some papers?"

"Alright doctor, Adrianne and Aaron, please stay here and don't go anywhere before I come back," said Mrs. Parker.

Adrianne and her brother sat on the orange couch in the waiting room, praying for a miracle to happen like their parents suddenly walking out of the emergency room and all going home to live happily ever after. She waited and waited. After realizing that it was impossible, Adrianne started crying silently. Aaron held back his tears.

"Adrianne, Aaron, come here darlings. It's okay, alright? I am going to help you guys through everything. Don't worry; everything is going to be alright," Mrs. Parker said as she hugged both Adrianne and

Aaron. "Come on, we're going home, and you're going to stay with me for now."

Adrianne and her brother didn't talk to anyone for a month; not even to each other. Every day, they did the same thing over and over again. Wake up, eat breakfast, go to school, come home, do homework, have dinner, and go sleep. They currently lived in a city in Shanghai. All this time, Mrs. Parker had been supporting Adrianne and her brother, giving them shelter, giving them food and providing for their education.

One day, Adrianne accidently knocked over Mr. Parker's antique and broke it into teeny little pieces of sharp glass. Mr. Parker got really mad and told his wife, "They aren't even our kids. Why are we paying for everything they do? Why can't we just send them to an orphanage and let people that want kids to take them? I don't want kids."

"You know it's really hard for them after what they witnessed. I'll talk to them about it," said Mrs. Parker.

Mr. Parker was a fairly old man and was really disgruntled around children. All of the neighborhood's kids learned that they should never mess with Mr. Parker.

"Adrianne! Aaron! Come down for breakfast!" Mrs. Parker yelled one morning.

"Kids, I have some bad news to tell you. Mr. Parker and I will be moving to South Korea because of his job at the factory. We can't bring you guys with us. So we're going to see if we can find your relatives to take care of you. If not, we'd have to find some other families that would accept you."

In a matter of a week, Mrs. Parker found Adrianne's Aunt Stacy.

That was it. Adrianne and Aaron were sent back to the United States-where they originate. They're going to Miss Shanghai. Their aunt arranged the trip. They went to live in their aunt's house in San Francisco.

Aunt Stacy's house looked perfect. It contained perfect furniture. Everything belonged in its own spot. In this spotless house, Adrianne and Aaron got their own room. They shared bathrooms though. The living room was huge. There was an attic, a basement and a garden.

Living with their Aunt Stacy and Uncle Charles was hard. Adrianne's aunt was a real perfectionist. Everything in her house needed to be perfect. One day, Adrianne made dinner for the whole family to show her gratitude for their help. She made potato soup. The soup smelled nice. Everything was good. Everyone enjoyed dinner. Then, Aunt Stacy found something in her soup... potato peels. She stood up and refuses to drink that eat again and walked away. Adrianne's heart turned sour, and she ran away to her own room and wept.

Things like this happened every single day. Adrianne chose to ignore her aunt. One other time, Adrianne helped to paint the fence because the paint washed away over the years. Adrianne painted the front and back of the wood plank, but she forgot about the sides. Aunt Stacy yelled at her for being careless and lazy. Adrianne ignored her scolding.

This time, she couldn't take it anymore. She told Aaron that she wants to run away. Aaron told her that there is absolutely no way for her to support herself. Aaron was very uncertain about his younger sister running away by herself that he said if she were to run away, he was coming with her. So the day came, their aunt and uncle went to the supermarket purchasing some grocery. Adrianne wrote a note.

> *"Dear Aunt Stacy and Uncle Bob,*
> *Thank you both so much for taking care of us for the past few weeks. We've really appreciated your help, but we think it is time to go.*
> *Love,*
> *Adrianne and Aaron."*

They left the house that night without their belongings, just some cash they discovered in various places in the house that their aunt had hidden. They ran and ran and ran, away from all their troubles. Adrianne enjoyed the feeling of freedom. She wanted it to last. She was so glad she made the decision to run away.

With limited money, they only supplied food for themselves for three days.

On the fourth day, reality struck them as they walked down the streets starving.

"Aaron! I'm so hungry! We can't keep picking off scraps from the ground. Come on, we can't survive without food," Adrianne complained.

They found only one way to solve this food shortage problem. They stole from grocery stores by hiding food in the huge pockets they have in their jackets when the storekeeper is not watching.

One day, they were caught.

Police officers brought them to the police station for an interrogation.

"Where are your parents?" one police officer asked. His name badge reads "Greg."

"We don't have parents," Aaron answered.

"Ah, so you guys are orphans?" another police officer asked, this time his name badge says "Thomas."

"Yes, we" said Adrianne without completing her sentence.

"No, we're not," Aaron interrupted.

The police looked rather puzzled, feeling that Aaron's lying.

"Contact the orphanage, immediately," Officer Greg whispered to Officer Thomas.

They put Adrianne and Aaron into the San Francisco Orphanage.

Although the orphanage appeared to be short, it actually held a lot of rooms. Slides, swings, and seesaws filled the large playroom. Rows of chairs and tables filled the room opposite from the large playroom.

Adrianne and Aaron lived a difficult life in the orphanage. All the other children did everything with them. Many orphans lived in the orphanage The children there weren't very nice at all. Bullies, kids that hated life, kids that cried all the time, all types of people came together here.

Adrianne and Aaron just stuck together for everything. They never left one another no matter what. They followed a schedule. Everyday, different activities occupied the orphans. Mondays, Adrianne attended a pottery workshop. Tuesdays. she had drama class, where the children had to act out different stages of their life. Wednesdays, Adrianne and her brother participates in group discussions about how to live a better life. Thursdays, they played different types of sports. On Fridays, they did activities that reminded them of their families or parents. Although losing their parents was a very unfortunate incident that happened in their lives, the people who ran the orphanage believes that it is important that they do not forget who their parents were.

One day, Adrianne saw some visitors that looked like people she'd seen every day in Shanghai. These Asian couples arrived at the orphanage and looked around. Adrianne overheard them talking to a worker that worked in the orphanage that would be giving them a tour around the crowded buildings. Apparently they were moving back to Hong Kong and wanted to adopt a son before they go returned.

Sometimes, the orphanage separated girls and boys into different rooms for the visitors to easier pick which child they wanted to adopt. The guide took the Cantonese couple to a room with all the boys. It just happens that Aaron was in the room too and he was making a sculpture with wires.

"How old is the boy playing with wires?" the Cantonese lady asked.

"Oh, he's turning fifteen this year. He's a pretty mature boy," said the guide.

"What's his name?" asked the Cantonese man.

"His name is Aaron," answered the guide.

"What happened to his parents?" asked the Cantonese lady.

"We aren't sure, they don't like to talk about it. But we are certain that they have already passed away," said the guide.

"Poor child. He must've had a lonely depressing childhood. He looks like a hardworking, sturdy, fine, young gentlemen," said the Cantonese lady.

At this point, you can see that the Cantonese couples are interested in Aaron.

"Does he have any siblings?" asked the man.

"Yes indeed sir, he has a sister named Adrianne," said the guide.

The Cantonese couples walked into a little corner and whispered to each other, but the guide could still hear them.

"I want to adopt Aaron, I think he'd do well in our family. But I'm not sure about his sister, I don't want too many kids in the house." whispered the lady to the man in the small corner.

"Yeah I agree, I think Aaron has a very good potential to take over my company when I get to that age. Yeah I don't want more kids in the house but don't you think it's too harsh for the siblings to separate? I mean, they only have each other in this world…" said the man.

"Yeah, let's meet Adrianne first, then we can decide if we want her or not," said the lady.

They walked back to the guide.

"Can we please see Adrianne too?" asked the lady.

"Sure no problem, I'll go find her now," said the guide.

After a while, the guide returned with a pretty little girl following closely behind her.

"This is Adrianne, Aaron's little sister." announced the guide.

"Hello there Adrianne. I'm Mrs. Lau and this is my husband Mr. Lau." Mrs. Lau took out her hand seeking for a handshake. Adrianne just ignored her hand and Mrs. Lau took her hand back. Mrs. Lau gave her husband an I-don't-like-her-so-far look.

"Well how are you today Adrianne?" asked Mr. Lau.

"Fine," replied Adrianne.

"Well that's good, how old are you?" asked Mr. Lau.

"I'm ten." Adrianne said.

"Oh, what do you like to do?" asked Mr. Lau.

"You know what? You're starting to creep me out." said Adrianne and she walked away.

"I don't think I want to adopt her, she's just going to make everyone in the family sad with that attitude with hers." said Mrs. Lau.

"Cut her some slack! Try putting yourself in her shoes!" said Mr. Lau.

"Yes I understand, but that attitude of hers is hard to live with, I cannot live with a girl that answers all my questions with one-word-answers!" explained Mrs. Lau.

"Okay, I really want to meet Aaron, he looks pretty happy when he was playing with the wire in the room just then, hopefully his attitude is better than his sister;s." Mr. Lau hoped.

"Okay I'll go get Aaron now," said the guide.

*   *   *

The guide returned again, but this time, it was not a pretty little girl, this time, was a well-built young man who owned a very handsome face. Mrs. Lau introduced herself again.

"Hello Aaron, I'm Mrs. Lau and this is Mr. Lau, my husband." She took out her hand again looking for a handshake and Aaron shook it.

This time, Mrs. Lau smiled at Mr. Lau, with a look on her face as if saying "he's the one I want!"

"Hey, I'm Aaron, nice to meet you. Can I help you?" he said with a smile on his face.

Mr. Lau was shocked that he turned out to be so friendly.

"Oh hello! How are you? It's my pleasure to meet you!" said Mr. Lau, still wide-eyed at the fact that an orphan at this age can be so warm and happy.

"I'm fine, how are you?" Aaron asked politely.

"Great! We are from Hong Kong. Where are you from?" asked Mr. Lau.

"Oh, I've been to Hong Kong a couple of times, I don't know where I'm from, I used to live in Shanghai . . . when my parents were still alive..." said Aaron.

Now, Mrs. Lau gave Aaron a hug.

"It's okay. It's okay. That is why we're here," she said as she patted his back.

Aaron broke away from the hug.

"Wait, what do you even mean?" asked Aaron while raising his eyebrow.

"We're moving back to Hong Kong and we want to adopt a boy before we leave," said Mrs. Lau.

"So you've picked me out of all the other boys in this orphanage? If you didn't know, I have a sister that needs to be taken care of and without me I don't know how she could survive. She's still young and she sometimes still gets really emotional about the loss of our parents," said Aaron.

"Yeah we have met her, she has an... attitude." Mrs. Lau whispered to herself.

"Excuse me?" Aaron glared at Mrs. Lau.

"I'm sorry, we want to invite you to come to Hong Kong and live with us, we promise you a bright future and we will offer the best education possible for we see real potential in you." said Mrs. Lau.

"I'll think about it, but what am I going to do about my sister?" asked Aaron.

"She'd have to stay here." said Mr. Lau.

*   *   *

Two weeks after Aaron moved to Hong Kong. Adrianne stared out the orphanage window.

She pictured her brother where she last saw him. He wore his blue sweater that Adrianne knitted for him for his birthday three years ago.

"I'll come back and bring you home."

That was the last thing Aaron had mouthed to her.

She was strong and tried holding back her tears but simply couldn't do it. She let her tears flow freely down her face.

It had been how long? Adrianne couldn't think straight. Flashes of her brother leaving her behind in this desolate place haunted her since the day he left. But she understood her brother; he had no other options, and wanted the best for her as well. The only thing she could do now was wait.

Living in the orphanage alone took a long time for Adrianne to adjust. She was not used to not having someone to go to when she has trouble dealing with emotional feelings. Now that Aaron, her only family member in the whole world left, she thought she really had no reason to continue living in this world.

Adrianne turned into a very violent girl. Whenever someone told her that she was not doing the correct thing she held up her fist and threatened to punch that person. No one in the orphanage wanted to be friends with her because of her behavior.

A tall building is located next to the orphanage, a fifteen stories high story building. One stormy day, rain was pouring from the sky. The rain drops shattered so hard that when they hit the palm of Adrianne's hand, it felt like sharp knives cutting into her flesh. She has waited to do this for such a long time. She has everything planned out carefully. This day was the perfect day to do it because with the darkness filling the sky and the pouring rain so heavy, no one noticed her running away. She left the orphanage when everyone else made their pot. She ran to the tall vacant building next to the orphanage. She raced up the steep stairs. Sweat gathered on her forehead. Tears spilled out her eyes. There was a balcony at the top of the building. She arrived at the balcony, walked over to the rim of the balcony and sat down. Her legs dangling below her and allowed the pouring rain wash away all her regrets and worries.

"Don't jump!" shouted a voice from behind her.

It was a boy from the orphanage. Adrianne recognized his face but couldn't recall his name. He looked just about the same age as her, both thirteen by that time. Long head, brown hair, light skin and he appeared fairly tall.

"Who are you?" cried out Adrianne.

"Do not jump off! Please!" the boy kept shouting.

"Stay away, whoever you are! Come any closer and I'll jump off!" yelled Adrianne.

"No! Please don't! You can talk to me!" screamed the boy.

"I don't want to talk to you! I am going to do this!" Adrianne shouted.

"Please! We can fix whatever you are not happy about if you are still alive! We will never be able to turn things around if you let your troubles overcome you !" the boy shouted.

"This is none of your business! Please! Just stay away, or I'll really jump!" Adrianne screamed at the top of her lungs now.

"You shouldn't kill yourself because something isn't going the way you want it to go! There's always a bright side to things and you should always think optimistically! Please! If you come back, I will be there to go through your troubles with you! I promise!" the boy, too, screamed at the top of his lungs now.

Adrianne sat there in silence for a long time. Thinking over and over what the stranger just said to her. The logic started to make a little sense in her head. Although life has been dreadful so far, it's not the end of the world. The more she thinks, the more it's starting to make sense to her. She shouldn't torture herself if something's wrong with her life. She should try to turn things around. She sat in the rain for awhile longer, noticing the stranger is still behind her. She didn't want to seem weak if she turned around. But she couldn't think of any other way to turn away, so she turned around and saw the boy smiling at her.

She walked over to the boy and said, "You're going to be by my side through all my troubles right? You better keep your promise!" said Adrianne with a slight smile on her face.

"Of course. I never break my promises." the boy said and a smile widened across his face.

Adrianne reached out her hand seeking for a handshake.

"Ha ha, after all this drama, I forgot to introduce myself. My name is Adrianne," said Adrianne.

"Yeah, ha, ha, I know who you are. Oh that totally didn't make me sound like a stalker," the boy said with a wink on his face. "My name is Ryan. Nice to meet you," said Ryan while returning the handshake.

"Wait how do you know about me? We've never met… have we?" asked Adrianne rising her eyebrow.

"No we haven't actually. But I've seen you around. I don't know why but you stand out from the crowd and I notice you. I noticed that you weren't there for pottery class. Then I saw this dark shadow running past the other side of the window in the rain. I ran outside when the instructor wasn't watching and saw you running up the stairs. I followed you and found you up here." answered Ryan.

"Oh. Well thanks. I guess if it weren't for you to come up here after me, I would've really jumped off this building. And that would not be a pretty sight! Ha ha." laughed Adrianne.

"Well I did what I thought was right and you really should live as a happy person like me." Ryan said with a smile.

"Yeah, I'll try. I'm already feeling a little better and less depressed. Maybe it's because the rain washed away all my worries and sorrows." said Adrianne.

"Yeah that's probably it. Speaking of rain. Do you notice that we're still standing in the rain? Ha, ha, I just realized that. Hmm, let's get you inside and dry you up before you catch a high fever." said the laughing boy.

They returned to the orphanage. No one noticed Adrianne and Ryan were gone. Everyone busied themselves while making their pot. Ryan and Adrianne joined in with the rest of the group.

*   *   *

Several months passed. Adrianne and Ryan became closer and closer. Ryan acted like the replacement of Aaron only Adrianne could relate more easily to Ryan because they came from the same age group.

Life went back to normal just like when Aaron was still here by Adrianne's side. Adrianne found someone to talk to, someone to play with, and they became "partners in crime." Adrianne has never been this happy in her life and it was really Ryan, who took out the best of her and she became an optimist.

One day, they went to a garden, on the swings on a sunny day.

"After all this time we've been friends. You've never talked about your childhood like when you were still a baby. I want to know about it!" said Adrianne with joy.

"It's a really long story, you're going to be half asleep after I finish with my life story," said Ryan.

"Oh, I promise I won't! I like long stories and besides, I've got time!" explained Adrianne.

"Okay, so I was born into a fairly wealthy family in Boston Massachusetts. My father was a doctor. My mother was a vet. My mother died when my youngest sister was born. I had five siblings, two brothers and two sisters. I was the middle child. My childhood was pretty fun, I had no worries, I lived carefree. Until the day when my dad turned into an alcoholic and when he came home, he beat us up for no reason. Then he met this woman, who he later married and she was horrible to us. She made my siblings and I do all the housework and she'd just relax or do whatever women's in their 40's do to waste time.

My dad doesn't care about us anymore. Since he started drinking, the less important we are to him. Once, my oldest brother got an award for something, my dad didn't even go to the ceremony, in fact, he came home all drunk and saw my brother's trophy and slammed it on the floor. I got very frightened after that. I had enough money to fly all the way here to San Francisco to live with my real aunt. She was basically like my best friend in my childhood because I could tell her anything with no regrets because she'd not let any secret slip out of her mouth.

"Then the day came when she was diagnosed with cancer. My uncle died a long time ago, he died in a battle in Vietnam. She only had me to take care of her now and I guess that's how I became more mature. I've really grown to appreciate life as it comes. Then she died and I was sent here. It's not that bad of a place, I met some really nice people here, like you. What is your life story?" asked Ryan.

"Oh… Well, my life was fairly smooth when I was an infant, nothing dramatic happened. I lived in Shanghai, China. Beautiful place, I must take you there someday! My "orphan" life started a few years ago, when both of my parents died in a car crash. I was there to see the whole thing happen, so it's still a pretty hard thing to forget. Then, my brother and I moved in with our aunt Stacy and uncle Bob. They were real perfectionists that I cannot stand AT ALL.

"So I ran away with my brother, Aaron by the way, and we couldn't stand the hunger so we stole from grocery stores and supermarkets and finally they caught us and we got sent here. Which was a pretty horrible place I must say. I hated it here when I first came. All the weird kids, teachers and those freaky visitors that smile all the time. My brother helped me cope with all the drama in my life up to that point. After a while, he was no longer available because some Cantonese couple wanted to adopt him. Then my life changed dramatically again and I was lonely for so long. I even thought of committing suicide and you were the one that talked me out of it. So I think, you should give yourself a pat on the back for being my savior." Adrianne said.

"Wow, I wonder what normal children do in their lives. I can pretty much say that both of our lives are pretty unique and abnormal." Ryan said.

They sat on the swings in silence for a while.

"Hey, wanna see something really beautiful?" asked Ryan.

"Sure," replied Adrianne.

Ryan hopped down his swing.

"May I take you hand please?" he said in a British accent.

This made Adrianne snicker.

"Of course, sir" Adrianne said with the same accent.

They ran, hand in hand, through the garden, which lead to a forest. Then they ran through the forest and ended up next to a beautiful lake.

"Oh my gosh." Those were the only words Adrianne could speak out.

"I know, I know, that was my first reaction when I saw it. Beautiful isn't it?" smiled Ryan.

"This is absolutely the most beautiful thing I've ever seen!" screamed Adrianne with joy.

"Yeah, I heard they have one just like this, or prettier in India. We should go there someday!" suggested Ryan.

"YEAH! And I can show you around China, and we can go visit my brother." Adrianne's eyes shined when she said that.

They walked together, hand in hand, back to the garden. Still planning the trip, which is bound to happen in just a couple of weeks.

Live To Surf

By

Alvin Yeung

Alex Hudson was a talented surfer. Unluckily, he was born in a family that lived in San Francisco. Alex's neighborhood didn't think that being in love with surfing was normal. They didn't accept Alex. Therefore, he felt like one of a kind, but that didn't stop him surfing.

One sunny day, as usual, Alex surfed in the waves, but he didn't know that a storm from the Philippines was heading his way. Soon, the sea would turn into a monstrous beast, and Alex's life would be in danger.

Wave after wave swelled from the endless sea, and Alex had the time of his life, gliding on the waves. Meanwhile, the sea got rougher and rougher. Alex didn't notice the storm headed his way until the sea became harder and harder to balance on the surfboard, and a massive dark cloud closed around Alex.

Struggling towards the shore, a wave knocked Alex from his surfboard. Waves slammed over him and made him choke. Life seemed so miserable. He took a last glance at the water.

"Wake up, wake up." A voice woke Alex. He found himself on the beach with his sister taking care of him.

"Hey, Cindy, what are you doing down here? Shouldn't you be at home?" his weak voice said.

"I heard a storm headed this way, and I knew that you would get yourself into some kind of trouble. So I came," Cindy said with a delightful smile. "Let's go home now."

Cindy and Alex walked home slowly. On their way home, Alex told Cindy how lucky he is to have a sister like her.

The doorbell rang. The sound of footsteps came closer and closer.

"What were you doing in the rain? Have you been surfing again?" Alex's mother yelled angrily.

"Why can't you just accept who I really am? I am a surfer," said Alex.

"Yeah, Mom." Cindy supported Alex.

"You are a girl, you stay out of this." Alex's **m**om stared at Cindy and said.

Dispute filled the house the entire night.

"Another day of my life. Is there a future in this?" Alex questioned himself. He sat on his bed and hesitated for several minutes. He stood up and started slowly, making his way down the stairs.

"You better get to work; you are late," Alex's mother said.

"Mom… I… I wanna talk to you about something," Alex slurred.

"About what? You are almost late for work. Make it quick." She replied.

"It's okay if our neighborhood doesn't accept me for being who I am, but you're my mother. I hoped you would understand!" Alex said and left without saying good-bye.

After work, Alex left for the beach to get some air.

The red sun shone on the water and reflected on the Alex's blonde hair, his blue eyes looked like the heart of a blue sapphire.

"Hey, what are you thinking about?" Cindy walked up behind him and asked. "You have been working the whole day. Don't you wanna go back home?"

"Not really, home probably is the last place I wanna go to right now," answered Alex as he turned to his sister. "Cin, I really need your advice."

"Sure, I'm right here, bro." Cindy replied.

"I am thinking of moving to Hawaii. We can start a new life over there. It is so much more suitable for us. Don't you think so?" said Alex excitedly.

"Yes, but are we just going to leave everything behind?" Cindy asked doubtfully.

"Yes, I am your elder brother. When you were born, I promised that no matter what, I would take care of you, and I will keep that promise," Alex proclaimed. "I will do the talking with Mom."

"Okay then," Cindy said with tears filling her eyes.

They walked to their mother's office.

Alex's heart beat faster and faster as he approached his mother. As Alex walked closer and closer to his mother, he was reciting the things that he was going to say repeatedly. Alex looked in his mother's eyes. After a few seconds, he finally had the guts and said. "Mom, Cindy and I are leaving since you know who we really are, and it doesn't seem like you care."

Alex's mother took a look at Alex and yelled. "You are right, you are twenty-two, and your sister is eighteen. Your guys are old enough to take care of yourselves. Staying here is just an imposition on me. Leave!"

"Cindy, let's go home and pack. We're going to Hawaii," Alex said firmly.

Packing his suitcase in his room. "What would my life be like from now on?" he thought. Alex took a glance at the poster hanging above his bed. It reminded him of how his father had always supported him before he passed away. He held back his tears reluctantly. "I've reached the point of no return," Alex thought while he lay down on his bed.

With all their baggage, Alex and Cindy walked out the door, got on a cab and loaded their baggage onto the cab.

"Sir, to the airport, please," said Alex.

"Okay," replied the cab driver.

"So, we are pretty serious huh? I'm scared!" Cindy's voice came from behind.

"It's okay, I'm going to take care of you." Alex comforted her.

*   *   *

"We're here, sir. It's ten dollars," said the cab driver.

"Here. Keep the change." Alex said as he handed the cab driver the money.

"Thank you, sir," the cab driver replied as he popped the trunk.

Alex and Cindy unloaded their baggage and headed for the counter.

"Good afternoon, Sir. May I help you?" asked the woman at the counter gently.

"Yes, I would like to have two tickets to Hawaii please." Alex said with a smile.

"Please wait a second, sir. I'll check if there are more spaces on the plane," the woman said. "There are two seats by the window in the last row. Would you like to take it sir?"

"Yes, please," Alex replied.

After paying for the tickets and checking in their baggage, they boarded the plane.

They plane took off about ten minutes later.

A girl with a book sat across Alex. She caught his eyes. Alex stared at her. He forgot everything around him. He felt like he had just met his dream girl-brunette, about twenty years old, five foot six, with blue eyes that attracted every moving thing on this earth.

"Alex," Cindy's voice interrupted his daydreams. "What were you looking at?"

"Nothing." Alex blushed and answered with a delightful smile.

Cindy leaned over, saw the girl, and said. "Bro, you should go talk to her. Girls like guys with confidence."

"But... What should I say?" Alex said nervously.

"Introduce yourself. Be smooth," answered Cindy.

"Oh, okay," replied Alex.

Alex stood up, and started slowing walking to the girl.

"Hi, I'm Alex," Alex said.

The girl looked at Alex, smiled and said. "After half an hour, you finally have the guts to come talk to me. I've been waiting."

Alex blushed even more, and he was speechless.

"I'm Petty. I'm single. I am moving to Hawaii, but I have no clue where I'm going. What else do you want to know?" asked Petty.

"Oh really?" said Alex surprisingly.

"I am basically in the same situation. That's my sister over there," Alex said as he pointed to Cindy.

Alex and Petty talked for the whole plane ride. They shared their common hobbies and expressed their pain to each other. Alex really felt like she is the one.

After knowing each other for three hours. They had decided to stick together.

"Passengers, may I have you attention please. Our flight has arrived in Hawaii. The local time is eight thirty in the evening. We will be landing in fifteen minutes. Wish you have a pleasant journey."

The plane landed at the airport of Honolulu. Alex, Cindy and Petty got their baggage, and hesitated.

"What should we do now?" asked Cindy.

"We should probably find a place to live first." Suggested Alex.

"Hm. Let's go then. What are we waiting for?" agreed Petty.

They went to the information center and asked the woman. "Excuse me, I'm wondering whether they are any cheap houses on the beach that are for sell?"

"I'm pretty sure they are some houses for sell on Hanauma Bay," the woman said as she handed him a map.

"Thank you," Alex said as he started to make his way out the door.

"By the way," a voice caught Alex's attention. She said, "Hanauma Bay is famous for surfing. Most of the people there are friendly but, some of them…"

"What about some of them?" Alex asked curiously.

"You will see when you get there," The woman said. "Wish you good luck."

"Thanks anyway," replied Alex.

Alex, Cindy and Petty walked out of the airport and got on a shuttle-bus to the Hanauma Bay.

As the coconut trees passed by, gradually, Alex's eyelids fluttered and closed.

"We're here!" Someone's voice woke Alex from his rest. A smell of fresh air and the sound of the restless sea freshened Alex.

The three of them got off the bus and walked into a house for sell. A man walked out from the kitchen. "Are you guys looking for a house to buy?"

"Yes, I'm wondering how much this house is." Alex said.

"Oh, I'm selling it for then thousand dollars. This house is not renovated. I don't want to sell it through an agent, and I want to get rid of it as soon as possible. That's why I'm selling it for only then thousand dollars."

"That's a reasonable price for a house like this I guess," Alex said as he turned to Cindy.

"Cin, I've earned about eight thousands from work and earned about a thousand from all the surfing awards. How much do you have?"

"I've got about two thousand from summer job," Cindy answered.

"Do you have any money?" Alex said as he turned towards Petty.

"Yeah. I've never told you about my family background." Petty turned away. "My parents are very rich. They own the Swith markets and the Swith factories. I think I should pay for this house."

"There is no way that I'm going to let you do that." Alex handed the man his credit card.

"But…" Cindy didn't know what to say.

*   *   *

They quickly sorted out the payment and went to the store to grab tools and materials for the renovation of the house.

The sun settled. It reflected on the restless sea as Alex prepared for dinner. It reminded him of too much.

"It has been a long day," Alex said at the dinner table.

"Yeah, I'm gonna have a good rest tonight," Cindy said.

Alex raised his cup. "I wanna purpose a toast," he continued. "To the start of our new lives."

Cindy and Petty gave Alex a smile, and both raised their cups. After dinner, they went to bed.

After flipping repeatedly on the sleep, Alex still couldn't seem to fall asleep. Petty's image was stuck in his head. He got up, slowly walked to Petty's door, and knocked on it. He opened up a little bit and whispered. "Hey, I hope I'm not bothering you. I just want you to know that I'm really glad that you can come along with us."

"Come on in," Petty said quietly. "I couldn't sleep as well. I've been thinking about someone." She said as she blushed.

"Same," Alex smiled. "Go to bed now, there's a whole new day ahead of us tomorrow."

A pillow slammed into Alex's face, and his sister's voice said, "Wake up. Wake up, you sleepy head. It's ten o'clock already. We have much work to do."

"I'm up! I'm up!" shouted Alex.

After cleaning himself up, he slowly walked down the stairs.

Waffles with maple syrup, butter, whip-cream on top of it, and some fruits on the side. Sound of cooking came from the kitchen. Alex took a peek and saw Petty cooking. He was impressed.

"You can stop peeking now. Come down and eat," said Petty.

"I wasn't…" Alex blushed.

He started slowly eating his waffles. "Mmmh. This is really, really good."

Petty smiled. "Thanks. I went to grocery store just now, and grabbed some food. On my way there, I saw a house on the mountain. Do you want to go check it out later on?"

"Sure," Alex replied. "But first, we should probably finish renovating the house."

After breakfast, they picked up their tools and started renovating the house again. Not long after that, Alex exclaimed. "We are officially done. Let's go check out the house now."

They found a path from the beach all the way to the top on the mountain. They walked all the way up there, and finally got to the so called "No man's house." Grasses and leaves covered the house. The one and only window faced the ocean, and a skull on the front door.

Alex went up to the door and lightly knocked on it.

"I'm coming. Just one-second," they heard a man say.

The door opened up. A man with black hair, about six foot and brown eyes came out. He was kinda chubby. " What do you want?"

"Nothing. We're just looking around. We just moved here." Alex replied with a gentle smile.

"Well, then, come on in," the man said.

As they walked in, they saw many surfboards hanging on the walls.

"Do you surf?" Alex asked curiously.

The man smiled. They sat down on a couch, drinking tea, and started introducing himself. "I'm Seth. I know that you guys might find it funny how I live all the way up here," he continued. "I live up here because I want to avoid the crowd, moreover have a better view of the restless sea."

"I'm pretty good at surfing," Alex interrupted.

Seth looked out of the window and pointed at a ten-foot wave and asked, "Are you sure you know how to surf?"

"Um…" Alex was speechless.

"That's what I thought," Seth said. "I used to roll in that kind of waves every day."

"What stopped you?" Alex turned to Seth.

"It's getting late, you guys should get going," said Seth immediately. He was trying to avoid the question.

"Tell me please," said Alex.

"I was the best surfer, until Luke Clayton showed up. He knocked me down in a yearly competition called Surf's Up. I've never shown my face after that." Seth tried to avoid eye contact. "I see some great spirit in you, Alex. But, you still have too much to learn. Starting from tomorrow, you should come to my place every day. I will teach you how to be a real surfer."

"Yes, Master," Alex answered with excitement.

When they got back home, Alex started to worry about their financial problems. He had decided to invest.

Early in the morning, Alex got up, prepared himself, and headed to Master Seth's place. He ate breakfast there and spent the morning with Master Seth.

"Before you surf. You need to make your own surfboard." Master Seth took out a saw. "I have a workshop and some pretty good woods on the other beach."

They took off and headed for the western beach. Alex and Master Seth walked in the soft sand that massages their feet. A small wooden hut stood in the middle on the beach.

"That's my workshop." Master Seth pointed to the hut.

"Let's start working then. What are we waiting for?" Alex rushed to the hut.

Master Seth taught him how to build a strong and smooth surfboard step by step. He easily took in all the techniques.

"Now, Let me see what you got, kiddo," said Master Seth.

Alex tied his surfboard to his ankle and started making his way out to the ocean. A big wave was about ten meters away from him. He quickly turned his surfboard around and started paddling. When he felt the wave lifted him up, he stood onto the board and tried to balance. He had the kind of feeling that he had never had before. He felt free. Suddenly, his surfboard lost control and he couldn't seem to balance. He fell off his surfboard and was taken down by the wave.

"You need a balance training of some sort," yelled Master Seth. "Paddle back to me."

Alex struggled back to the beach, lay there, and tried to catch his breath.

"Here are some tips. Loosen up, relax, and try to let the wave take you." Master Seth headed back to his house.

"I have to do this." Alex thought.

He ran toward the ocean and gave it another try. After trying repeatedly, he got exhausted and fell asleep on the beach.

"Alex . . . Alex." Cindy's weak voice woke Alex from his dreams.

"Yeah?" Alex replied.

"Why didn't you tell me that you weren't coming back home? Petty and I worried about you for the entire night!" Cindy shouted.

"I'm sorry, Cin," Alex continued. "I was too focused on surfing. I totally forgot about everything."

Cindy sighed. "Let's go back home and eat breakfast." She said as she dragged Alex back home.

For the entire morning, Alex told Cindy and Petty how amazing it was to surf in the big waves. "I think I'm ready to surf on this side of the island and show the people here that I have skills." Alex said proudly.

"Congrats," said Petty.

"Have you told Master Seth about his yet?" asked Cindy.

"Not yet. I will," said Alex.

Alex quickly finished up his breakfast and headed up to Master Seth's place.

"Master Seth?" he shouted as he knocked on his door.

"I'm coming, I'm coming. What's with the hurry?" Master Seth said as he approached the door.

"I think I'm ready to show the people that I am ready," said Alex.

"You do? Do you mind showing me first?" asked Master Seth.

"Sure. Let's go then," said Alex.

They hurried off to the western beach. Alex grabbed his surfboard and rushed out to the sea. A wave came up behind him. He started paddling. He stood up as the wave approached. "Yeah, Master Seth. I think I'm really ready," he yelled.

"Come over here," Master Seth yelled back.

Alex surfed to the beach and picked up his surfboard proudly.

"You are not ready to prove to the people yet," Master Seth looked Alex in the eyes. "You are just done with the first stage of the training."

"What?" Alex was shocked and disappointed at the same time.

"Here, come with me." Master Seth walked towards his workshop. He brought Alex into his workshop and pointed at a picture. It's a handsome and fit man in the picture.

"Who is that?" Asked Alex.

"That's me," answered Master Seth as he pointed to himself. "I don't want you to turn into this. Get it? That's why I'm training you. Don't let me down, kiddo."

"I won't," Alex said with confidence.

"The next stage, which is the final stage. You need to know how to go up and down on a wave smoothly, and you have to know how to accelerate on a wave. To be able to gain control on a wave, you need great balance skills. To be able to accelerate, you need to bend down, and lean your center of gravity forward. That's all I can tell you, kiddo." Master Seth left Alex some alone time to work on his skills.

"Great balance. Lean forward." Alex repeated to himself. Falling into the ocean decrease Alex's faith in surfing. Every time he fell, the harder he tried. "I don't score until I sore." Alex said to himself. The violent sun rose. Alex had decided to take a break. He went back to the house to see how Cindy and Petty did. When he walked by the beach, he saw people gathered around, cheering and shouting. He went closer and saw a strong guy extorting another guy.

"Hey, you. Stop this nonsense." Alex yelled at him.

"Who are you supposed to be, punk?" Laughter poured from the crowd.

"I'm Alex. Who are you? What gives you the desire to pick on other people?" Alex said with anger.

"Who am I? Ha, ha, is that a joke? I'm Luke Clayton, the best surfer known in Hawaii. You're messing with the wrong guy, boy!" Said Luke.

"So, you are Luke Clayton. The foolish and arrogant man." Alex teased.

"What did you say!" Luke's anger exploded, and punched Alex in the face.

Alex felt blood coming out of his month. He spat out the saliva along with blood. "Solving problems with your fist," Alex smiled. "You loser."

"I'm going to kill you." Luke rushed toward Alex.

"Knock it off, boys." The beach patrol approached.

"This is not the end of it. I will remember you." Luke pointed at Alex.

"First of all, I want to welcome you to Hanauma Bay. I am Kuno, a member of the beach patrol. If those guys pick on you again, let me know," said Kuno.

"Thank you for the offer, but I think I can handle this myself." Alex shook Konu's hand, looked him in the eyes, and walked back home.

"Oh my gosh, are you okay?" Petty said when Alex walked in with blood on the edge of his lips.

"I'm fine. Master Seth was right about Luke," said Alex.

"Cindy and I are always worrying about you," Petty said.

"Where is Cindy?" asked Alex.

"She won't be here for the night. She's meeting some friends" Answered Petty.

"Let's watch a movie tonight then. It will be our first movie in Hawaii." suggested Alex.

"Sure." Petty went through the DVDs they had. "Let's watch *Avatar.*"

"Anything would do." Alex smiled.

During the movie, Alex slowly put his arm around Petty when it got to the scene where the main characters kissed, Alex pulled Petty closer and kissed her on the lips. It made Petty's heart fluttered. The two lovebirds enjoyed their evening alone. As the movie played, Alex and Petty fell asleep on the couch.

Cindy walked in the door quietly. She didn't want to wake Alex and

Petty. Surprisingly, she found them on the couch. She giggled and went to the kitchen to make breakfast.

"Breakfast for the happy couple." Cindy laughed.

"What?" Alex opened his eyes with Petty was in his arms. He didn't know what was going on. He looked at Cindy and mumbled. "Wait, I don't want to wake, Petty." He slowly set Petty's head on the couch and got up.

"So, do you want to tell me anything?" Cindy said as they walked to the dining table.

"Since when did you and Petty started going out? You never told me," said Cindy.

"Oh, about that. We are not officially going out," Alex continued, "or maybe we are. I'm confused."

"I'm even more confused," said Cindy. "Anyway, all gossips aside. On my way back, I heard people talking about the yearly surfing contest. Do u think that you want to join? If you do, I have some friends that can sign you up."

"Yes, of course. I would love that. Thank you, sis," said Alex.

"More than you love Petty?" Cindy teased. "Just kidding."

Petty came up from Alex's back, slipped her hands around Alex's waist, kissed her neck, and said: "When did you wake up?"

Alex held Petty hand. "I guess we are officially going out now."

"Yeah," Petty smile. She walked in front of Alex and started kissing him.

Cindy cleared her throat. "Do you guys mind?"

"Good morning, Cindy," blushed Petty.

"You guys have fun. I'm going to practice," said Alex.

"So, I will sign you up?" asked Cindy.

Alex nodded and went out.

Cindy and Petty washed the dishes. They saw people working and decorating the beach through the window. They went out and asked one of the workers. "What are you guys working on?"

"Surf's up." The man said with surprise, "You guys don't know?"

"The contest is tomorrow. Is Alex ready?" Cindy questioned Petty.

"I believe in him." Petty gave Cindy a sweet smile and walked back to the house.

Rain dropped from the sky. Alex thought it was a good opportunity to practice in the rain because, the rain made the sea rougher. He practiced until late night.

At about ten o'clock, Alex got home. He shivered as he rang the doorbell. Cindy opened the door, saw him soaked in water, and gave him the "You made me worry." Look.

"I'm sorry; I'm sorry. I thought that I was a good opportunity to practice in a rough sea," explained Alex. As he walked in, he saw Petty giving him the same look. "I'm sorry, babe. I'm going go dry myself up," he lightly kissed Petty on the cheek.

"Go to bed now. The contest is tomorrow," said Petty.

"It is?" Alex didn't seem surprised. "Okay then, I'll go right after I take a shower."

The fresh sunshine of the morning shone on Alex's face. He took a look outside. There were many people preparing for Surf's Up.

"Here I go." Alex thought. "Time for me to prove myself."

After Alex bushed his teeth, he walked downstairs for breakfast. Petty looked at him surprisingly. "You're up early today."

Alex smiled and looked at his surfboard. "I'm going to decorate my surfboard before I go."

"Can I help then?" asked Petty.

"Only if you want to." Alex quickly finished up his breakfast and took his surfboard to the basement. Alex decorated his surfboard with fire and wrote his name on it. Petty gave him ideas as he worked. They finished decorating it within half an hour.

Alex walked out the door. Petty dragged him back in, and gave him a kiss. "Be safe out there, okay?"

"I will try," smiled Alex.

Alex walked to the sign in counter. "What's your name?"

"Alex Hudson." Alex said as he showed the man his surfboard. The man went over the list and allowed him in.

"We have no time for the laggards. Let's start our first round. Surfers who had signed in, please get ready." The sound came from the speakers all around the beach.

Alex rushed to the sea. There were about twenty surfers. Luke was the one in the middle. Alex joined the line, and they all started paddling toward the ocean.

"Here comes a wave," someone shouted. All twenty surfers hopped onto their surfboard and tried to go faster than the wave. Two people from the far right got taken down because they weren't fast enough. Luke tried to push as many people down into the water as possible.

"Hey, it's you. Told you I'm going to take you down someday," said Luke as he approached to Alex. Alex started to accelerate and doge Luke from pushing him into the water.

"Impressive. You know how to accelerate," said Luke as he went faster and faster. Before he reached Alex, they were back to the beach.

"We have fifteen surfers taken down. Now, it's time for second round."

"You watch it, boy. No one mess with me. No one," said Luke before they took off.

The big wave brought the surfers to their surfboards. This time, Alex wasn't fast enough. He was in the wave tunnel while Luke took out all the other surfers. It was the first time for Alex to be in a wave tunnel. He was amazed by the vision he saw. He got out of the wave as the wave went smaller and smaller. He and Luke were the only ones left for the final round.

A massive fifteen-foot wave headed towards Alex and Luke. Luke had never surfed in such a huge wave before but Alex had surfed in a similar wave. The sight terrified Luke. He had no clue what to do. He hopped on to his surfboard and tried to balance. The furious wave buried him. Alex noticed and surfed quickly to where Luke struggled. Wave after wave, Luke couldn't catch his breath, and passed out in the wild ocean. Alex jumped off his board, swam to Luke and dragged him back to the beach.

"Are you okay? Luke, are you okay?" Alex's voice woke Luke.

"Am I in heaven?" asked Luke.

"You wish," Alex smiled.

People gathered around and gave started clapping their hands.

"Thank you," Luke said. "And I'm sorry."

Alex gave Luke a smile, "Don't mention it." He put his arms around Petty, stroked her hair, and sat on the golden beach as the sun set. The way that the sun shone on the sparkling sand and reflected on the endless sea created a gorgeous view. Alex, Cindy, and Petty relayed on each other like a family. Alex felt something that he hadn't felt in a while, happiness.